SEASIDE

THE
WORLD OF
THE MIRROR

VIANLIX-CHRISTINE
SCHNEIDER

Disclaimer:
This is a work of fiction. All characters, locations, and businesses are purely products of the author's imagination and are entirely fictitious. Any resemblance to actual people, living or dead, or to businesses, places, or events is completely coincidental.

To my parents and all their endless love
and support in everything I do

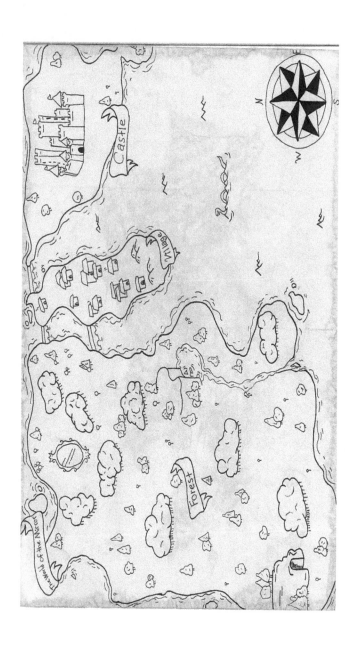

Prologue

1943

IN A MAGICAL WORLD

erlin's eyes passed over the village people who had gathered around the table. They were dressed in their best for him, their king.

The castle never seemed more alive than when a banquet was held. From the large windows lining the wall, sunlight softly spilled in. Sounds of laughter and conversations around the long table filled the great hall. Lunch sat under food domes in front of each seat, and smoked lamb and fresh salad held a strong scent that made Merlin's mouth water.

He stood tall at the end of the table with confidence and a kind smile. He had a dark skin tone, and his dark brown hair was always neat no matter what time of day. He dressed fairly humble in a nice white shirt and a beautiful burgundy vest, along with cream trousers and shiny black boots. Maybe that was why the village people loved him so: he never acted as if he was better than them, and he treated everyone the same.

****

Looking around the room, he scanned the crowd one last time as everyone took their seats. *She had promised not to be late this time*, he thought with a sigh. He picked up his gold chalice that was filled with ale and tapped his wand against its side. Three taps was all it took for the room to fall silent.

"I am truly enthusiastic that we can share this afternoon with each other," Merlin said. "As usual, I have opened my doors to you, my people. Without you, this kingdom would not be what it is today. So, let us drink, eat, and enjoy our time together."

Every day, he held a banquet at the castle for his people. He always looked forward to it, planning meals with the cooks to make sure everything was perfect. For some banquets, he had a singer or a jester perform.

"I want to—"

His eyes moved to the large wooden doors as they opened halfway. The guards standing nearby turned to see who came in before moving aside. Zuly and Athena made their way into the room without a sound.

Zuly slowly closed the door behind them. He was pale with a slick black man bun and always held himself with confidence. He was still a fairly young man even though he was the captain of the guards.

Merlin smiled at Athena as she arrived at last. Her story had always broken his heart. While walking through the village's outskirts with Zuly four years ago, many screams had filled the calm morning air. A home was burning at an alarming rate, and everyone had desperately tried to control the fire with their magic, but it was past the point of control. No one else had dared to go in to save those who were still inside. Without a second thought, Merlin had raced inside to find a young Athena choking on the smoke. Her parents had been lost in the flames, but he took her to safety.

Quickly, Merlin's and Zuly's roles in her life had become something like a father and an older brother respectively. Merlin gave her a place to stay in one of his many rooms at the castle and gave her dresses like she was a princess. Mostly because he treated her like his own. Zuly gave her piggyback rides around the castle, her laughter filling the halls. In that first week, Merlin had noticed just how strong her powers were and started to train her. She became his loyal apprentice.

Merlin's smile faded as he saw mischievous grins on both Zuly's and Athena's faces. "One moment," he said to the crowd as he set his chalice down. He walked over to his captain and his young apprentice.

"Sorry she is late, my King," Zuly said with a bow.

Merlin brushed it off with a smile. "Not to worry. I am just glad you both made it. Do I dare ask what you both were up to?"

"Zuly said it was okay," Athena said, her right dimple showing. She smiled up at her master before rushing to her seat next to his.

"Do not worry, Merlin," Zuly added. "I did not let her do anything you would not want her to do. I just let her drop off water to Christopher, the new guard, with her magic."

The other man smiled. "I see no harm in that. It is a hot day out after all."

Zuly shook his head with a grin. "Well, I shall leave you to enjoy your meal. I will make sure everything is running well, my King." He placed his fist across his chest and bowed.

"Please, you can eat here with us tonight."

He gave his king a surprised look. "I am not sure how it would look if I was not doing my job. I—"

"I do not care what they might think of such a thing. Come and have dinner with us, my good friend." Merlin gestured to the empty seat across from Athena, who looked back at the two men.

Zuly stayed where he was.

"I know you must be hungry," Merlin added as he rested his hand on his friend's back.

He smiled. "The food does smell great."

"Good. The guards can take care of themselves for one night."

They made their way to the empty seats. Zuly sat as Merlin picked up his chalice once more.

"Sorry about the wait," he said, speaking to everyone. "I will make this shorter than I had planned. Thank you for coming. Bless tonight and this meal."

"Merlin the Great!" everyone called out, lifting their glasses before the room fell into conversation once more.

Zuly looked across the table to see Athena lift the food dome wearily. "It is just lamb, Athena. You will be fine."

Merlin looked over, having forgotten that she disliked the meal. He picked up his wand and tapped her plate with it.

"Thank you," she said with grateful eyes as the lamb and salad turned into chicken and cold pasta.

"How have you been, Zuly?" he asked, turning to his friend as he cut a large piece of meat. "I feel as if I had not seen you much of late."

Zuly looked down at his food. "I-I have been busy training the new men."

"I hope they are doing better than the last time I stopped by to see them," Merlin said kindly.

"Just a bit." He shook his head. "They are messy, but I know they will be much better soon. I can only hope."

"You are training them. They will be fine."

After chewing a bit of chicken, Athena looked up at the two of them. "When do you believe they will be ready?"

"Soon, I hope," Zuly said.

They ate in silence for a few minutes.

"Merlin, did you see the jester when he came in?" Zuly asked, keeping his voice low.

"No. What happened?" Merlin asked after taking a sip of ale.

"When he came in through the main gate, some child told him that he was not funny."

Athena smiled.

"Not again," Merlin said lightly as he put his hand to his head.

Zuly laughed. "It gets better. He yelled at the kid until he cried, declaring he was the funniest man in the land. It was sad to watch, but I cannot lie. I found it hard not to laugh."

Merlin shook his head. "Only you would find that funny. Making a poor child cry is not amusing."

"Oh, you should have seen it," said Athena, obviously hiding her laughter. "I do not think he is that funny either." She lowered her voice. "But I would never dream of saying that to his face."

Zuly reached across the table and took a piece of chicken from her plate. "For the next banquet, I think we should stick with music. At least a singer has never made anyone cry."

The three of them laughed, but Zuly stopped short and took a deep breath. Merlin watched, knowing that his friend could smell anything for miles.

"Something is not right," Zuly whispered.

The castle shook hard, and the room fell quiet.

"What was that?" Athena asked, looking wide-eyed from Merlin to Zuly.

Merlin grabbed his wand. "I do not know. Zuly, come with me." He cleaned his lips with his napkin as he stood. "Do not worry," he told the crowd as they looked to him for reinsurance. "Enjoy your meal. We shall be back soon." He moved over to Athena and spoke in a low tone. "I will come get you if I need your help."

Once out of the great hall, Merlin turned to Zuly. "Something is not right. I can feel it."

They both paused, waiting for the shaking to come back or for a strange sound.

"What do you think it could be?" Zuly asked, resting his hand over the wand on his belt.

The castle shook again.

A guard ran over to them, seeming flushed. He bowed to Merlin before addressing his captain. "Sir, there is an intruder in the castle."

"What do you mean?" Merlin asked before Zuly could speak.

"A man broke in. So far, we do not know how. He has killed anyone who has gotten in his way. He is going towards the gem."

"What?!" Merlin gasped, feeling faint. "Who is he?!"

"I do not know, but he has strong magic."

He turned to Zuly, who looked much paler than normal. The gem was the reason everyone in this land had magic, some stronger than others. In the sunlight at the highest point of the castle, it had never moved in the history of the kingdom. If gone, magic would disappear, leaving everyone powerless.

"Zuly, do whatever you can. I need to get Athena," Merlin said.

"What about the villagers?"

Merlin looked at the guard. "Please advise them to teleport away from the castle immediately. Stay safe!"

Both Zuly and the guard bowed before Zuly left, and the guard stayed. Merlin took a deep breath and opened the great hall's door with the guard following close behind.

Merlin and Athena made eye contact. He gestured for her to come.

****

The sun's rays came in through the stained-glass window of Merlin's office. It filled the room with various colors. Many books, wands, and other items that any magical person might need filled this large room. A light ink smell lingered in the heavy air. On a normal day, this room was filled with life and magic. Merlin could sit behind his large oak desk for hours, ignoring the world. This room was his favorite, the one place that was truly *his*.

A room filled with wonder that was now empty.

It stayed calm until the heavy wooden door opened with a loud creek, and Merlin ran in. "Hurry!" His heart beat fast in his chest. "We do not have much time!"

His apprentice ran in after him, her face a light color of red from trying to keep up. "Yes, master!" She bent over, resting her hands on her knees, as she breathed heavy.

He looked around the room, his hands pushing objects all over. He searched for anything that could help them. His mind rushed as he looked through the mess of books and papers on his desk.

The castle shook once again, throwing them off-balance. Dust and pebbles fell from the ceiling and landed on Merlin and Athena as they shared a look of panic.

"What do we do, Merlin?" she asked.

He pulled a wand out from a bag by the window before turning to look through a spell book. He noticed how both of her hands fidgeted with her dress' hem. Her green eyes darted everywhere.

Never in all his life had someone broken into the castle with such bad intentions. But he could not let fear take over his young apprentice. "Athena," he said, "we are going to be fine!"

She released the hem, letting it drop back down, she moved her hands to her long, light orange hair that was done into a neat braid. She nodded to him.

Before he could tell her anything more, the castle shook again, much stronger this time. It knocked her off her feet. She landed on her side, catching herself with her hands. He grabbed onto the desk, making himself sturdy as everything shook around him. More dust and small stones fell. Athena coughed.

Merlin needed to do something fast. Once the shaking was not as bad, he let go of the desk and helped her back to her feet.

"Are you all right?" she asked with a shaky voice.

"Athena, we cannot let that man take the gem. We must do whatever it takes to keep it out of his hands."

She nodded as he handed her a wand. The shaking stopped, but the great wizard knew it was only temporary.

"What spell are we to do?" she asked.

"We should try Hucabufs and see if that one works. Stay close to me!" he said, hoping she would listen. She had never disobeyed him before, but he wanted her to understand that she must do as he said.

She nodded.

Zuly ran to the doorway, out of breath. "Your Highness!"

Merlin and Athena turned to look at him. His uniform that had been so neat a few minutes ago was now in disarray. The front metals had flipped over, his dark brown boots were scuffed, and his hair stuck to his forehead with sweat.

"The intruder has killed all my men! He made it to the gem!"

Merlin's eyes went wide. "What?!" he yelled out, not daring to believe it. *How can that be? They were trained by the best!*

"If you are going to do something, I think it should be now."

Merlin closed his eyes. The time of action was now; he only wished that no one had died. He met Zuly's panicked eyes, a rare emotion from him. "We are going now!" he said, taking Athena by the shoulder. "If things get bad, I will teleport you away from the danger."

"No! I want to stay with you!" she protested, holding her wand tightly.

"No, you must not! Athena, you will do as I ask. You must stay away till I come and get you," he said, meeting her eyes before looking up to Zuly. "If needed, Zuly will get you. You will not be alone again. I promise." He guided her out the door, passing their captain as they made their way up to the tower.

"Your Highness," Zuly called, making the pair pause to look back at him. "I will take this man by surprise. Distract him, so I can come in when he least expects it."

Merlin nodded. "Good plan, my friend."

"Stay safe, you two," he said, looking from Athena to Merlin.

"You as well!" she said, smiling at him before Merlin put his heavy hand on her shoulder once again.

"Stay safe, Zuly. I will see you after," he said, and they turned to head up to the gem.

Once they traveled up the tower, they found the man they were looking for. But the strong winds seemed like they might just knock them off the side if they were careless.

"There he is! The great wizard and his pet!" the man said over the wind as he turned around to face them. A white mask covered his face. "I thought you were just going to let me take the gem, but I see you *do* want to fight me for it. The great king of this land…" He raised his eyebrow, it peeking over the mask. "Should I feel honored you graced me with your presence?"

Merlin gripped his wand as he stared at this man. Athena looked up and copied her master, standing the same way he did.

"I do not know who you are, but I know what you want!" Merlin said in a stern voice, his eyebrows drawn. "I cannot let you have it!"

The man laughed, giving Merlin chills. "You will not let me?" he asked, mocking Merlin's voice. "Let me tell you something." He stepped closer to the gem that sat between them. The gem was large, the size of a nightstand. "When I, Achilles Remis, want something, I always get it."

"Back away from the gem!" Merlin called out sternly as anger filled his body. He did not want to talk to this man any longer than he needed to. His wand pointed at him.

Achilles brought out his own wand. "I'm not leaving here without this gem." He lifted it and shot a strong power toward Merlin.

Merlin launched in front of Athena and flicked his wand back toward the man.

Achilles laughed as he flicked his wand, moving the spell away. "Be careful, King. Or your pet might get a boo-boo."

Merlin shot a strong lightning spell toward the man. It hit his arm. With a yell, Merlin created a strong wind that sent Achilles back a few feet. Achilles flicked his wand, making Merlin lose his footing. He tumbled back till the back of his feet touched the air, having no more flooring to stand on.

"Merlin!" Athena yelled as he disappeared over the edge.

Merlin held onto the tower's edge with his fingertips. His wand dug into his palm. He was getting ready to teleport back up when Athena's head popped up from above him. She lay on her belly, reaching her left arm toward him.

"Merlin!" she yelled as she reached her arm farther down.

"Athena, you need to teleport out of here!" he yelled, fearing for her safety.

"No! I will not leave you!"

"Athena!" he yelled as she grabbed his hand. He saw the man in the mask come up behind her. "Athena, look out!"

She let go of Merlin, standing to face Achilles. "Stay away from me!" She used her wand to lift herself into the air and shot her powers down to him.

Since Achilles was busy fighting her, Merlin let go of the edge and used his wand to teleport. Pushing away his frustration, he stood back in the tower as she lowered herself down next to him.

Achilles laughed as he looked at the pair. "For such a powerful wizard, you sure let this child fight your battles for you."

Merlin knew that he was trying to get under his skin, but he was not going to let him. He and Athena were a team. He flicked his wand toward him, making him jump out of the way and move next to the tower's stairs. Away from the gem. Just like he wanted.

"Sorry, old man, but the powers of this land are mine!" Achilles hissed.

Merlin could tell that Achilles was getting blinded by his own anger, which he could use to his advantage. He stood between the man and the gem, and Athena followed him, not pointing her wand away from Achilles. Merlin hit the man again with pure power.

At the same time, Zuly came up the steps with his body low. He held his sword in one hand and his wand in the other. They made eye contact before Merlin looked back at Achilles, not wanting him to know that Zuly would attack from behind. He noticed Zuly's stare and poked Athena's back with his finger, so she'd look away from Zuly.

"Ready to die?" Achilles asked as he looked at the pair in front of him.

Merlin held his breath, waiting for Zuly to make the final blow. Zuly's eyes were set, but something on his face looked off to Merlin. Like he was overthinking it. *Do it!* He seemed like he was frozen with his sword up, ready to run it through the other man.

But then he lowered his sword and brought his wand up, pointing it away from the man's back. He turned to where Athena stood. Her eyes went wide. A second later, his spell flew toward her so fast that she did not have time to move or fight back. Merlin watched in horror as the spell hit the middle of her chest, making her scream. A scream he would never forget.

She dropped to the stone floor like a lifeless doll, one hand over her chest and the other reaching for him. Her eyes weakly opened as she looked toward him. She lifted her outstretched arm before her eyes closed again, and her arm dropped back down to the ground. Her wand rolled out of her hand.

"NO!" Merlin yelled, dropping to her lifeless side. His heart sank. He took her small hand in his while running his other hand down her innocent pale face. "Zuly, how could you?!"

Achilles and Zuly now stood next to each other, side by side.

Zuly's face had no remorse. "I let him into this world!" he said with pride, holding his wand tightly.

Merlin felt like an ice dagger stabbed his heart.

"Now, I serve him and only him. I do not listen to your orders anymore!"

"How could you?!" Merlin yelled, letting go of her hand as he stood. He did not want to leave her, but his anger pushed him. He and Zuly had been there for each other many times. How could he just turn on him so easily? How long had his trusted friend wanted this to happen? "Zuly," he muttered, "I trusted you. *She* trusted you." He pointed at Athena, but Zuly's face stayed hard like a stone.

"I have been planning this for longer than you could ever know. You were wrong to trust me."

Before any other words could be shared, Achilles flicked his wand, hitting Merlin with a spell that pushed him back hard. He fell out of the tower once more. He tried to grab the edge again, but this time, he missed.

His nails felt like they were ripping off as they clawed at the tower's side. While in the air, he used his magic to slow his fall before landing on the ground below. He landed harder than he would have liked, and pain shot through his body.

Everything had happened so fast that his mind still tried to take it all in.

The worst pain in his life swelled inside as his powers drained. It felt like his life force was being pulled from his soul. His whole body weakened. He dropped to the ground, resting his forehead on the cold stone and finding no strength to keep his head up. He breathed in heavy, knowing Achilles had just removed the gem.

"My kingdom!" he cried, looking to his land that no longer had the bright colors it used to moments ago.

In a matter of seconds, the land had turned into a nightmare. The trees' green leaves changed to the darkest grays, browns, and blacks. The grass around him also became a dark brown color. The sky darkened along with the clouds. The moat around the castle turned black like tar. It looked like something right out of his darkest nightmares.

"No," he whispered. "What have I done?"

His mind went back to Athena. Her endless joy and contagious smile were now gone forever. He would mourn her till his last breath!

But it was also no longer safe. He would continue the fight—to get the gem back—but his body seemed as if it would give up on him. He had to get off the castle grounds.

He grabbed his wand that he had dropped and hoped it had one more spell left in it. "Teleportsheam." It took everything in him, but he removed himself from his castle and landed in the middle of the woods.

He dropped to the ground with a rushing mind and a broken heart as he let out a sob.

Chapter 1

1954

Night was falling on the small, peaceful town of Duck, North Carolina. The warm sun had shone on the town all day, but now it lowered as the moon rose in the cool air. As the pink sunset turned into a night sky full of bright stars, lights from each shop and house turned on. Behind each light was a life, someone with their own story. It was always such a lovely sight to take in, something so peaceful.

But for fifteen-year-old Caroline Smith, these lights meant she was late. *Extremely* late. She had promised her grandmother to be home before the town lights turned on and long before the sun went down. But here she was, biking through town with Sal by her side. He tried to keep up with her fast pace on his own bike.

Tonight, she had to be home for dinner. It would be a late dinner, but Jewel, her grandmother, had insisted that they have a grand meal to celebrate. Today marked the one-year anniversary of when Caroline had moved in with her grandmother and her whole magical journey had started. The path was a hard one, but she wouldn't give it up for anything. Learning magic was a gift she held dearly to her heart. She loved the family she had found in Duck.

As she biked faster, her legs burned, and she took a deep breath, breathing in the salty air. Her brown hair flowed behind her in a low ponytail. Sal now trailed her, breathing heavy. He had started out as her friend when she got to Duck but had soon become so much more.

"Keep up!" she called, looking back as he started to fall behind.

"Why…can't…we…just…teleport?!"

"Because," she called back, "I get to spend more time with you this way!"

The house she called home was in the back of the neighborhood with the big blue ocean in front. Throughout the whole day, she could hear the waves breaking on the shore. It was one of the many things she loved about the house. She didn't even know if she could sleep without the sounds of the waves anymore.

Once she made it home, she put her bike away. Sal stood next to his bike, looking at her. She looked back as she fixed her ponytail. His hair was surprisingly neat, and his face was a light shade of pink from the bike ride.

She smiled. "What?" she asked as he smiled back at her.

"Oh, nothing. It's just that you've never biked that fast before." He put his bike's kickstand down and walked up to her.

She laughed, taking his hand in hers. "I told you I was late."

"I told you we could have gone to see the lighthouse another day."

"I know, but I've been here for a year, and I hadn't seen one up close yet," she said, recalling the view from the lighthouse. She had felt as if she was on top of the world.

"Well, go eat your dinner. I don't want Jewel to get mad that I kept you." He slowly approached her and kissed her lips. They shared a smile as he kissed her hand. He turned to get back on his bike.

"Good night," she said as she watched him leave, smiling the whole time. *Gosh, he's so handsome.* She looked down at where he had kissed her hand.

She took a second to look at the beach and hear the waves crashing on the shore. Though it was late, a few families were still out on the beach, talking and laughing. She looked up to see all the stars appearing one by one in the darkening sky before closing her eyes to take in the waves' crashes one more time.

One newer sound that had become present was gleeful screams as little crabs came out from the sand for the night. The long winter had seemed so quiet without that sound. This year already seemed to have more crabs than the year before. Those who visited Duck stayed out a bit later to watch them crawl out. Dutch tried to stay off the beach instead since he hated the idea of crabs crawling around him.

She walked up the few steps to the front door. Lights were on in the living room, along with lights in the kitchen where Jewel had been cooking for what seemed like an entire day. She had started when Caroline had woken up at seven a.m. and had insisted that she wanted no help. But she only knew how to cook with her magic. She would use her wand to make amazing meals in seconds. Without magic, it took her twice as long and was twice as messy.

Caroline opened the door. "I'm home!" As she walked in, she heard the radio. A smell filled her nose, but she couldn't tell what it was or if it was good.

Jewel popped her head around the corner. She had a big smile on her face along with what looked like mashed potato on her right cheek and a green bean stuck in her brown curly hair.

"You have a green bean in your hair," Caroline pointed out as she walked past her and into the kitchen.

Jewel stopped smiling and patted her head. "Oh boy." She pulled out the green bean and threw it into the trash.

"Do you need help, Grandma?" Caroline asked as she saw the mess. More mashed potatoes lay out of the pot than in it. A mess of seasoning bottles were on the counter, some open and spilling out onto the floor. She looked down and noticed that some bottles had rolled off the counter. She picked them up, not wanting Jewel to fall over them.

"I'm almost done cooking," Jewel said, walking back over to the stove and pulling a wooden spoon out from the mash potatoes. She pulled with force since the potatoes acted like a sticky paste.

"You made my favorite?" Caroline asked as she saw what looked like meatloaf on the table.

"Yep!" Jewel said. "That's why I made it today." As she spoke, she never looked up from what she was doing. She stayed focused as she put butter in the pot with her tongue sticking out the corner of her mouth.

"Hey, youngin!" Dutch called out from behind Caroline, making her turn to see him sitting where he sat every night at the table for dinner.

"Hi, oldie," she said.

He had lived next door long before Caroline was even born. Jewel and Dutch had been friends for even longer, but this past year, their friendship had become something more, something sweeter. Jewel liked to say they were sweethearts, but Caroline knew they would get married one day. When he looked at Jewel, Caroline saw love in his eyes. It was beautiful to see, and she hoped that she and Sal would have that type of love for each other one day.

"What did you do today?" he asked, pulling out a chair for her to sit next to him.

She took the seat, folding her hands on the table. "Well, Sal wanted to do something fun today, so he took me to see a lighthouse."

Jewel turned back and smiled. "Was this the lighthouse you had been asking me to take you to?"

"Yes. We should go together one day. The view was amazing." A part of her was glad that it had been Sal who took her. The thought of them holding hands at the lighthouse had been lovely. "Do you need help, Grandma?"

"No, sweetie. I'm done," Jewel said, cleaning her hands. "But you can help me set the table."

The dinner was better than Caroline had thought it would be. Jewel even looked surprised by how good it tasted. The only thing Caroline didn't like was the mashed potatoes; they were gummy somehow and tasted like school glue. Though no one dared to say it, it was clear that no one liked them because they were the only things that remained on their plates.

Once they finished eating and cleaning up, Dutch suggested they play charades together. He and Jewel moved the coffee table out of the living room, so they had more room to play. Caroline turned on the record player, putting Nat King Cole on low. The music lightly filled their ears.

Jewel pulled out the cards, holding them facedown. "All right. Who wants to go first?" she asked, sitting on the sofa.

"I think the girl who changed our lives a year ago

should go first," Dutch said as he winked at Caroline with his light blue eyes.

Caroline smiled and took one of the cards from Jewel's hand. It read *seagull!* She knew this card would be easy since she had seen them fly every day. She stood in the middle of the room, facing Jewel and Dutch. She flapped her arms up and down as if she was flying. She thought it was clear, but it was not.

"Plane! Fanning a fire! Flaring!" he called out loudly.

Caroline jumped, flaring her wrists hard. She tucked her arms in like a bird on land, walking around the way she had seen them on the beach. She even bobbed her head as she moved.

"Kid, what the heck are you?" he asked as Jewel laughed.

"Caroline, stop," she said. "You're going to hurt yourself. Time is up."

Caroline stopped and looked at Dutch. "How did you not know what I was?" she asked, sounding a bit irritated.

"How could I?"

"It was a seagull!"

Jewel laughed even harder. "No, it was not!"

Caroline made her way to the sofa with her arms crossed. "Whatever. Whose turn is it?"

As they played for a bit longer, no one really kept points. They were all just having fun and learning that Caroline was no good at this game, which frustrated her. She sat on the sofa with her arms crossed as Dutch picked up the last card.

He smiled. "Okay. Here we go," he said as he put it back. He moved to stand right in front of Jewel as he reached into his back pocket, pulling out a small box. "Jewel," he said as he got down on one knee, "will you marry me?"

"What…" Jewel muttered as she put her hand to her chest. A smile grew on her lips. She covered her mouth with her hands as the diamond sparkled back at her. "Dutch…"

Caroline smiled as she looked between Dutch and Jewel. She knew he had wanted to ask Jewel this question for what had felt like the longest time. A few months ago, he had told her all about the idea after he had picked her up from school. He had wasted no time to ask her if she was fine with it.

She had stopped walking and looked up at him with the biggest smile. "Are you kidding me?! Of course!" She gave him a hug. "Oh, I am so happy for you both! When are you going to ask her?"

"I'm happy too. One reason I wanted to pick you up today was because I want you to help me pick the ring," he had said as they started walking to the car again.

"This is so exciting! You're going to be my grandpa!" She could not stop smiling. "When can I start calling you grandpa?!"

Dutch smiled as he opened the door to his Bristol 401 for her. "I would like that but not until I ask your grandma. I don't want her to have any idea it's coming."

Each day that went by, Caroline had waited for him to ask Jewel the big question. She would look across the table at them and wonder if today was the day. And at last, the day had come!

As she watched the pair, excitement coursed through her. She looked at her grandmother and waited for her answer.

"I'm sorry, Dutch," Jewel said shyly.

Caroline froze. *What?*

Dutch's smile fell. "Jewel?" he whispered.

"Dutch, we have only been going steady for almost a year."

Hurt was written all over his face. "But we've known each other for years, longer than I even know."

"I know, but—"

He stopped her, raising his hand. "I-I don't get it." He stood. "I love you, and I've stayed by your side when you needed me the most. So what if it's only been a year? We have been through more than anyone has."

She sighed, looking away from him.

Caroline no longer smiled as she looked back at Jewel. She had thought Jewel would be jumping and hugging him. Not this.

"Dutch, it's too soon."

"I don't understand why—"

Jewel raised her hand to stop him, making both him and Caroline look at her in shock. "I think you should go home."

Caroline's body went numb.

Dutch looked as if his heart had been broken into two pieces. "What? Jewel…"

Jewel walked away and then slowly turned back to him. "Please go."

His arms dropped to his sides.

"Grandma?" Caroline called softly.

But she left the room and headed up the stairs.

"Good night, Caroline," he muttered before turning toward the front door.

"Wait!" Caroline said, moving fast to get in front of him. She put her hands up to stop him from leaving. "She'll come around."

He didn't look her in the eyes.

She followed his gaze to the ring box still in his hand.

"I'm sorry," she mumbled as the weight of the night fell on her. She looked up to find tears building in his eyes, making her heart break.

"Good night, youngin." He sighed, resting his hand on her shoulder before he headed out the door.

Chapter 2

The next week went by slowly. Each day clawed by as if it lasted a lifetime. Dutch had not come over once to work on Caroline's magic like they did every day after lunch or to eat dinner with her and Jewel. Even Jewel stopped training her, leaving her alone most afternoons. Caroline missed him already. *Are things never going to go back to normal?*

After a few days had passed, Caroline had asked Jewel what had happened, why she had said no so harshly, but she would answer in ways that really had no true answer. Or she would change the subject, leaving Caroline to feel like an outsider.

"Grandma, I'm your granddaughter. You can tell me anything," she had said one night, while they had a quiet dinner.

"Caroline, please understand I need time to think."

"What does that even mean?" she had asked, putting down her glass hard.

Jewel had taken a large bite of her dinner before answering. "So, how was your day?"

"I'm not going to tell you! I MISS DUTCH!"

"I went shopping today. I found the cutest thing for the kitchen."

Each night, Caroline would look out the kitchen window to find Dutch sitting in his living room. He'd read a book or just sit, looking deep in thought. It was clear that he was broken by everything that had happened.

Once, he raised his head, looking toward her. She gave him a small wave. How she wished she could tell him how much she missed him. He weakly waved back before leaving the room, out of sight. It seemed that even seeing her brought him painful thoughts. She sighed before getting what she needed out of the kitchen.

****

"I just don't get it," Caroline said, sitting next to Sal on the sofa.

"It's a big mess," he said, looking at her with understanding eyes. "Adults know how to make everything so complicated."

She nodded. "Hold the training wand like this." She held hers.

"Like this?" he asked, copying her.

Shortly after Achilles—her parents' murderer—had died, Sal wanted to learn how to use magic. He had told her that he was fascinated with everything she could do with her powers, and they had agreed that she would teach him some. They would meet up whenever Jewel was not home, which almost never happened, but these days, she was gone for hours.

Though he was not the best at magic and would get frustrated, she enjoyed sharing her gift with him. He had some magic in him but not enough to make training easy. Still, she found herself looking forward to the days when Jewel was out.

As far as she was concerned, Jewel didn't need to

know. A very small part of her wanted to tell Jewel—wondering why she found the need to hide this from her—but she thought Jewel would get mad at her for teaching magic to someone *normal*. Not even Dutch knew. She would let them know when the time was right.

"They haven't talked in a week," she said, looking over at Sal. "Hold it like this." She showed him how to hold the wand right once more.

His face looked like he was in deep concentration. She took a second to look at it, a small smile growing on her own.

His eyes never looked away from the training wand. "Like this?" he asked again, changing his hold.

"Yes, that's right."

"Jewel and Dutch just need something to do that will get them to work together again," he said as he stood.

Work together? "That could work! They just need something to do together. They're not even training me at the moment. I know Achilles is gone, but I would still like to know some new things."

Sal nodded. "Don't worry about training for now. Try to do something new with them."

"Sal…" she said as he raised his eyebrows. "You. Are. A. Genius! Maybe I can get them to meet at the donut shop or something."

A playful smile grew on his face. "I know I'm a genius. That's old news." He tried to read the spell book that was open on the coffee table but seemed confused. "What does this spell do again?"

"It's to teleport. Like from room to room or from city to city." She stood next to him. "Think about where or who you want to go to."

He nodded. "So, what do I think about?"

"Since it's your first time," she said, looking around, "just think about my kitchen table, and you'll teleport to that room."

His eyebrows moved closer together. "But you're not the only person with that table."

"What?"

"I'm just saying what if a neighbor has that table? Or the president?"

She looked puzzled. "I doubt Eisenhower has the same table as we do."

"But what if I teleport to someone else's house by mistake?" He spoke with such worry that it made Caroline scratch her head.

"What?!"

"I'm just saying what if I think of the wrong table?"

"Sal, you're overthinking it," she said. She tried to keep her voice at one level, not wanting him to think she was getting frustrated, but she was. A part of her wanted to laugh too. "Just think about the table."

"What does your table look like again?" he asked with a shy smile.

"Okay…" She looked around the room for something that would not stress him out. "The stairs. Teleport to the stairs," she said, pointing to the staircase.

"But what if—"

"Ohmygosh. Just do the spell!" she said with a frustrated laugh.

He held his wand out in front of him. He flicked his wrist, keeping his eyes on the stairs, and for a second, she was worried he would go to someone else's stairs like he had said. "Teleportsheam."

She held her breath, but after a few seconds, nothing happened, and she let it go. Out of the blue, Sal's wand seemed to explode in his hands. They both jumped back as smoke filled their lungs.

With a wave of her wand, she made the smoke disappear before looking back to see that he was nowhere to be seen. "Where are you?!" she called out in full panic. She looked around with millions of thoughts running through her mind.

"Bathroom!" he yelled out, sounding far away.

"How?" she asked as he walked back into the room.

His hair was pushed back, out of his face, and he had ashes on his forehead. "What happened?" he asked, looking at the broken wand in his hand.

"You did something wrong."

"I broke the training wand." He held it so she could see. "Has that ever happened to you?"

"No," she said. As she looked up, she noticed that his face had turned a light shade of red. "Sal, it's okay." She rested her hand on his shoulder.

"This is so hard!" he exclaimed. He moved away from her, and her hand fell back down to her side. "I have been doing this crap for almost a year, and I still can't do one spell right!" He threw what was left of his wand at the floor, making it bounce.

Caroline looked at him, surprised. She had never seen him this worked up before. "Let's calm down," she said sternly, not liking that he had thrown his wand and yelled. Her smile was long gone.

"Fine!" he said, putting his hands up in defense and throwing himself onto the sofa.

She picked his wand up from the floor and put it on the coffee table. "I won't train you again if you act like this, Sal."

"You make it look so easy," he said, still sounding mad as he took a cookie from the plate on the coffee table.

"It's not easy. I also had the hardest time at first. I lit Dutch's shoes on fire." Her heart tugged at the thought that she had not seen Dutch in days.

"Let's call it a day," Sal said. He looked out the window as if he didn't hear her.

"Calm down. It's not that serious."

To her surprise, he laughed. He looked back at her, his face much softer than before. "Sorry. I got frustrated," he said, putting his arm over her shoulder after she sat next to him.

"With me?" she asked.

"Never. Magic is just harder than it looks. You know I suck at school. I thought this would be easier. Sorry I yelled at you."

"Please don't do it again. I don't like yelling. It brings up bad memories from my past." She leaned her head on his shoulder.

"I promise I won't. Sorry."

"Thank you. But hey, you'll get it at some point." She looked back at him and lifted her wand, fixing his hair and cleaning his face.

She looked deep into his eyes. The house stilled as they stayed that way for a few seconds. She could feel his breath on her cheeks, making her heart beat faster. She had not realized how close he had gotten. He moved even closer, leaving a kiss on her lips. She put her hand through his soft hair as he caressed the back of her neck.

"I'm home!" Jewel called from the front door.

Sal and Caroline jumped away from each other. Her heart beat even faster now, if possible. He moved to the chair next to the sofa.

"Hey guys!" Jewel called as she stepped toward the room with a few shopping bags.

Caroline covered the spell book with a few of Jewel's *McCall's* and *Life* magazines, Marilyn smiling up at her. She also pushed the wands under a pillow. "Hey, Grandma," she said, acting like she was not just kissing Sal or teaching him magic. She held her breath as her grandmother walked into the room.

Jewel set her bags down by Caroline.

Caroline saw Sal let go of his breath, clearly thinking the same things she was. "What did you find at the stores?" she asked, turning her attention to the small bags at her feet.

"Oh. Hi, Sal," Jewel said, seeming to just notice him.

He smiled. "Hello."

"I got some fall decorations and a necklace I liked," she said, sitting where Sal had been moments ago.

Caroline brought the bags up to her lap, pulling out what was inside.

"Wow. Fall stuff already? Summer just started," Sal said with a laugh.

She looked over and noticed that he had her lipstick on his face. Her eyes almost came out of her head. As her grandmother looked into one of the small brown bags, she made hard eye contact with him and moved her thumb over her bottom lip as if she was wiping something off. Thankfully, he noticed and wiped his lips.

"I know it's early," Jewel said as Caroline made a mental note to wear a lighter shade of lipstick. "But this scarf was just too pretty to leave behind."

"I agree," Caroline said as Sal nodded. She looked at her grandmother, and something in her heart felt that seeing her grandmother happy was wrong after what had happened.

"So, what are you two up to? If I had known Sal was coming over, I would have invited you both to come with me."

"We were just talking," Caroline said.

Jewel looked over at Sal. "Would you like to stay for dinner?"

He smiled. "I would love to, but my grandfather wants me home for dinner because he needs help with something after we eat. We bought a television, and he wants my help setting it up. Grandma also just wants me to be there when we turn it on for the first time."

"No way!" Jewel said. "I would have never thought Bob and Patti would get something so futuristic."

His smile only grew. "I know! I talked them into it. Been talking their ears off about one since 1950!"

Caroline smiled, remembering what a big deal it was when Uncle Edmund had bought one. Everyone had been bursting with anticipation for the little black screen to come alive. Norna and her older brother had made so much popcorn, filling the memory with a sweet smell.

"Maybe another night for dinner then," Jewel said. "Oh, before I forget, Mayor Scott was passing out a flyer that said he will be doing a speech tonight." She pulled two flyers out of one of the brown bags. "The flyer said it's nothing super important, but he would like it if everyone could be there." She handed one to Sal.

"I'll give this to my grandparents," he said.

"Who knows if you can go?" Caroline laughed. "Maybe you'll be watching the stars on your television all night."

He chuckled. "The television turns off at midnight."

He then stood, grabbing his leather jacket off the back of the chair. "I hope to see one of those broadcasted shows. Like a series on Walt, the man who drew the famous mouse."

"I heard he bought one hundred and sixty acres to open a theme park in California," Jewel said, making Caroline and Sal gasp together.

"Really?!" she asked. "Can we go?" She grabbed her grandmother's arm. She had watched Walt's movies and the broadcasts with Jewel and Dutch. It would make her year if she could go to such a magical place.

"We'll see," Jewel said with a smile. "I don't even know when it's going to open."

"It would be so much fun to go with you and Dutch."

Jewel's eyes dropped at the mention of Dutch.

After an awkward silence, Sal spoke up. "I'm going home. I'll see you both later."

"Bye, Sal," Caroline said as he closed the door. She turned back to her grandmother. "I have a question."

"What's wrong?" Jewel asked.

"You try to act like nothing has happened, but I know you." She pointed to the shopping bags, knowing Jewel was hiding her pain with shopping. "You miss Dutch. Why are you acting like my age and not talking with him?"

Jewel looked down at her hands in her lap. "I didn't say no."

"You said no in the worst way."

"Look, I don't know why I did what I did. I've been thinking about it, and I still don't know what to think of it." She got up to leave.

"Why do you keep leaving me like this? Why can't we talk about it?" Caroline asked, following her out of the room and into the kitchen.

"It's not that simple. I can't just go and talk to him. Not yet," she said, turning to face Caroline.

"Why not?" she asked, crossing her arms. Sal had been right. Adults could make messes out of nothing. Jewel and Dutch had never fought that she knew of. So, this seemed as if it came out of nowhere.

"Look," Jewel said, "can we talk about something different?"

"No. We have to talk about this. Dutch is really sad."

"Have you talked to him?" she asked in a strange voice.

"No, but I've seen him through the window, and he looks broken. You did that!"

She took a deep breath. "Caroline," she said with her voice full of emotion, "how was your day?"

"AH!" Caroline cried out. "It was fine! Thank you! But one day, you're going to have to talk to either me or him about this! You can't keep running from this! I'm your granddaughter! We always tell each other everything!"

Jewel acted as if she didn't hear her as she went to start dinner.

Caroline sighed. "Fine. I'm going to get ready for the meeting tonight." She left the room, leaving her grandmother alone.

Chapter 3

Soon, people filled the courthouse to hear the mayor's speech. With so many vacationers visiting the town, it was easy to forget how small the population was.

Caroline and Jewel walked toward the middle of the crowded room. After she had been out in the hot summer night, the cold room filled her arms with goosebumps. More people than she had thought had shown up at such a short notice. She looked through the crowd for a familiar face, getting on her tiptoes.

"Who are you looking for?" Jewel asked. Since she was a foot and a half taller, she bent over, trying to see what Caroline was looking at.

Caroline looked at her grandmother, smiling. "I'm looking for Dutch. He never misses a meeting."

"Caroline…" She stood straight again. "Can you drop it please? I don't want you stressing over—"

"Dutch!" Caroline called out, cutting Jewel off. She waved at him.

He was talking to Elena and Hector, the owners of the donut shop in town, but he looked back, scanning the room. Once they made eye contact, he walked over, making his way through the crowd. "Hey youngin," he said, giving her a hug. Then his voice flattened, and he put his hands in his suit pockets. "Jewel."

He was dressed in a brown suit with a white-collared shirt, his black tie laying on his chest. He also had a hat that matched his suit, and even though he looked so well put together, his eyes told a different story.

Jewel just gave him a half smile. Even with those talking around them, silence sat heavy between them, painfully noticeable. Caroline's eyes darted from his to her grandmother's face, waiting to see who would speak first.

Before anyone could share a word, Scott walked out onto the small stage, making the crowd clap and shout with joy. Caroline jumped at the sudden noise. Dutch turned back to face the stage while moving next to her. She now stood between Jewel and him.

"Hello, my good people!" Scott said with a warm smile. His bright yellow tie stood out from his gray suit. His umber skin blushed at the applause. "How is everyone doing on this fine night? We are having some great weather."

Scott Dickerson had won last year's election for town mayor after going against Achilles all last summer. A few days before the voting, Achilles had died, leaving Scott to happily take the position. It seemed as if everyone had forgotten Achilles much faster than she thought they would. It helped that Scott was a good mayor.

He rested his hands on the podium. "Thank you for coming. I wanted to share with you all a last-minute event that will happen next Sunday here at the courthouse. We will be hosting a small party. Nothing big but something fun for the summer that all ages will enjoy. There will be food, music, and a good time. On the way out, grab a flyer from my assistant, so you don't miss it."

Everyone looked at one another, seeming excited at the promise of a fun night. Caroline imagined herself dancing with Sal, making her heart flutter.

Scott smiled as he fixed the cards in his hands. "Also, as most of you might know," he continued, "Achilles left this town almost a year ago."

At the mention of Achilles' name, Caroline's body filled with chills. Because of him, she had lost so much and almost lost Jewel. She had many nightmares about him, like he had died just to haunt her dreams. She could no longer sleep in the dark; she always needed a light on. If not, she would see his face in the darkness. Though so much time had gone by, it was still hard for her to think about him.

"We all thought he would come back to us," Scott continued, hiding a smile. "But as his absence continues, we see that he will not. So, I must ask something of you. I was taking a walk the other day, and I happened to pass his old home. It looks abandoned and does not represent our town well. I would like to ask some of you to clean out his house."

Everyone in the crowd looked at each other and muttered.

"I'm not doing that," someone mumbled.

"It would only take a few days," Scott said, raising his hands to hush the crowd. "I made plans to remodel it, so families can rent it out for vacations." He paused. "I know what I am asking is a lot, but it would be a great act to your town and to me."

Caroline could not even imagine a family staying in his house. The thought of sleeping in it gave her the creeps.

She glanced over to her left and spotted Sal standing a few feet away with his family. Then she looked over to

Dutch and Jewel. Sal's words from a few hours ago played in her mind. *They need to do something together!* This was perfect. Plus, no one else should clean Achilles' house. He had a whole room filled with magical things. If someone found that stuff, it could be bad.

"ME!" she called out loud enough for everyone to hear. She raised her arm up high.

Everyone looked back at her with glad faces, and Scott smiled. But Jewel seemed surprised. Dutch stared at Jewel, sharing the same confused look.

"I will do it!" Caroline took Jewel's and Dutch's hands in hers. "With my grandma and Dutch. We will clean out Achilles' house."

This was what Jewel and Dutch needed. Something to get them working together again. Things would go back to the way they were in no time. And maybe she could even take some things from Achilles' magic room and learn how to use her powers more.

"Caroline!" Jewel whispered, trying to act calm.

"Wonderful!" Scott said happily. "Caroline, that is such a kind thing to do. Thank you."

Everyone clapped.

Everyone but Jewel, who looked at her. "Caroline, why?" she asked.

Caroline kept her voice low. "We'll have fun."

****

The next morning, Caroline, Jewel, and Dutch headed over to Achilles' house with many trash bags.

"I wish we didn't have to do this!" Jewel said for what felt like the millionth time as they walked up to the house. All night and morning, she had been whining like a young child.

The house was just as Caroline had remembered it: dark and spooky. Even though the man who had lived in it was no longer there, she could still feel him.

Just by the outside alone, it was clear that no one had lived there for some time now. The tall grass looked dry as it came almost up to Dutch's knees. Pushing her way through the grass and the weeds, she feared something hid in them, just out of sight. Some vines climbed up the side of the house as if nature was trying to pull the house under the earth.

Anxiety made her heart beat fast. Taking a deep breath, she told herself that this was not like the last time. No one who would hurt her was waiting inside.

"I still can't believe you talked me into this," Jewel said a few feet behind her.

"Grandma, just think about all the magical things he owned that no one else can see." She stepped up onto the small porch and turned to look back. "We have to do this."

Jewel sighed, stepping up next to her.

Dutch walked up next as he dusted his pants off. "Tonight, we'll have to check if we have any ticks from walking through that jungle."

"Good thing we wore pants today," Caroline said with a smile.

Each of them were dressed much more comfortably than they normally would be. Dutch wore light-colored jeans that folded at the ankles, showing off his white socks. He also had a white short-sleeved shirt. Jewel had on gray and green plaid pants with an off-white blouse. Her cobbler apron had flower prints with large pockets, where Caroline knew she hid her wand. Her curly hair was neatly pinned up, out of her face. Caroline wore peach pants with her favorite pastel short-sleeved shirt and her own red cobbler apron. She pushed back a lock of brown hair that had fallen out of her ponytail.

Dutch went to open the wooden door, but as he tried to open it, he walked straight into it. He grunted as his body made a thud against the door. He tried again, but nothing happened. "It's stuck." He tried once more.

"Do we need a spell?" Caroline asked, reaching for her wand in her apron's pocket.

"Hang on," he said as he backed away from the door.

Jewel looked at him, raising an eyebrow. Caroline flicked her wand, and the door opened just as he ran up to it as fast as he could. He fell inside with a loud bang. Dust lifted from where he landed, making them cough and sneeze.

"Sorry," she said, trying to cover her laughter.

Jewel chuckled under her breath.

Dutch stood, dusting himself off. They all looked around to find a dark and dirty home. No one moved for a moment.

"Oh boy," Jewel said as a strong smell met them even before they walked in.

One by one, they slowly made their way through the front door and looked at what had become of Achilles' house. With their trash bags in hand, they walked through a hallway. A thick layer of dust covered the floors, and the stale air felt heavy. The dust in the air tickled Caroline's nose. A smell like nothing she had ever smelled before added to everything she saw. Since an open window had let in rain from past storms, mold grew on the wall and floor by the window.

A large rat ran right over Jewel's foot. She yelled, kicking as it ran from her. Both Dutch and Caroline jumped.

Jewel jumped, flaring her arms. "That is so nasty! It touched me with its little rat feet!"

Dutch held in a laugh. "It's okay. It's okay," he said kindly as he continued to walk through the house. "This place is gross!" He covered his nose as he found a small mountain of rat poop. "Poopoonono." He waved his wand, and the poop disappeared. "There will be none of that!"

Jewel sighed. "That spell made parenthood so much easier."

He then turned to the window, pointing his wand at the mold. "Restoration." It disappeared as well.

"You okay?" Caroline asked, walking up to her grandmother.

"Not really! A rat walked on me!" Jewel cried, holding the bags in her hand tight. "Did you see how big that thing was?!"

Caroline laughed.

Jewel lightly pushed her. "It's not funny! We had contact."

She left Jewel to deal with what had happened. She walked past Achilles' magic room and froze. As she looked inside, memories filled her mind. She saw the chair that Achilles had her tied up to the year before. She remembered how a big part of her thought she was going to die that night. She took a deep breath as Jewel walked up next to her.

"Are you all right?" Jewel asked as she tucked a lock of Caroline's hair behind her ear.

"I believe so," she said, taking her eyes off the chair to meet her grandmother's.

She walked past the room and toward the rest of the house.

Dutch poked a dead roach with his wand. "Where do we start? This place is a mess."

"Don't touch it!" Jewel cried out.

The closer Caroline got to the kitchen, the worse it smelled. The leftover food had become rotten; that much was clear. Jewel and Dutch followed her. Jewel gagged, covering her nose and mouth with her hands. Her face turned a light shade of green.

"Jewel, you can go home if you'd like," Dutch said.

"NO!" Caroline said, making them both look over at her. She awkwardly smiled. If Jewel went home, this would all be for nothing. "We need all the help we can get."

"Fine," Jewel said, sounding displeased. "Let's start where the smell is the worst to get that over with."

"Go team!" Caroline said, trying to sound excited about the day ahead of them.

Chapter 4

The three of them got to work, and many trash bags were filled with old food and trash that they had found in the kitchen alone. Caroline cleaned the counters, while Jewel cleaned out the refrigerator. Dutch used his wand to make all the cups and plates float off the shelves and into a bag for the poor. Jewel had used her magic to bring the broom and duster to life, so they had little helpers as they cleaned.

Dutch opened the oven, and a few cockroaches waddled out, making him jump back. "Oh gosh!"

Jewel jumped up onto the counter. "Shut it!" she yelled, and he did.

They watched as the large red bugs hid under the refrigerator and stove.

"Why?" she cried, sounding like she wanted to cry. "As a child, I never cleaned such a thing! We had money."

Caroline looked over at her. "Your family had money growing up?"

She nodded. "I was born and raised in Charleston." She looked down as the last cockroach hid under the stove. "My father was the town mayor, so we were well looked upon. I never had to clean!"

Caroline didn't know that. "That's really swell. Did you have maids and butlers?"

"Yes." She screamed as a rat came up next to her on the counter. She jumped and went toward Dutch.

"Are you all right?" he asked as he rested his hands on her shoulders.

She looked up at him. "I've been better!"

He looked at her kindly for a moment, but then his face hardened.

"I'm going to clean the hidden room," Caroline said, leaving them alone to talk if they wanted to.

"I'll go with you," Jewel said, making her freeze.

How hard was it to keep them together? She just wanted them to talk. She looked over to Dutch. "Hey! Dutch, come with us. It will be faster if we all work together."

He didn't look like he wanted to, but she smiled, and he sighed, following them into the hidden room. As they got there, they all looked around, not too sure where to start.

"The mess from the fight is still here," Dutch said.

"Yeah," Caroline mumbled.

Holes lined the walls, things were knocked over, books lay all along the floor, and thick layers of dust covered every surface. Caroline spotted a large map on the wall as a spider crawled across it. The desk in the back looked as if spiders lived within it, covered in many spiderwebs, and a large mirror she had not noticed before had cobwebs around it.

The beautiful gold framed mirror called her attention. It was so big that she was unsure how she had missed it the last time. She saw herself in the reflection and felt like someone was looking back at her. It gave her chills the longer she looked at it.

"I've had it with the dirty looks! Why are you so mad at me?" Jewel asked, putting her hands on her hips.

Caroline looked over to find Dutch cleaning off a table and ignoring Jewel.

"Dutch!" she said.

He still didn't turn to face her.

"Stop ignoring me!" she yelled, sounding frustrated.

His eyebrows were drawn down. "Fine!" he snapped, turning to her and raising his voice. "You want to know why? You want to know why I'm mad at you? It's because you hurt me!"

No one spoke, making the tension thick. Caroline didn't want to just stand there and watch them fight, so she picked up a few things, like trash and books, from the floor.

"Dutch, I'm sorry," Jewel said after a few seconds. "But you can't just ask me such a big thing and then—"

"Then what?!" he yelled, cutting her off.

"You have no right to yell at me!" she said sternly.

Caroline held her breath. She thought that maybe she should leave the room but feared Jewel would use her as an excuse to leave.

"Dutch, the other night…" Jewel looked flustered as she spoke. "It scared me, and I don't know why."

He rolled his eyes.

"Y-you can't just ask me something like that and not think about what I am feeling!"

"You don't tell me what you're feeling!" he yelled, throwing his arms up. "You never do! Not anymore! After your accident, you closed yourself up!"

Caroline looked up at the pair, waiting to see what Jewel would do. It was clear that Jewel had changed since the accident last year. She held more things to herself, not sharing as much.

"Since your fall, you haven't talked to me like you used to! Have you thought about how that makes me feel?"

Jewel's eyes filled with tears, but she blinked them back. "Do you think it's easy? Caroline healed me, but I still remember how horrible those weeks were. I feel so guilty when I think of all I put you through. I am the one who is supposed to take care of her, not the other way around! I just don't want to put you through anything more."

Dutch's face fell.

A tear rolled down Caroline's cheek. Still talking about it hurt.

"Jewel, I really care about you," he said, speaking much softer than before. "You can tell me anything, and I will hold your hand. You've never been a problem to me. Or to Caroline. She never once complained while taking care of you."

Caroline nodded as her grandmother looked over at her. "It's true."

Jewel looked back at Dutch. They both stayed quiet for a few moments till she said, "Did you think I was going to say yes after only a year of going steady?"

Caroline sighed as she picked up more books. The back of her foot landed on a corner of a book, which slipped out underneath her. She lost her footing, gasping as she fell back. She hit the wall and the large golden framed mirror and yelped. Jewel and Dutch looked over just in time to see her body hit the mirror's glass.

She disappeared as the glass pulled her in, glittering for a second before looking as if nothing had happened at all.

****

45

Caroline hit the ground, her face slamming into the dirt. She lifted her head and spat out a blade of grass. The trash bag she had been holding had fallen out of her hand, landing next to her. *Where am I?* She pushed herself up and took notice of her surroundings.

The first thing that caught her eyes were the tall, dark trees with dark-colored leaves. She looked up to see if she could find the treetops, but they seemed to go so high that they became a part of the sky. The leaves moved in a light breeze, making a soft sound as they pushed up against each other.

Caroline stood. The mirror she had fallen through floated in place with no reflection. It dawned on her that there was another world hidden behind the glass.

Her heart beat faster. "What just happened?!" she asked, not daring to step away from the mirror in fear that it would disappear. Anxiety grew within her, making her chest tight. A breeze lifted her hair off her neck, and the leaves moved again.

She looked up at the sky. Unlike her usual sunny morning, this dark sky looked like a storm was coming.

She dared to take a step forward, making the grass crunch underneath her like it had never been stepped on before. Everything in this forest looked so untouched by humans. Not one leaf lay on the ground. The dark plants looked so unnatural; she had never seen something so oddly beautiful.

"Hello?" Caroline called out, slowly walking a bit farther into the forest. She didn't want to go too far from the mirror, but something pulled her forward.

A cold but welcoming wind pushed past her face. She wondered why Achilles would hold onto such a lovely and peaceful place.

A soft voice from far away spoke. At first, she couldn't make out what they were saying, but she stood still, holding her breath.

"Someday, she will find us."

Caroline's head snapped to where she thought the sound came from. The male voice was deep, filled with care. It sounded so warm and comforting. But who? Who else was in this world, and who were they talking about?

She thought about running back to the mirror, praying it would let her go back home. But she stayed right where she was, waiting for the voice to speak again.

"I have faith in my girl," he continued.

Is someone else stuck here? Am I stuck?! She took a few steps closer to where she thought the male voice might be but stopped. A voice in the back of her head sent off warning signs. Maybe following a random voice in a strange place was not her best idea. She put her hand over the apron's pocket, feeling her wand.

"Caroline will find us."

Her head spun. She backed up as she realized why the voice sounded so familiar. Her breath caught in her throat. "Dad?"

But her father had been killed. Achilles murdered him eleven years ago, along with her mother. Yet this voice was the one she had heard in her dreams and in the magical books that took her to her memories. It had to be her father.

She walked forward, forgetting about the mirror and her fear. She went faster with every step. If her father was alive, why was he here? Or was this a trick by Achilles?

The voice spoke again. "She will find us someday."

Caroline's eyes filled with tears. "Daddy!" she cried out.

A strong hand grabbed her shoulder, holding her tight. She gasped as it pulled her hard, making her fall back through the mirror before she could even realize what was happening.

The voice spoke one last time. "Caroline will find us."

Chapter 5

"Are you all right?" Dutch asked Caroline as he helped her to her feet.

Her hands were cold for reasons she didn't know, which made his warm hands welcoming. Her mind was confused and dazed as she looked from her grandmother to Dutch. "What happened?"

"I just went in and pulled you back." He sounded out of breath.

Jewel pulled Caroline into a hug, holding her tightly. "Are you okay?!" she asked, cupping her granddaughter's face.

Caroline grabbed her grandmother's hands. "I'm fine." She looked back up at the mirror on the wall with so many thoughts running through her mind. Once more, she felt as if someone was looking back at her through the glass. "I heard my dad's voice."

"What?" Jewel asked softly, sounding distant. She looked up at the mirror behind her, their eyes meeting in the reflection.

Caroline walked over to the mirror and rested her hand on the cold frame. "I heard his voice as clear as day!"

Dutch and Jewel looked at each other, sharing a confused gaze.

She saw their doubt in the mirror and turned to face them. "He's in there! He said my name. I didn't see him, but I know it was him. He said I would find him." She turned back to the mirror. "He needs me."

"How do you know it was him? What if it is a trick?" Jewel asked, sounding unsure.

Caroline saw concern in her eyes. "I didn't see him, but Grandma, it was him." She put her hand on the glass. It was colder than the frame, and it pulled like it was trying to take her back in. How she wished it would.

"Caroline," Dutch said, making her look over to him, "I went in there to get you." He paused as she held her breath. "I didn't hear anything."

Her heart dropped.

"It could be a trick. One last trick from Achilles," Jewel said.

"But…" she muttered as she looked down at her feet. "I heard him." She wished she could run into her father's arms and give him a loving hug.

"Let's go back home." Dutch lightly grabbed her arm. He waved his wand with his free hand, and a jacket appeared on her shoulders.

She looked up, trying to hold back tears. "You don't believe me." She looked from Dutch to Jewel as they both had eyes full of pity. Her heart felt as if someone had run a knife through it. "You. Don't. Believe. Me!" she repeated, each word with more hurt written within it.

"It isn't that we don't believe you," Jewel whispered.

Dutch spoke up. "What if we go home?"

Caroline looked back at him.

Jewel nodded. "We can think this over and make a good plan."

"Yes, we just need to think this over first, all right?"

No other words were shared. Caroline left, feeling as if she was leaving her father behind all over again.

****

Once Jewel and Caroline got back home, Jewel told her to rest and take it easy. But instead, she sat at the top of the stairs, listening. She wanted them to make a plan. Now.

"Keep an eye on her," Dutch told Jewel.

"I will. Have a good day, Dutch," Jewel said, making Caroline sigh at such a formal goodbye.

Not only did they not make up, but they lied to her. Nothing was planned. She always thought the three of them could conquer anything together. But now she stood alone.

Jewel smiled at her as she walked up the stairs. "Dinner will be done soon."

"All right."

She now stood next to her. "I want you to rest." She gave her another pitiful smile.

After dinner, Caroline lay in bed with her mind going a million miles per hour. Her hands fiddled with the buttons of her nightgown.

If the voice was her dad, did that mean her mother was there with him? Was that a possibility? If that was true, had Achilles *not* killed them with no mercy? But if they were in that mirror, why hadn't they gotten out? Caroline and Dutch had gone in and out, so why couldn't they do the same? Each new question overwhelmed her.

She knew she should not put all her hope on one thing; she had learned that early in life. She had put her hope in living with Edmund forever, and he moved her out. She found out later that it was to keep her safe, but it still hurt to think of.

51

A thick foggy night rolled in, not allowing Caroline to see the ocean from her bedroom window. Looking out her window, she only saw faint lights from other houses and heard the loud high waves. Not only had a fog filled the night sky, but a strong wind had come with it.

She closed her eyes, listening to the sounds around her. The house was quiet, meaning that Jewel had fallen asleep. Which gave Caroline the perfect idea.

Tiptoeing past Jewel's bedroom, she tried not to make a sound. The door was wide open. She looked in and saw her grandmother lying in her bed with a book in her lap. She was up against the pillows and under a blanket, breathing steady. The lamp next to her bed gave the room a light-yellow glow.

Caroline watched where she stepped, not wanting the floor to creak. She stepped down the stairs. Going down the stairs at night always reminded her of bad memories, making her fear she might find Achilles waiting for her like he had that one night all those months ago. But tonight was different. She needed to know if she had indeed heard her father's voice. And no fear was going to keep her locked in her room.

She now stood in front of the door to the magical room in the back of the house. It was the only door that was always shut, away from unwanted eyes. No one other than Jewel, Caroline, and Dutch could come in. Filled with wands, spell books, and—best of all—books that took her through time, it was easily her favorite room in the whole house. Every book promised her the past and an adventure.

She pushed the door open as quietly as she could before closing it behind her. The room always had such a strong scent of old ink and paper. It added to the charm.

The shelves that held many books made the room feel even cozier.

Caroline snapped her fingers, making the candle on the table in the middle of the room light up. Once the light reached all the corners, she walked over to a book she knew her parents would both be in. She reached up and took it down with both hands.

She set the large brown book on the table by the candle. "All right. Here goes nothing," she said, her mouth dry.

A loud sound made her jump in her skin. She held her breath, waiting for Jewel to come into the room. The noise happened again, but then she recalled how strong the wind was blowing outside. She relaxed, looking back at the book.

Hope and fear built up in her. *If it is him, I need a plan! Should I wake Jewel and head back to the mirror? Or should I go alone? Should I only tell Dutch since he is more understanding?* She pushed those thoughts aside as the wind howled again.

She let a deep breath out as she opened the book. Looking through the pages, she took her time to find just what she wanted.

Within each page, a day was shown—with Caroline, with her family, and from Jewel's childhood. Some books were only half filled, meaning that life was still being lived, and the book was not yet finished. Each page had lovely artwork for each day, magically made with the beauty of a watercolor painting. They were like the world's best photo albums! One flick of a wand, and she was back in the day the page showed. The only downside was that she could not be seen or heard.

She took out her wand from the pocket of her

nightgown and set it on the table. Her palm lay flat on it. Taking a long breath, she picked her favorite memory from this book: her fourth birthday, the last one she had spent with her parents. Whenever she missed them, she would recall the day with a smile. As she looked at the page, she saw her father holding her in his arms and her mother holding her hand as they sang to her, the candles on the cake lit. Looking at it now, she could not believe she would lose them in a matter of months.

Caroline put her hand on the picture, smiling at the family she missed with all her heart. She grabbed her wand, closed her eyes, and whispered, "Pastgona."

Chapter 6

Caroline opened her eyes and put her hand above them, letting them readjust to the light. She looked around as she lowered her arm. A light breeze lifted her hair as chills ran down her spine. Winter in Washington was colder than the winter air she had lived through back on the East Coast. She put her hands together, blowing air into them.

She looked around and saw the house she had lived in with her mom and dad. It always seemed smaller than she had remembered, but she was only four when she lived in it. Everything at that age seemed so much bigger than they really were.

She walked up to the house, her feet crunching through the leftover snow. Her footprints disappeared before anyone could see them. The earthy smell of Calluna flowers welcomed her as she stepped up to the front door.

The best part about traveling through books was that she could walk through things. It was a funny feeling at first, but it was fun to do. She looked at the door before stepping right through it.

Delicious cookie smells filled her nose. It made her mouth water. Her mother always made sugar cookies for parties, and she had always loved the recipe, trying to make the same yummy cookies again. But she never could master it.

Laughter and conversations filled the house. She smiled at each person she cared deeply about as she made her way past them. Uncle Edmund, who she loved like a father and had lived with for seven years, stood in the living room, laughing. Her cousins, who were like her siblings, laughed with him. She smiled as she saw a younger Norna with her dirty blonde hair pulled back with a pink bow. She had always seemed to have one in her hair when she was seven. Her sweet face beamed as she talked with her aunt, Caroline's mother, in the kitchen. The two had gotten along very well.

Edmund's laughter grabbed her attention. He now sat with his wife, who had the same hair color as their daughter. They both looked younger, their hair a bit brighter. Even as the years went by, they still held that strong love for each other in their eyes. It was always something Caroline loved about them and wanted for herself one day.

"Ed Moon!" a four-year-old Caroline called out as she ran up to him.

Caroline smiled as her younger self ran past her, wearing an old favorite outfit: a plaid blue and white dress that stopped a few inches above her knees. Black Mary Jane shoes shined on her feet with white socks coming up to her ankles. As she ran, her brown hair in two pigtails with two blue ribbons bounced.

Edmund picked the four-year-old up with ease, sitting her on his lap. "Birthday girl!" he said, hugging her tight.

"How old are you now?" Caroline's aunt, Mary, asked her.

The little girl shyly smiled, showing her aunt four small fingers.

"There's no way," he said jokingly. "That's too big."

"That's what I told her!" a familiar voice from behind Caroline said.

It was the same voice she had heard in the mirror. Her breath seemed stuck in her throat, and her eyes filled with tears. She told herself to stay calm as she closed her eyes. The voice was not filled with hope like the last time she had heard it but with joy and pure happiness. Delight grew on her face as she opened her eyes to see her dad, who had joined his brother.

He picked up the four-year-old Caroline, who jumped into her father's waiting arms. "I told her there was no way she could be turning four today."

A sob caught in her throat. It *was* the same voice she had heard. She had been right. Her dad needed her!

"Daddy!" she cried, even though she knew he could not hear her. "You're *alive*." Happy tears ran down her cheeks. She looked at him so full of life, now knowing that he was waiting somewhere for her. Somewhere right this minute, he was alive. And after all these years, he still had hope that she would come and find him.

She could not believe it. "I've missed you so much." She wiped away the tears. "I will find you like you said, and I will bring you home."

It was a big promise, but she would do whatever she had to do to bring him back to her.

Many new questions filled her mind, but she pushed them all aside as she thought about what she would do next. A part of her didn't want to wait for Jewel to decide what they would do. She wanted to act as soon as she could.

Norna walked by Caroline as she made her way to Caroline's younger self. "Caroline." She looked up to where her cousin sat in her uncle's arms. "Time for gifts."

Dilandro set her down.

"Come here, sweet girl!" Caroline's mother called from the other room.

The birthday girl jumped, sharing an excited look with Norna before they both ran over to her mom.

"Mom!" Fifteen-year-old Caroline sighed as she watched herself run. Was her mom with her dad in the mirror world as well? Maybe when she had heard him, it was her mom whom he had been talking to! The thought that maybe both of her parents had been alive the past eleven years overjoyed her. She had to find them.

She looked back over. Her younger self sat in her mom's lap on the floor as she opened a box. Her mother kissed the top of her head.

Tears formed once more. "I will find you," she said with determination.

****

Once out of the book, she made her way up to her room, lifting her nightgown to not trip. She had to change and grab some things for her journey.

A part of her wanted to talk to someone, to have them tell her that she was doing the right thing. She knew Jewel would not want her to act yet, and she was unsure how Dutch would respond. She stepped into her room, looking around at the faintly lit space. She then noticed the date on her wall calendar. "Edmund!" she whispered.

Edmund came once a week to enjoy a cup of hot chocolate with her. She could not believe that she had forgotten he was coming tonight.

She turned around without a second thought and ran to the kitchen, turning on the light and grabbing two mugs, milk, and chocolate. Pulling her wand out of her pocket, she waved it over what she had set on the table. Everything moved on their own as if they had puppet strings. Once the milk and chocolate were in each mug, she flicked her wand, warming up the drinks. Grabbing her own mug, she put her wand away and sat.

"Sorry I'm late!" Edmund said as he appeared in the seat across from her.

She smiled, acting like she had not forgotten he was coming. "I'm really glad you are here tonight," she said as he took a sip of his hot chocolate. "I need advice."

He looked slightly concerned, his blue eyes meeting her brown ones. "Are you all right?" he asked, setting his mug down and accidentally spilling some.

After taking a deep breath, she told him everything that had happened in the past twenty-four hours, but she left out that Jewel had wanted her to wait.

He raised his eyebrows. "Are you sure it's Dilandro you heard?" he asked softly.

"I went into a book, and his voice was the same. Uncle Edmund, I want to go get him."

"What did Jewel say?" he asked.

She took a long sip out of her mug. She had never really lied to him before, especially about something so important, but she had to find her parents. "She supports the whole idea. She just wanted to see what your thoughts are. Grandma wanted to talk to you, but she had a headache and went to bed early." It scared her how easy that lie came out, but he seemed to buy it.

"All right," he said, moving a lock of his brown hair out of his face. "I would hate for you to go alone, but I can't go with you." He moved the liquid around in his mug.

"Why not?" she asked, trying not to sound too disappointed. It would have been amazing to have him with her in the strange world.

He stared down at his mug. "Norna insisted that I start training her after she heard about how powerful you have become. She was kind of mad that I had never shown her how to use her own magic. And she is a slooooowww learner."

Caroline smiled.

"She would be very mad if I left her. She doesn't believe in taking days off."

"Do you think I should go into the mirror?" she asked, setting her mug down to let him see that she was dead serious about it.

"If you believe your dad and maybe even your mom is in there, I say yes."

His words lifted her spirits. "So, you're giving me the okay?"

He nodded. "Yes, Caroline. But please be wise on your journey."

A huge smile grew on her face. "Thank you, Uncle Edmund!" She stood to give him a hug.

He laughed as he wrapped his arms around her. Because of his large body, his hugs were like big bear hugs. "Wait!" He grabbed his wand off the table. "I'll be right back!" He teleported away before she could say one more word.

She put the mugs in the sink before jumping with joy. It was so much better knowing that an adult believed her. Especially being Edmund.

With a pop, he was back in his chair with a small bag in his hand. "Come here."

Caroline went to his side. "What is that?"

He pulled the string that kept the bag closed, revealing many marbles of different colors. "I want you to take this with you," he said, closing the bag.

"What are they?" she asked, confused.

"When you need me," he said, handing her the bag, "grab a few and throw them at the ground."

"So, we could play mancala?" she asked, making him laugh.

"No! They're magic! You throw them, and I will appear wherever you are."

She held the bag close to her chest. "Wow. That's amazing."

"Each marble is a minute. So, how many you throw is how long I will stay. You have fifteen."

This was the best thing he could have given her. "Thank you," she said as he stood, pulling her into another hug.

"Just be smart. Don't do anything that will hurt you."

She hugged him back, looking at the bag. "Wait!" She pulled out of the hug. "What happens when they are all gone?"

"Don't let that happen. Just save them for when you really need me, all right?"

She nodded.

"I should get back. Norna wakes up early." He gave her an awkward smile. "I mean, she's up before the sun." He seemed horrified by that.

"Tell Norna I believe in her," Caroline said.

"That will mean a lot to her. Now, go get your dad and be safe. I'll see you soon." He kissed the top of her head.

"Love you," she said as he grabbed his wand.

"Love you more." With a wave of his wand, he was gone.

She looked down at the bag with a smile.

Chapter 7

J ewel didn't mean to fall asleep when she did. After a stressful morning and a busy day, she had wanted to relax with a good book and some nice hot tea. But four hours had sneaked by unnoticed.

A part of her knew that if she had not rolled over, sending the book in her lap to the floor and making a loud sound, she would have more than likely slept through the night. Her mind felt heavy with sleep. She moved a curl out of her face and stood, spotting her book on the floor. Taking a moment to rub her eyes, she sighed before looking up at the clock on the wall. It was 12:33 a.m.

Now that she was awake, she wanted to check on Caroline. Within the year they had lived together, Jewel had learned fast that if Caroline didn't get enough sleep, her brain could not work properly the next day.

She grabbed her long light blue silk robe, sliding it over her matching nightgown. She walked over to Caroline's room and softly opened the closed door to not wake her. Noticing that the nightstand's lamp was still on, she made her way over to turn it off. As her fingers reached for the switch, she saw Caroline's form lying under the covers. She decided to bend over and give Caroline a kiss on the forehead like she did every night before shutting the light off. She then pulled back the sheets and froze.

"Caroline!" she gasped, finding pillows where she thought her granddaughter had been. "What in the world?!" She looked around the empty room. "Caroline!" She moved to the door. "Caroline!" she called again, confused.

A piece of paper on the dresser caught her attention.

"Oh, no no no!"

Jewel picked it up with a racing mind. *What did Caroline do now? Where is she? I'm too old for this crap!* She loved Caroline very much, but at times, she did things Jewel was not the biggest fan of. Like this! Her daughter, Lucy, used to leave notes in this very room growing up, and it was never a good thing.

"Could she be more like her mother," she cursed under her breath.

Hi, Grandma!

I know you will be mad that I left in the middle of this windy night with a thick fog, but I have a good reason. My father—and maybe my mother—is in that mirror! I know you said to wait, and I know it could be a trick, but I can't imagine not knowing for one more moment.

Please don't be mad. I left at ten p.m. with my wand and a plan since I knew you'd try to stop me, which is fair. That's why I didn't wake you. I hope I don't make you worry too much. I'll be gone for a few days! Don't worry though! I was trained by the best. See you soon!

Lots of love,
Caroline =)

"Caroline!" Jewel looked back up at the clock, seeing that it was almost one in the morning. It had been hours since Caroline had left. She looked out the window as the nearby trees moved with the wind, making a whistling sound. Her mind spun. She could not believe that her own granddaughter had dared to get dressed, walk out into this weather, and take off into the night alone. *Did she teleport?* She put her hand on her face, sighing deeply.

Jewel put the letter in her pocket, turning to leave the room. She had no time to waste; she had to go get her granddaughter. She reached her hand out. "Wand to my hand."

Her wand came to her hand in seconds. She waved it over herself, making her outfit change from her nightgown to something better suited for the journey ahead of her: pants with a light shirt and boots.

"Caroline, what have you gotten yourself into?"

****

Long before Jewel woke up, Caroline left the house, trying her hardest to not make a sound. She didn't want to open the front door and risk Jewel hearing it, so she used her wand to help with that part. She teleported herself out of the house and then to the front of the neighborhood. She had thought about waking Dutch up but feared if he came along, Jewel would get even more upset with him. So, he was out of the question.

But she was still worried about going in alone. No one knew what that world had to offer and what dangers waited for her inside. She needed someone who understood, who had lost their parents as well. And that person was Sal!

Months ago, he had told her that his parents had died in a car crash when he had only been a few months old. After that, his grandparents took him in.

As Caroline walked, the fog made her skin damp. She

found the house that Sal and his grandparents called home in no time. Their house was one of the first homes in the neighborhood, standing out with its soft blue color and white framework. Lots of plants covered the porch, letting a strong flowery smell fill her nose.

One of them reeked though; she always thought the Valerians smelled like dirty socks. The first day Patti had put the plant out, it smelled so bad that Sal and Bob had looked all over for some animal that had died. After they found out it was the Valerians, Patti didn't let them throw it away because they were her favorite. But Caroline could not stand the smell.

She walked with her hand over the pocket with her wand. The dark street made her fear that someone could be watching her from the shadows. Having her hand near her wand gave her a bit of comfort. The wind blew harder, making the trees move wildly. Her hair slipped out of its ribbon and fell loose around her face. Pulling her wand out, she walked below where Sal's bedroom window was. No light shined behind the closed curtains, meaning that he must be sleeping. She sighed. *Should I let him be?*

Making up her mind, she pointed her wand at the pebbles by the porch, lifted one up to his window, and flicked her wrist. The pebble hit the window, not hard enough to break anything but strong enough to be heard. She held her breath as she waited for him to pop his head out. A chill filled her body from the cold wind.

The pebble made a noise like she wanted, but it also made each dog in the house bark. The large house only had three people, so Bob and Patti had filled the space with dogs. They had four cocker spaniels that Caroline knew didn't like her. When she would come over, each would yap or growl if she got close to Sal.

"Sal!" she called not too loudly, not wanting to wake anyone but him. But she knew anyone could hear the dogs. She flicked her wand again, sending more pebbles to the window. No sign of Sal. Sighing with frustration, she flicked her wand harder. Right before more pebbles headed toward the window, Sal opened it, popping his sleepy head out to be welcomed by the fast-moving pebbles. One hit his forehead with a loud thud.

"Ah!" he cried out, putting his hand where the pebble had hit. That woke him up for sure.

"Sorry," she whispered, trying to hold in a laugh. *I cannot believe that just happened.*

"What do you want?!" he asked, sounding a bit annoyed, and she could not blame him.

"Grab your wand and please come down," she said, trying to speak louder, so he could hear her over the barking dogs.

"Nugget, Onix, Lady, Ginger! Stop it!" he scolded, looking into his room. Each dog listened, calming down. He then turned back to her. "Fine! Let me get dressed! I'll be right down." He closed the window.

****

"Do you want to train now?" Sal asked as he stepped out the front door, still fixing his bedhead. His face looked swollen as he walked down the porch to meet Caroline by the steps. "And why did you throw that rock so hard?" He pointed to the red spot on his forehead.

She smiled shyly. "I'm sorry about that one. At least it wasn't the window."

"I think you would have broken the window," he said with a sleepy laugh.

"I need your help."

His eyes went wide. "Are you all right?" he asked, sounding worried as he put his hand on her arm.

"I need to tell you something. When we were cleaning Achilles' old house, I found something." She told him everything, not leaving out one detail.

Sal stayed quiet for a moment, deep in thought. "How do you know the mirror is not bad? I didn't really know Achilles as a villain, but he did so many bad things."

She smiled. "You believe me?!"

"Of course I believe you," he said, giving her a loving smile.

"I don't know if it's a trap. But I need your help."

"How can I help?" he asked with no hesitation in his voice.

"Well, I want to find my dad. So, I'm going back to the mirror, and I'd like you to come with me to help me find him."

"If you think your parents are in there, I'll help."

Caroline smiled at his words and gave him a hug. "Thank you so much!" He hugged her back, making her forget about the wind, the smelly flowers, and the fear of the unknown. "Let's go then."

He let go of her. "I have to tell my grandparents."

Fear built up in her. "No, you can't!" She grabbed his hand, stopping him.

"Why not?" he asked, looking confused.

She didn't let go of his hand. "What if they stop you? I didn't tell my grandma."

"Wait. I thought you told Jewel."

"I left her a note. It's like the same thing." The wind blew her hair into her face.

"So, can I leave a note for my grandparents?" he asked.

"Yes, but don't take too long," she said, letting go of his hand.

"I won't," he said, turning to the door. He fought his way into the house without letting one cocker spaniel out into the dark night. About ten minutes went by until he came back out, blocking the dogs from leaving the house. "All right. I'm ready."

She stood. "What took you so long?" she asked lightly. "Did you write a whole book?"

He laughed. "No, just a long letter. I've never done this before. I don't want to freak anyone out."

She grabbed her wand, planning to teleport them to Achilles' house. She had no plans on walking so far in the middle of the night. "Do you have your wand?"

He nodded.

"Give me your hand," she said, holding out her free hand. His hand in hers was always a comfort she didn't know how she could live without. "Teleportsheam!" In no time, they both stood in front of the tall mirror.

"That felt wild!" Sal laughed. "Is this the mirror?" he asked as he looked up at it, their eyes meeting in the glass.

"Yes. All we have to do is step into it." She watched him as his eyes took in the mirror.

"You know…" He laughed lightly. "When I met you, I had no idea I would be walking into mirrors with you."

She smiled. "Ready?" she asked, looking back at her own reflection.

Sal grabbed her hand a bit tighter. "Ready as I'll ever be."

They both took a deep breath and took the first step into their long journey together.

Chapter 8

"**O**h my goodness! That was unbelievable!" Sal said, rolling onto his back and looking up at the gray sky.

"We just did that!" Caroline rolled over as he stood and helped her to her feet.

Going through the mirror had felt as if she was normally walking but in slow motion. Like they were in it forever, but if she blinked, she would miss it. They had both dropped to the grass, gasping for air. Once they both stood, they took a moment to look around, taking in the many trees and the fairytale-like woods. Even though everything was a weird, faded color, it still was one amazing sight to take in.

"This is groovy. I feel like I just went colorblind," he said.

Caroline noticed right away how the night in this world was calm, not filled with high winds and a thick fog. The air was cold, and stars shined over them. A shooting star shot across the sky, making them both lightly gasp at the sight.

"Where do we even start looking?" he asked, turning back to her.

Her mind slowed as his words sunk in. "I-I...don't...know." This hit her hard. She came to this place with no real plan other than just finding her parents. She had not thought of what she would do to make that happen. *I hate it when Grandma is right!*

He stayed quiet, giving her time to think as she looked out toward the many trees that went on for miles. From where she stood, it seemed impossible to know how long the woods went on for. If they traveled too far into the woods, could they find their way back to the mirror? She turned, looking at the mirror. *Can we even go back through after some time has passed?*

"Sal," she said, looking back to him, "I didn't think of a plan. I just thought about finding my parents. I don't know how or where to start looking."

His face was unreadable, making her heart beat faster. He opened his mouth to speak, but loud footsteps took their attention away. They were getting closer with each passing second, rattling her with fear. He looked toward the unseen sound as she put her hands on his tense shoulders and walked up to his back.

"Look over there," he whispered. He pointed toward something moving through the trees a few feet away.

Caroline's mouth went dry as she saw many men dressed in dark armor, making them hard to see in the night. Guards. With the small moonlight, she saw that they all had long swords leaning against their shoulders, and they moved with purpose, looking at everything.

Sal took one last look before taking hold of her arm. "Come on," he said so quietly that she was not even sure he had spoken.

He held her hand tight as they made their way away from the guards. She watched where she stepped, not wanting to snap a twig that would reveal them. The grass crunched underneath them, making her bite her tongue.

"Get down!" Sal whispered.

She held her breath and lay in a deep ditch with him. The wet mud soaked through her clothes. It was cold, but it didn't even register in her mind as she hoped the guards had not seen them. It seemed almost impossible to catch her breath. She put her head down, feeling the mud stick to her face. Sal did the same and put his arm over her back.

All went still and quiet. Only the trees rustled in the wind. Caroline and Sal locked eyes, both wide with uncertainty. The silence didn't last long as loud footsteps came closer once more. She wanted to get a better view of who they were hiding from, so she lifted her head and saw more than ten guards walking through the forest as though they were looking for something.

One guard stopped walking, looking in their direction. She saw something on his helmet that took the air out of her lungs: a mark that matched the scar Achilles had had. She put her head back down fast, mud covering the side of her face once more. She hoped the darkness was her friend, so they couldn't be seen in the limited light.

Her mind raced a million miles an hour. Achilles used to have a scar running across his face that went from his forehead and down to his cheek.

"Are you sure you saw a girl walking through here earlier?" a man asked, sounding close to the mirror.

"Yes, I am sure, Zuly, sir," someone answered in a deep voice, sounding much closer than the other man. "She was a young girl. Maybe thirteen or so."

Caroline looked at Sal, meeting his wide eyes.

"Is she still here?" the one called Zuly asked.

"Well, I did not see her leave," the other man said, sounding unsure.

"So, what you are saying is you brought us out here in the middle of the night for uncertainty." He sounded angry with a stern voice, moving closer to the other man. By the way he spoke, it was clear that he oversaw them. "It has been years since anyone has come in from the other world. So please let me know what makes you think someone came in."

"I believe it was the girl Achilles wants."

Caroline froze. They were looking for her! "Let's teleport away," she whispered as she reached for her wand.

"Now that is a big thing to say with no proof," Zuly spoke again.

Sal and Caroline peeked up, making sure no one was looking their way. Zuly was not dressed in armor but in a leather outfit. His shirt outlined his muscles. He was tall, and his light skin looked even whiter in the dark. He had his dark hair pulled back into a slick man bun. Some gray hair shined in the moonlight.

"Yes, sir. I know!" the other man said. "But I can promise—"

"Shut up!" Zuly said, putting his hand up in a fist.

Each guard stood ready. Sal and Caroline lay back down fast.

"What is it, sir?" a guard asked, sounding close.

Zuly took a deep breath in through his nose, smelling the air around him. "You were right." He took another long breath. "Caroline Smith is here."

"I think we should run," Sal muttered under his breath.

"You think?" she whispered, but she also feared that running would make too much noise, making them easier to find.

"She is with a boy in the ditch," Zuly said.

The next thing she knew, it sounded like each guard was running toward them.

"RUN!" Sal yelled as he grabbed her hand and stood. He practically dragged her for a moment until she could get her feet under her. He ran like he was trying to win a race, pulling her arm hard.

The guards raced after them with a great might that could be heard for miles. Caroline looked back to see how close they were.

Zuly was running out front, leading his men. "Do not let them get away!" he yelled.

Sal reached into his pocket, grabbing his wand despite not knowing many spells. He kept running but turned to point his wand at the people chasing them. "Pastgona!"

Magic sparks flew toward the guards, making them all yell out. But the sparks landed on the ground, not slowing them down.

"Sal!" Caroline called from behind him. She had never run with such fear before. It made it hard to even talk. "What the heck…are you…doing?! That spell only w-works with a magic book in front of you!"

"I don't see you trying anything!" he yelled back.

She grabbed her wand. When she half turned to shoot magic at them, she noticed that Zuly had stopped his guards with a hand signal.

Why are they stopping? She looked back ahead and saw why they had stopped. "SAL!"

He looked back at her for reasons she would never understand. She dug her heels into the dirt, trying to stop them, but it was too late.

His body weight pulled her forward before his hand slipped out of hers, making her scream. She watched in horror as he fell down the deep cliff. His own scream gave her chills as it cut through the air.

"SAL!" She moved to the edge, trying to see where he had fallen. "SAL! No, no, no!" She looked back, spotting the guards coming up behind her. "Stay back!" she yelled as she flicked her wand at them. "Fire itera!"

A strong fire lit at their feet. Some yelled out, and others backed away.

She turned back to the cliff, looking for a way down. Teleporting was not an option since she didn't know where Sal had gone. On her right, she noticed what looked like a path down. Without a second thought, she raced down the path.

"Sal, please answer me!" Twigs and branches hit her legs, but she hardly noticed. She went as fast as her feet could carry her. "Sal!"

A sob caught in her throat. This could *not* be how their story ended. *What if he's dead?* Her chest went cold. There was no spell to bring someone back. She pushed that thought to the back of her mind.

Where he would have landed, water flowed with so many rocks. She tripped on her last steps down the cliff. "Sal!" she called out, running to the water. As she jumped in, the cold water welcomed her. She pushed herself up and took a big breath after her head broke through the surface. She looked around for any sign of Sal, but he was still nowhere to be seen. "SAL!"

She put her hands to her head, not knowing what to do. Why would he not answer her? "Sal!" she sobbed, fearing the worst.

She looked across the water, spotting his shoe floating a few feet away by the rocks. She made her way toward it.

"No, please." She grabbed his shoe, waiting now to find his body.

"Go down and get her!" Zuly, pointing at her, ordered from the cliff's edge.

Her eyes widened as the guards made their way down the cliff. She swam to the lake's edge, tripping as she pulled herself out of the water and pushed herself off the ground. She ran. Her wet hair stuck to her face. She made it to the woods again before one of the guards had made it down. She wondered if they had any magic since they didn't use any.

She hid behind a tree, turning to see if any guards had seen where she had gone. While trying to steady her breath, she saw the guards walk around the water, clearly not knowing where she had escaped to. But she knew this would be short-lived. The one they called Zuly had smelled her! *How is that even a thing? I know dogs do that but not people!*

Caroline thought of leaving this whole mirror world behind her, but she could not leave without Sal. He was in this mess because of her. If she had just waited for Jewel or even Dutch, maybe she would not be running for her life while not even knowing if Sal was alive.

She put her hands above her head as she tried to calm herself the best she could. Sal needed her, and if she freaked out, what help would she be? She looked back at the water. If he needed any kind of help to save his life, she could not reach him in time. Tears slid down her face as each breath became shallower in her tight chest. Getting caught didn't matter anymore. She needed to find Sal.

She took a step forward, but a large hand covered her mouth.

Chapter 9

"**D**utch!" Jewel called as she shook him in his bed. She had teleported to his house, something she had never done before. But she didn't care to wait for him to come to the front door. "Wake up!"

His eyes snapped open. He looked at her, confused.

"I need your help," she said with a shaky voice.

"Are you all right?!" He sat up on his elbows, his face flushed. "What happened?!"

"She left me a note." She pulled the note out of her pocket with a shaky hand.

"Caroline?" he asked, taking it.

"Yes. I need your help!"

"She ran away?" he asked with panic in his voice. "She *does* know we can just teleport to her, right? You can't run away from sorcerers."

"Dutch, it says she went into Achilles' mirror to look for her parents."

His eyes widened. "What? All by herself?!" He put his hand through his hair.

"That's why I need your help. I can't let anything happen to her because she is chasing after a dream. I can't believe she did this!" Jewel looked down to organize her thoughts, but she noticed he had bunny slippers beside the bed. They were white with pink noses.

Dutch followed her gaze. "Caroline g-got them for me," he muttered.

"Forget the slippers. Read the note!"

He took a few seconds to read over it. "You don't think her parents are in there, do you?" He looked back at Jewel. "I have a really bad feeling about that mirror. There is no way something good is waiting for her on the other side."

"As much as I would want this for her, it's been more than ten years since they have died. Why would they be in a mirror in *his* house?"

Dutch nodded as he looked down to read the note once more. "Let's go get our girl back," he said, looking back at Jewel.

He stood, grabbing his wand from the nightstand. He waved his wand over his body, changing into something that worked more for the journey: jeans with a white and blue striped short-sleeved shirt. She looked at his biceps that poked through the tight fabric.

"Look, even if what you are saying is true," he said, making her eyes meet his once more, "I won't stop supporting her till she learns it for herself."

Jewel nodded, blinking away tears. Caroline was lucky to have him in her life. She had to have been excited for him to be her grandfather. And Jewel had taken him away from her. "The note said she left around ten, and it's almost two in the morning now."

Dutch held his wand with both hands, calling out, "Say no more. Teleportsheam!"

****

Within an instant, Jewel and Dutch stood in front of the mirror.

"What is it like in there?" she asked, looking at him.

"It was like a whole other world."

They both stayed quiet for a moment.

"Who knows if we can even find her right away?" she asked, looking at her reflection in the mirror. "If she's been in there as long as she has, she might have walked so far that we won't even know where she went, Dutch. And what if we can't teleport in there?" Their eyes met in the mirror. "What if we can't find her…"

He took her hand in his. He looked down at it as he rubbed it with his thumb. "Hey," he said, squeezing her hand, "we will find her, and we will bring her back home. Then you get to ground her."

Jewel nodded. They held each other's gaze for a moment before Dutch cupped her face and leaned over, kissing her forehead tenderly. Her heart melted at his touch, but a part of her thought she didn't deserve it.

"Ready?" he asked.

She took a deep breath. "Yes," she said.

They both took a step into the mirror. Jewel waited to feel the cold glass as she walked into it, but before she knew it, they were both within the mirror's world. She stood on the crunchy grass with Dutch as she looked up at the high trees. Everything looked dark and odd. Brushing off her pants, she could not believe that Caroline was out here alone in the dark.

"Any idea where we should start looking?" she asked. "This place is huge."

"I don't know," he said, pulling his wand out and giving it a flick. Its tip illuminated their area faintly, and Jewel noticed how the grass was black. "But we can fly over

79

these trees and look from there if teleporting doesn't work."

"Great idea," she said, pulling out her own wand. "But let's stay together till the sun comes up. This place gives me the creeps."

Dutch looked down at the ground, seeming deep in thought.

"What's wrong?" she asked.

"I hear something." He looked around, and Jewel tried to follow his eyes. "Turn off your wand." He flicked his wrist, leaving them in the darkness with only crickets chirping.

"Hey, you!" an angry voice yelled from somewhere unseen.

Dutch and Jewel turned to where the voice came from.

"Put your wands down!"

They both pointed their wands toward the voice.

"No one will get hurt if you do as we say!" the voice demanded.

We? There were *more* of them. "Who are you?" Jewel called out into the darkness. "Show yourself!"

A figure walked into the moonlight, letting them see a man dressed in black armor with a long sword hanging off his belt. If he was an inch shorter, the sword would have touched the ground. He held his helmet by his hip. Scars filled his tan face, and his intimidating eyes looked Jewel and Dutch up and down.

Dutch stepped in front of her. Seven other men dressed the same way came out from behind the trees with their swords in hand.

"Put. The. Wands. Down," the first man said sternly.

Dutch flicked his wand at the seven men. "Stonesoul!" He froze them all as Jewel pointed her wand at the first man.

"Do not try me!" he said, spitting.

They both pointed their wands at him as he lifted what appeared to be a whistle.

"Give me one good reason!" Jewel said, her eyebrows drawn.

"With one blow," the man said, showing them the whistle, "a warrior elf will come at my command, and your story will end here."

Jewel slightly lowered her wand in confusion.

"Unfreeze my men, and maybe you both will live."

Dutch sighed and flicked his wand. "Sundfulle."

Jewel slowly put her wand down, looking at Dutch to do the same. The man put the whistle away.

"Look, fellas," Dutch said, putting his hands up. "We're not looking for any trouble."

The first man spoke with a hard tone. "Then why are you on our land?"

Jewel rested her hand on Dutch's shoulder to give him some comfort.

"We're looking for a young girl," he answered.

Each man pointed their sword at them regardless. A few stepped forward.

"Wait!" he said, backing up. "My granddaughter came here. She's about this tall." He raised his hand up to Caroline's height, by his mid-arm. "She has brown hair! Her name is Caroline Smith."

The guards all stopped walking.

"So, it is true…" the lead guard muttered.

Jewel watched them with fearful eyes, unsure what would happen next.

He turned to his men. "Zuly was right! The girl is here!" An evil smile took over his face.

"Wait!" Dutch said.

"I bet if we bring them in, Zuly can get information out of them." He turned back to Jewel and Dutch.

Dutch rolled his eyes and spoke with a harsher tone. "Are you not listening? We came here *looking* for her!"

"And even if we did," Jewel said, "we would never tell you!"

The main guard pointed two fingers at them, making the seven men march toward them.

Dutch grabbed Jewel's arm, pulling her behind him again. "Touch her and you die!"

The guard in charge waved his hand again, and one of his men grabbed the wands off the ground. "Take care of him and take them both back to the castle."

Dutch tried to fight the seven guards off, but one ran his sword up Dutch's arm, making him scream. Jewel yelled out at the sight and lifted her hand to call her wand to her. Once it was in her hand, she blasted one of the guards back, slamming him into the ground. But pain filled her head as one of the guards hit her with something hard. She dropped to the floor, her vision blurring. Someone removed her wand from her hand as another guard hit Dutch with his sword's handle, knocking him out cold.

"DUTCH!" Jewel screamed. As she ran over to him, a guard put his sword to her neck.

"Take one more step, and your fate shall be far worse than his!"

She put her hands up as a tear rolled down her cheek. She didn't know what was going to happen to them; this was worse than she had feared. She looked at Dutch, laying so close yet so far. One of the guards tied her hands behind her back.

"I won't tell you anything!" she said as they pulled her away to follow them.

Chapter 10

"If I move my hand, you must not scream," a man's voice whispered over Caroline's left shoulder, his breath brushing against her ear. The hand itself smelled as if it had never been washed. Actually, the whole person smelled like he had never showered in his life.

She just wanted this person off her, so she nodded.

He removed his hand, allowing her to turn around and face him. He had a long pepper beard that reached his mid-chest. A few leaves and dried mud hung in it. His long, messy hair was pulled back, away from his face. It was also very oily and filled with other items from the woods. Dirt and mud caked his legs, but his face was surprisingly clean. His dark skin was clear, while the rest of him looked as though he had lived in the woods all his life.

"Who are you?" she asked, keeping her voice low.

He put his large hand back over her mouth, making her head hit the tree behind her. He then gestured that she should be quiet with his free hand. His eyes looked somewhere behind her to where Zuly's men searched for her. By the sound of their far away voices, they were still by the lake. He looked around at the trees, making her wonder if he was hiding from them too or if he would kill her. Either way, she didn't want to make this wild looking Santa mad.

"Sir!" a guard called out, sounding a bit closer than the lake. "We have lost them!"

Caroline felt a bit more at ease but looked back at the man holding her up against a tree.

"The water washed off her scent," Zuly said from someplace above the cliff. "You imbeciles!" A sound like a slap filled the air. "I must speak with his lordship about this."

She heard the guards make their way back to where they had come from.

"Come with me," the man covering her mouth whispered.

"I will do no such thing!" she said quietly as she removed his hand from her face.

His breath smelled almost as bad as he did. "I am one of the good guys," he said, pointing to himself. He pulled a wand out from his broken poncho. "Trust me. I will take you somewhere safe."

She didn't want to go anywhere with him. She wanted to find Sal. "Why should I trust you?" she asked angrily.

"Because I have your friend."

"What did you do to him?!" she asked, making him put his hands up in defense.

"I mean no harm. He is safe. Your friend. I teleported him away when he was falling." He grabbed her hand, making her pull her arm back. "I have no more magic left in me today. You have to teleport us to him."

"How do I know you won't try to hurt me like those men back there? And where did you take him?"

"Trust me," he said, reaching his hand out for her to take the wand. He didn't grab her like before but instead left his hand open, waiting for her to take it.

She took a deep breath, looking back at the lake one last time. If this man was lying, she'd lose Sal forever. But maybe he really had Sal safe. She looked back at the man, who still waited for her. She grabbed the wand.

"Just think of your friend," he said.

She flicked her wand at them both, hoping with all her heart that she didn't just make a deadly mistake.

****

Caroline opened her eyes to a well-lit cave. It was damp and cold with a large fire in the middle. The fire warmed her a bit from where she stood. She looked around, seeing a space where one might sleep with lots of leaves in an attempt to make it somewhat soft. She looked over to the other side and saw Sal looking at her, perfectly fine.

"SAL!" she cried as she raced to him. She dove into his open arms. "I thought I had lost you." She never wanted to let him go.

He rested his hand on the back of her head. "I got you. You're all right."

"Are you all right?!" she asked, looking up at him.

His face looked like he was trying to hide any pain he felt. "Yeah. Just a little stunned," he said, meeting her eyes.

She handed him back his shoe.

"Of course, he is fine," the man said, walking up behind her. "I was walking by the cliff when I heard this boy yell and saw him fall to the rocks below. So, I used my weak magic to teleport him here to my humble home." He gestured to the cave.

Caroline realized why this man smelled like he had never showered before. He lived here! She didn't know how someone could live in such a place. She looked up at the low roof and saw water dripping down into a pot, making a soft sound as it bounced off the bottom.

"I could not get to you in time, young one," the man continued, pointing to her. "But I did go back for you. I cannot be seen by the guards. Besides, using too much magic at one time is hard on me. I tend to pass out from how tired I get." He grabbed the wand from her and put it back in his poncho.

"Who are you?" Sal asked, staring at the hairy magic man.

"I am no one anymore," he admitted, looking off to the cave wall.

Caroline looked back at Sal, and they shared a confused look.

"I once was the king of this land." A deep sadness shined in his eyes. "This land used to be peaceful. Full of magical people. I used to be the most powerful wizard in all the land." He paused, looking away. "I had everything I ever needed and did not even know it."

"So, what happened?" Sal asked, breaking the silence after a few seconds.

Caroline watched as the man looked back at them. "Everyone here has magic?"

"Yes. That was until Achilles found the mirror."

"Achilles?" she muttered. *How many lives had he wrecked in his life?*

"He took the gem of power! The mirror you more than likely came through is the only way into this land. Magic comes from here; it is born here." He ran his hand through his long beard, seeming unbothered by the leaves falling out.

"Magic comes from a gem?" Sal asked.

"Yes, young man. It came from the gem in my castle."

He pointed out the cave door, where the castle could probably be seen from where they stood. "The gem holds so much power, and sometimes, it gives the gift of magic to those in your world."

Caroline was a bit confused, but to know where her magic came from was something she found amazing. She had always asked Jewel why they had magic, but her grandmother never really knew.

"You have to know," she had told her grandmother once after dinner.

"I really don't. But not everyone can be taught," Jewel had said.

"So, we have magic because it's in us?" Caroline had asked.

"I really don't know, my love."

Now, this literal caveman seemed like he could answer all her questions. "How does magic get to my world? And why only some people? How do I still have magic here, but you say you're weak?" she asked.

She knew she had asked far too many questions by the look on his face. It was much like the one her grandmother, Dutch, or even her teachers gave her when she asked too much at once.

"Well," he said, seeming to think of the best way to answer everything, "magic can go through the mirror's cracks at times. You do not need the gem like we do to keep the power in your land. The magic is in your blood. Like the gem is to us. With the gem gone, it no longer sends any magic to us in this world."

"How long ago did this happen?" she asked, hoping he didn't mind her questions.

"Let us see…" He walked off to one of the cave walls

that had many lines on it. In fact, the whole wall was covered with them.

Sal looked back at her. "Are those dates?" he asked quietly.

As the man counted under his breath, she mouthed, *I don't know.*

The man turned around. "Looks like it has been ten or eleven years since the gem was taken."

Caroline nodded. "My whole family has magic."

He laughed, filling the whole cave with its echoes. "Child, no whole family has magic in your world. More so now with no magic coming through. There was one family actually, but they must all be dead if he had his way."

"Can magic be genetic?" Sal asked.

"Yes. Yet it only happened once in your world. To the Smiths. But they have been dead for years, I would believe."

She smiled, knowing the Smiths weren't going anywhere anytime soon. "I'm a Smith!" She lifted her right arm, showing him the birthmark her whole family had on the inside of her wrist.

The man's eyes widened. "You are a Smith?" he asked, scratching the top of his head. "That cannot be. They are all gone. Or I thought so…"

She smiled and shook her head.

A grin grew along his face. "My word. Look at you, a Smith in the flesh!" He got closer and walked around her to get a better look. "Never thought I would ever see one of you in person."

"How do you know about my family?" Caroline asked, going in circles to follow the man.

"I know everything," he spoke as if it should have been obvious. "I had a book that I used to read to the young ones." He stopped walking, took hold of her arm, and ran his thumb over her birthmark. "I read about the gift the gem gave the Smiths centuries ago." He looked at something on the wall, seeming to be in his own sad thoughts for a moment. "I used to read about your strong family to my apprentice."

It was wild to think that people Caroline didn't even know—in a land she never even knew existed—knew about her family and would read about them like legends.

"Now that I know who you are, I can see it in your eyes. Yours are bright and full of magic."

"What happened to the gem?" she asked, sad that something so amazing was gone.

"Achilles." He gestured toward the fire, and they all sat around it. Its warmth made the cold cave cozy. He looked at Caroline before he continued. "He took the gem's power for himself, leaving this whole world without any powers. No one here can use their magic."

Sal looked at him, seeming lost. "How did you teleport us if you don't have magic?"

"You see, my boy, I was a great wizard. *Very* powerful. So, when Achilles stole the gem, it did not take all of my power. But I hardly have any left. I must be careful when I use it because I get tired easily. It is very weak and pretty much useless." His face dropped.

Caroline could not believe what this man was telling her.

"Is that why you live here?" Sal asked, looking around the damp cave. "Because of Achilles?"

"I lost everything that damn day. He took my crown, my castle, my magic, and—worst of all—those I cared deeply for!" He looked down at his hands in his lap and took a deep breath.

"Who's in charge now?" Caroline asked.

He paused, seeming confused by her question.

"I mean, Achilles is dead. So, what's stopping you from taking back your crown? I know there are guards, but who is the king now with Achilles gone?"

He looked back at her as if she had spoken in another language. A loud bang outside the cave made them all jump.

"What was that?" Sal asked.

The man shook his head. "A creature. Do not worry though. We are safe in here."

He nodded. "Is there a way to put the magic back in the gem?"

"Yes. You must take it to the castle's highest point and put it back in its stand. That is in the highest tower. Once the sun runs through it again, it should work like before, taking back all the powers Achilles stole from it and giving it to the people."

Achilles is dead, Caroline noted, *but this man speaks of him like he's still alive.*

"Where is the gem?" Sal asked.

"I heard it is hidden somewhere in the castle, or they might have broken it. I really do not know. I have only heard whispers." He looked at the two young faces. "Why are you here?"

"I came here by mistake this morning when I fell into the mirror," she admitted. "I heard my father's voice, who I thought was dead."

The man ran a hand through his messy beard once more. "Who was your father?"

"Dilandro. Dilandro Smith."

"The youngest Smith brother," he said, making her smile. "You know, sometimes Achilles puts people in this world instead of killing them. So, maybe your father is being held in the castle's dungeon."

"What do you mean? Why would he do that?"

"When the person he fights breaks his wand, Achilles would rather you live here locked up than him losing a fight."

Caroline thought about the time she had broken his wand and how he had done some strange magic with his hands. Was that what this man was talking about?

"So, her parents could be locked up here?" Sal asked, smiling.

"If you heard his voice," the man explained, "there is a good chance that he got out of his cell and used some leftover magic to send you a message. But the longer someone is here, the weaker their magic becomes."

Her heart leaped in her chest at the thought of her father alive in this world, pushing her to find him. She looked at Sal, and they shared a smile as she stood.

"How long do we have until we lose our magic?" Sal asked, standing next to her.

"Well, you will feel it bit by bit each day. But it becomes useless in about six days."

That was more than enough time for her to find her family and get back home. "Then I'll go to the castle and get him." She walked toward where she thought the cave exit might be.

Sal started to follow her, but the man grabbed her arm, stopping her.

"No!" he said, raising his voice. "You will do no such thing!"

Chapter 11

"No?" Caroline grabbed the man's dirty hand and pushed it away from her. Who was this man to tell her what she could or couldn't do? "Cut the gas!" she said as he opened his mouth to answer back. "I just found out that my dad could be here, and you want me to do nothing? Who the heck do you think you are? I don't have to listen to you!"

"Listen," he said with a flat tone, which only angered her further. "The castle is nearly impossible to get to. And if they find out you are a Smith, the guards will kill you on sight."

After a heavy sigh, she spoke with a much softer tone. "I understand what you're telling me. But I came into this world for my dad, and I'm not leaving without him."

The man sighed, glancing at Sal before looking back at her. "You will die a foolish death if you look for him!" the man said in a harsh tone that she didn't care for.

Sal looked at her with worried eyes, but she was too frustrated to care. This man was once a king or whatever he was, but she didn't live here, meaning she didn't have to do what he said.

Sal rolled his eyes. "Come on, Caroline. We'll go find

your dad. We have a lead now at least." He shrugged, looking at the stranger. "We don't need his help anymore."

Caroline walked away with Sal but stopped, pulling him close. "Do you think he will help us if we ask?" she whispered.

"No. He made it pretty clear that he doesn't think you should go to the castle," he said in a hush tone.

But Caroline knew this man could be a great help. They didn't even know where the castle was. "It will save us time if he comes with us. We only have six days of magic here."

Sal stayed quiet for a moment, thinking. "Ask him if you like," he said, glancing at the man who was warming his hands by the fire. "But I don't think we really need him."

Maybe that was true, but she didn't want to get lost in this mirror world. She already didn't know where she was or where the mirror was. "Let me at least try. If he says no, we can do it ourselves."

He nodded. "Do it fast."

She turned back to the man. "Look," she said, walking over to him. "It's clear that you're not happy here and that you know a lot about where my family could be at." She smiled. "And you used to be the king! You can get me to that castle!"

The man said nothing, only looking up at her.

"I want my mom and dad back..." The thought made her throat tighten. "So, going there is something I must do no matter the risk." She lowered herself, getting to his eye level. "And you need your gem back. By putting the gem back, you can be a powerful king once again and take back your land, right?" She saw the wheels turning in his head. "You said there is a way to put your gem back, right?"

"Yes but—"

"So, come with us to the castle and help us find my family. Then we will help you bring magic back to your land."

She stuck her hand out, but he jerked back as if she would hit him.

"Deal?" she asked, smiling.

"I do not understand why you want to help me," he said, keeping his hand near his chest.

"Well, like you said, the castle guards make it dangerous to go there, but I don't even know the way to the castle. But *you* know that castle better than anyone does."

He raised an eyebrow.

"I would like your help very much, and as a thank you, Sal and I won't leave until we put that gem back." She kept her hand out, waiting for him to take it.

"This is a reckless mission," he said, looking at her hand.

"I know, but if this works, we both get what we need." Her arm was getting heavy, but she refused to put it down.

"You two just need me as a map," he said, looking back at Sal.

Caroline sighed. "Yes, you're a map in a way. Do we have a deal?"

"I am sorry, but I have never even thought about putting the gem back. I have no powers. It would be deadly for me to try."

"Well, now you have me: a Smith."

He looked from Sal to Caroline. "You have yourself a deal," he said, taking her hand in his. His hands were still warm from the fire.

"Groovy!" Sal said.

Caroline smiled. This was great and so much safer. Now they had someone who knew the land on their team. And all they had to do in return was put a little gem in a tower. Easy.

"My name is Caroline, and this is Sal," she said as Sal nodded.

"I don't think you have told us your name yet," he said, standing by her.

"Merlin," the man said, standing with more confidence. "My name is Merlin."

****

The cold and damp dungeon only had a few candles lighting up the cells. Jewel sat alone in the cell she had been placed in, staring at the cold stone floor. There were others in the other cells, but she paid them no mind. Instead, she held her hands in her lap. Her hair was no longer pulled back; it now framed her face as she thought through everything.

Her heart ached for Caroline, not knowing if she was okay. The men who had brought her and Dutch to the castle had acted as if they didn't know where Caroline was, which meant she was out of harm's way. For now. *Maybe if I had listened to her—if I had paid attention to what she had said—she would still be at home.* Her vision blurred with tears.

She had not seen Dutch since the forest. She didn't know what the guards had done to him. He had been so mad at her, but when she needed him, he put all that aside and helped her without any of the anger she knew he still felt. She closed her eyes, willing her tears not to fall. But she couldn't stop them. She put her hands up to her face, crying into them.

As the guards had brought her to this castle, the world she saw had taken her by surprise. The forest had not been as big as she had thought it would be. It had opened to reveal a large, dark lake that didn't let anyone see through it. Over it, a long bridge had led to a village.

Houses had filled the village. Everyone had been dressed as if they lived back in the sixteenth century, but some village people had looked at her as if she was the one dressed strange. Some had looked past her and to the guards with pure terror. Even the youngest children playing with a ball in the streets had stopped, letting the ball roll away as the guards passed. Most villagers had looked at her with pity though, which had made her worry since they must have known that where she was headed was not good.

After so much walking, Jewel's feet had hurt, and her back had stung from the guard who kept hitting her to move faster.

As the walk had continued, they had traveled over another bridge that led to a large castle that took her breath away. It was built out of stone, glittering in the sunlight, with a backdrop of mountains behind it. It had many windows that looked as though they had their curtains closed, not letting any natural light flow in. The highest tower went up so high that she couldn't see its top with the bright sun behind it.

The castle had looked welcoming, but the moment she had been pulled inside, she had felt just how dark it was. It smelled stale, like Achilles' house had. The sun had not been welcomed inside for quite some time, and dust lingered everywhere. She only saw the main part of the castle for a few seconds before a guard shoved her to the lowest part and locked her away in one of the cells.

A loud noise clanked, taking her out of her thoughts. A guard, who had his dark hair pulled back into a man bun, pushed Dutch into the cell. He lost his balance, falling to the ground right before the man shut the door behind him. The dungeon echoed the banging sound.

"Dutch!" Jewel cried, moving toward him. She threw herself onto him, wrapping her arms around him. After a moment, she let go just enough to let him sit up before embracing him once more.

He held her close. "Are you all right?" he asked, pulling out of the hug and cupping her face with his hands.

"Yes. W-what about you?" she asked as he wiped away a tear from her cheek.

"Touching. Old love," the guard said in a mocking tone. He put the keys on a hook on his belt.

Jewel and Dutch looked back at him. "What do you want from us?!" she asked, wishing she had her wand. She noticed that his left cheek had a bruise.

He laughed. "In time, you will see. I spoke with his lordship, and he already has plans for the both of you."

His tone made her uneasy.

Dutch put his arm over her, speaking through clenched teeth. "Touch her, and you're a dead man."

The guard smiled before walking away, banging on each cell as he left. Once the door closed, she turned to Dutch.

"I won't let them hurt you!" he said.

"Never mind that." She held his arms, noting that he seemed unharmed for the most part. "What did they do to you? Why did it take so long for them to bring you here?"

"I woke up tied to a chair," he said in a low voice. "Zuly—the one with that thing on the top of his head—asked me questions."

Jewel swallowed.

"Strange things too. Like what I knew about Caroline, where she could be, and how I knew about this place."

"Dutch, why do they want her so badly? How would they even know she's here?"

"I don't know. When I wouldn't tell them anything, Zuly brought me here."

"At least they didn't hurt you."

"For now," he muttered under his breath.

Jewel rubbed his arm nervously. "Wait. Why didn't they just use magic to make you tell them what they wanted? Now that I think about it, they didn't use magic at all. But they knew what wands were when they saw us."

"I don't think they have magic here, but they do seem to know what it is. It's odd."

"Dutch, we came in here to help Caroline! Not to get trapped!" she said, trying to keep her voice even.

"I know, but Caroline is a strong girl. She should be all right." He pulled her into another hug. "Copper," he said as he let her go, looking around the cell. "The cell is made of copper."

"I know," she said, looking around her. How had she not noticed the copper? It was the only metal that could take away someone's magic when they were close to it. Sorcerers tended to stay away from anything made from it, including pennies. "I'm scared, Dutch."

Dutch grabbed her hand. "We will be fine. I promise."

Chapter 12

The next morning, the warm sun beat down. Merlin's cave got humid due to the lack of circulated air. Once the cave got far too hot, Sal and Caroline woke up on the floor at the same time. Merlin had offered what he called his bed, but the mess of leaves didn't look as welcoming as he must've thought it was.

She put her hand to the back of her neck, trying to make it pop.

Sal wiped sweat from his brow as he looked around. His eyes widened. "Merlin... He's not here!" he said, sounding alarmed.

Caroline turned to where Merlin had slept. Empty. Her eyes searched around the large room, but she couldn't see him anywhere. She wondered if he had left, leaving them all alone to fend for themselves in this strange land.

"Do we go on without him?" Sal asked as he stood.

She ran her hands through her hair as she stood too. "Yes, we must keep going. I just can't believe he left. Some king he was." She tried to hide her disappointment from her voice. She really had thought that Merlin had wanted to help them. She sighed, knowing she could only truly trust herself and those she held dear.

"But what about the gem?" he asked, fixing his hair.

"Forget it. That's not our problem anymore. We'll go to the castle and find my parents."

"If you find your parents," he corrected.

"If?" She rested her hands on her hips, staring at him. His face froze, looking as if he just realized he had messed up. "What do you mean *if?*"

"Where is Merlin?" he asked, looking around the cave as if he hadn't just done so.

"He'll be back, Sal," she snapped. "We're in his house."

"I am right here!" Merlin said, walking into the cave.

He didn't look like himself—or at least not in the way Caroline had known him. He had washed his face and looked much cleaner with glowing skin. No stench followed him around. The most noticeable thing was that his hair had been cut by the top of his neck, and his face only had a shallow beard of what had been there before.

"You look great!" Caroline said as he walked over.

"Thank you," he said, running his hands down his clean poncho and smiling. "I thought that since it might be the first time my people have seen me in years, I should look the part."

"We should get going," Sal said, not meeting her eyes. "It's getting hot in here."

"We should! The weather is perfect for our journey." Merlin walked over to a bag sitting by his bed and pulled it over his shoulder. "Oh, I almost forgot!"

He pulled out a large map from under some leaves and rolled it out on a rock for them all to see. It looked old with stains and rips, but it would get the job done.

"Here is where our journey will take us." He pointed at the castle and dragged his finger over the map. "Today, we shall walk through the forest. And tomorrow, we will exit the forest and head into the village."

Caroline's eyes went wide. "Wait! We're not just going to teleport to the castle?" She found that it was the easiest thing to do; walking was unnecessary. "Why can we just do that?"

"In my life, I have learned that magic is not the only answer," he said, looking over at her. "That we are more than our magic."

Sal looked up to Merlin like he was a wise teacher, and maybe he was, but Caroline was too stubborn to see it. "But Merlin—"

"What if we teleport to the castle and someone sees us?" he countered, raising his eyebrows. "We cannot risk anyone seeing us. It will be safer to walk there."

"That makes a lot of sense," Sal said.

"Well, how long will it take us to get there?" she asked. "You said that I will lose my magic in six days. I have already been here for one."

"So, now we have five days!" Merlin's tone was not mocking, but his words got under her skin. His plan sounded like so much work when she could be there with a flick of her wand. "It should take us four days if we do not stop."

Sal gasped. "Wow!"

"The village will take us almost a day to get through if we go the long way; there are almost no guards that way. Well, the last time I dared to go there, I did not see many guards. Once we make it through, we should stop to rest if needed. On the last day, we shall cross the lake before making it to the castle. We find a safe way in, get the parents, and put the gem back."

Caroline and Sal nodded.

"The last part does not need to be in that order," he said with a smile. "I am more than happy to put the gem back first. Oh! And one last thing." He put the map in his bag and pointed at them. "The way you two are dressed will never do."

Caroline looked down at her jeans and blouse. She thought she looked quite fashionable for her age.

Sal fixed his leather jacket and looked at his black Converse. "What's wrong with the way we're dressed?"

"Well, I have never seen anything like it in my life!" Merlin seemed as if he was trying to hold back his laughter. "Caroline, I can see your legs and ankles!" He pointed down without looking.

She looked down, spotting the small space of skin showing. "Is that a bad thing?"

"No, not now," he explained. "But once we get to town, you will both need new clothes to not stick out so much. If we do not, Caroline, you will have to marry the first chicken that crosses your path." He turned to leave.

Caroline looked at Sal, sharing a face of puzzlement.

"Let us go!" Merlin called. "We do not have all day!"

****

After giving Merlin a moment to say goodbye to his cave, they started their long journey.

He didn't look back once, walking ahead of them. "Since Achilles took all that was once mine, I never thought I would take it back." He looked over. "With two children."

Caroline smiled, hoping to lift his spirits. "I was trained by the best. And Sal here is still learning, but he is very powerful."

Sal laughed.

"Why are you laughing?" Merlin asked, looking over.

He walked faster to be beside him. "Well, I can't do many spells well."

Caroline shot him a look, willing him to shut up.

"Oh," Merlin said after a long moment of silence.

"But I can still help," he said.

"It's true," she added, keeping her tone light.

"Like I had said before," Merlin said, looking toward Sal, "magic is not what makes one strong."

"So, Merlin, how did Achilles even find this place?" Caroline asked, making the wizard turn toward her as they continued to walk through the forest. She kept her eyes down, not wanting to trip on any branches.

"This land's only doorway is through the magic mirror," he explained. "Achilles somehow got ahold of it and came in much like you did. But he came in with ill intentions."

"Could you leave if you wanted to?" she asked.

She saw an opening in the trees with a creek up ahead. The sun was not as bright as she thought it would be as gray clouds moved above. The creek's running water gave off a peaceful aroma. As they neared it, she noticed that the water was black, causing her to wonder if it was safe to drink and whether that was normal here.

Once Merlin leaped over the creek, he answered her. "The people here have no interest in going to your world."

Sal hopped over, tripping as he made it to the other side. He then reached for Caroline's hand to help her jump. "Why not? Our world is pretty groovy." He still held her hand after she made it to the other side.

"What is this word you keep saying?" Merlin asked. "Groovy?"

"It means fashionable, enjoyable, exciting, excellent…"

"I see, but why not just say that?"

"I don't know. It's cooler to say groovy," he said, shrugging.

"Have you ever been to our world?" Caroline asked, going back to the topic from before.

"Why would I want to go to your world?" Merlin asked as he stepped over a fallen tree. "Who would want to go to a place where there are wars, illnesses, hate, violence, killers, and no magic? I mean, sure, Achilles has taken over this world, and my best friend killed my apprentice." He stayed silent for a moment. "But before that, we had no violence. Before Achilles showed up, we only knew peace."

"You do know that the second we came here, we were almost killed right?" Sal asked lightheartedly.

"That is because of Achilles."

"But Achilles is dead," Caroline said. "So, why are his guards staying here if he is not the king of this—"

Merlin quickly turned around and put his hand over her mouth, making her jump.

Why does he keep doing this? "What?" she asked from behind his hand, her voice muffled.

Merlin looked at her strangely before looking up at the sky.

"What's wrong?" Sal asked as Merlin removed his hand.

He didn't say a word. Instead, he looked up at the sky for something they couldn't see. He bent down to the ground, picking up something. Caroline couldn't tell what it was.

"What is that?" Sal asked.

The wizard held it up. It was about the size of a dinner plate and a dark purple color. Caroline looked at Sal, not understanding what was happening.

"It is a scale," Merlin said, speaking in a much quieter tone than moments ago.

She looked toward the path ahead and saw a few more scales on the ground. Whatever they were from, the creature was quite big.

He set the scale down. "There is a dragon flying around."

"WHAT?!" Sal and Caroline asked in union, panic in their voices.

"Did he just say *dragon*?" Sal asked in a shaky voice. He stood a bit closer to her, but she didn't know if it was because he was scared or if he wanted to keep her safe. He grabbed her arm. "Did he just say *dragon* like it was no big deal?"

"There are dragons here?" she asked.

"Yes!" Merlin said quietly but intensely. "They cannot see well since they are pretty much blind; they can only see a few feet in front of them. But they have amazing hearing, so just stay quiet, and it will not know we are here."

Sal stared at the wizard. "Why are there dragons here?"

"Achilles put a few in this land to instill fear in us."

"It's working..." he whispered as his face turned a light red color.

Why is Achilles' magic still here if he is gone?! Her mind puzzled with the question.

"Now is a good time to let you know that they smell fear as well," Merlin admitted.

Sal's eyes went wide.

"So, relax." He continued walking like this was something he was used to.

Sal and Caroline looked at each other and then followed Merlin.

"Wait, Merlin," she said, walking faster to get next to

him, while Sal stayed close behind.

A loud rustle in the trees made everyone stop walking. They looked up. The ground shook with a loud bang, making birds fly away. Then it became deadly quiet.

"Do not move," Merlin whispered to the pair.

Caroline held her breath as her heart raced. She tried to stay calm, but it was not working. She didn't come to this place to be eaten by a flying monster she couldn't even see.

Merlin put his finger to his mouth, signaling them to be quiet. Sal took a deep breath, and his shoulders dropped a bit. She took his hand, hoping to feel some sense of calmness by knowing he was with her.

The temperature spiked as bright orange fire shot out in front of them. Impacted trees fell, slamming into the ground. Near the fire was the hottest she had ever felt in her life. Fear built up in her, and Sal jumped at the sight. Merlin backed away as his body tensed. The fire stopped, leaving ashes floating in the air. The knocked-over trees burned, making loud popping sounds.

Caroline looked to where the flames had come from, seeing two large eyes through the trees as clear as day. Sal's eyes went wide.

The dragon made its way into the open field they were standing in. Caroline swallowed as it stood in front of them. It looked about the size of a large dinosaur with its purple scales shining in the sun. She hoped that they were safe where they stood for the time being.

The dragon took a step toward them, its sharp claws digging into the earth. The ground shook, making everyone off-balance. As it walked, its wings expanded, letting them see just how huge the beast was.

Merlin looked at it without any fear on his face,

something she wished she could have done. She was terrified, and she knew the monster in front of her knew that. It walked toward them faster and opened its large mouth. A light formed in the back of its throat. She already felt the heat.

"RUN!" Merlin yelled.

****

Caroline and Sal wasted no time, running off like Merlin had told them. In the panic, they ran in two different directions without even noticing. Fire filled the spot where they had just stood, heating up the forest again.

She tripped over a log, landing on her stomach. The beast more than likely heard her. She looked over her shoulder to see if Merlin or Sal had been burned, but she could not see them anymore. Pounding footsteps got closer to where she was at. She stood and ran, hiding behind a nearby tree and holding it close. *Calm down, Caroline! Calm down!*

She patted her pockets for her wand, but it wasn't there. She looked around the tree and spotted it on the ground where she had fallen. Smoke from the dragon's fire filled the air, making her hold back a cough. She covered her mouth with her shaking hands, trying to hold it in.

She needed to calm down, but the ground shook as the dragon walked around. The trees around her swayed. She didn't dare move to her wand or call it to her. All was quiet once again, but she anticipated the worst. Resting her forehead on the tree, she waited.

Seconds later, fire shot past her on both sides of the tree. She screamed out. The only thing keeping her safe was the tree she pressed her body to. The unbearable heat seemed as if it went on forever as her skin and throat burned. The tree filled with smoke, starting to fall on her.

"Wand to my hand!" she coughed out, stretching her arm out behind her. Once she felt the hot wand in her hand, she said, "Teleportsheam."

Soon, she was out of harm's way, but it was not far enough. The dragon stopped breathing fire as it turned its head toward her. More fire built up in its mouth. She pointed her shaky wand at the beast.

Sal's voice cut through everything. "Hey, over here!" he yelled as he ran out of the woods and back into the field. "Hey you!" He waved his arms over his head.

The dragon stopped and turned to face him as Merlin ran up behind him. They waved their arms and shouted.

Her vision became blurry as the dragon's tail slammed into the side of her head. Her whole mind clouded, and a buzzing sounded. Pain shot from her neck to her head from the ground's impact. Her breathing became heavy as she tried not to let the black dots swimming in her vision take over.

"Get up," she whispered.

Sal didn't have strong magic, and Merlin was pretty much powerless. She couldn't let this dragon burn or eat them.

A chill went down her spine as black dots filled her vision once more, far too many to see straight. She felt the bag of marbles on her hip. With a shaking hand, she reached inside, pulling out five and throwing them as best she could.

In less than a second, Edmund appeared in front of her. "What happened?!" he asked, sounding horrified.

Blood slid down the side of her face as she looked up at him. "Help them," she said, pointing to Sal and Merlin.

He looked at her with panicked eyes.

"I'm all right. Help them!" She forced herself to sit up a bit more to prove she was fine.

He looked at her one last time before taking off to where she had pointed.

****

Edmund was *not* expecting to see a dragon at all. "What in the world?!" he muttered under his breath. He saw Sal and an older man he didn't know do whatever they could to move the dragon away from Caroline. Without a second thought, he ran up in front of Sal and the other man.

"Who the hell are you?!" the older man asked.

"Edmund?!" Sal said, sounding surprised.

Edmund knew he only had minutes, so Caroline would have to answer their questions later. Flicking his wand, he made lightning fly toward the dragon. It cried out, fire embers still growing in the back of its throat. He sent fire next, making it madder. It released its own fire toward the three of them. Grabbing his wand with both hands, Edmund made a force field around them. The fire hit the outside, but he could still feel the heat.

"Where is Caroline?" Sal asked.

"She's hurt," he said, trying with all his might to hold the force field as the dragon continued to breathe down fire.

"Strange man," the older man said as he tapped Edmund's shoulder, "teleport me to her."

Edmund looked at Sal. "Who is he?"

"He's on our side," Sal said.

With a flick of his wand, the older man disappeared. "Get ready!" he said as he removed the force field. "Stone-soul!" The fire froze in the air. "Gepsic!"

****

Merlin saw Caroline laying on the ground with her face in

the dirt. "Caroline!" he said once he was by her side.

"Edmund?" she asked as she lifted her head.

"You are bleeding," he noted as he bent down to her. He put his hand on her head, feeling a large bump that was moist with blood. "I am going to do a spell." He put pressure on her head as he muttered a healing spell.

After a moment, she looked back up at him, seeming more focused. "Are you all right?"

He nodded. "Do not worry about me! Let us go!" He picked up her wand, handing it back to her. Without another word, they made their way to Edmund.

****

"My time is up!" Edmund yelled, and in a second, he was gone.

Caroline shot strong magic toward the dragon, angering it more.

The dragon opened its wings and lifted into the air.

"Holy crap!" Sal screamed as the wind from its wings pushed him back.

Everyone was knocked off their feet, while the dragon flew into the sky. If it was even possible, it looked so much bigger in the air as it stared down at them.

"Say *sizable* and point your wand at the dragon!" Merlin ordered Caroline. "Do it!" He backed away from her.

She pointed her wand at the dragon and did just as he asked. "Sizable!"

The power hit the dragon with a bright light, blinding the group.

"What did I do?" she asked Merlin, who said nothing.

As they opened their eyes, the dragon was not in the air anymore.

Merlin pointed to the middle of the field. "Look at the dragon now," he said much calmer than before.

Caroline and Sal looked. The dragon now stood about the size of a small house cat.

"Oh," he said.

This was the last thing she thought would've happened from the spell. "Well, okay..."

It looked up at them and walked over to them with short stubby steps. Its little tail waved with each step.

"Aww! Look at it!" Sal said as he bent down to pet it.

"Do not touch it!" Merlin ordered.

The dragon backed away from Sal's hand at first as it came toward its head, but once Sal petted it, it moved closer, wagging its tail softly.

"Can we keep it?" he asked.

"Um, no."

"That thing just tried to kill us!" Caroline said as she looked at the dragon.

"Are you all right?" Sal asked, sounding panicked as he stood and looked at her. His worry showed in his eyes. "Edmund said you were hurt."

"I got hit by the dragon's tail," she said. "But I'm okay now. Merlin's spell helped."

"I did what I could with my weak magic," Merlin mumbled, "but it looks like you are still bleeding. If I had my true powers, you would be fully healed."

"My neck doesn't hurt as much anymore," she said, putting her hand to it.

"Once I feel stronger, I can do the spell again and heal the cut and the sore muscles." He turned back to the dragon, who still looked up at them. "It cannot hurt us now. I suggest we keep going."

As if to prove a point, the little dragon spit a small amount of fire on Sal's leg.

Sal jumped back and patted down his pants. "So, we're not keeping him? Come on! Look at him! He is adorable! He can't hurt us much anymore."

Merlin shook his head.

"Will the spell wear off?" Caroline asked as it sat and looked up at them. It *did* just try to kill them, but she hoped it would be okay once they left.

"No. You can undo the spell, but it might try to eat us again," Merlin said, turning to leave. "Let us continue. We have a long journey ahead of us."

Sal took one last look at the dragon before following Merlin.

"Come on," Caroline said, taking his hand in hers.

"Who was that man by the way?" Merlin asked. "The large one."

"He is a Smith! And he is my uncle Edmund," she said and explained what she had in the bag.

Chapter 13

J ewel looked over at Dutch, who pulled on the bars
hard. They had tried almost everything they could to
get out of the cell. But everything they tried ended
in frustration. So far, it had been a cold night, and they
both were tired and hungry.

"Dutch," she said, walking over to him from where
she had been sitting. "Just give it up."

He let go of the bars, breathing hard as he put his hand
to his face. "I just can't believe this happened."

She put her hand on his chest and looked up to him,
to his lips. She got on her tiptoes to kiss him, but he turned
his head away. "Dutch…" she said so quietly that she was
not even sure he had heard her.

"Problems in paradise, I see," said a hidden person,
their voice filling the room in an unsettling way.

Jewel and Dutch looked around their empty cell.

"Who's there?" he asked.

The dungeon stayed silent for a few seconds. He took
a step closer to her. She saw no one, which confused her,
until she noticed a shadow just out of sight.

"My men," the voice said, sounding much closer now,
"told me that she was here, but I didn't believe she would

be reckless enough to come into *my* world."

The voice sounded too familiar to Jewel, sending chills down her spine.

"Who are you?" Dutch asked with no fear in his voice.

A candle lit from where the voice came from, revealing the person behind it. His pale face lined with a scar that stretched across his nose to his cheek, appearing like a backward *L*. His cold purple eyes, filled with hate and rage, never looked away from her.

She gasped. "Achilles!" Chills filled her body as she looked back at the man she thought she had killed last year. "How are you alive?" She stood tall with her head held high and her fist held by her side. She moved forward, wanting this man to know that she didn't fear him, even though she was terrified.

Achilles put a thin smile on his face, one she had definitely not missed. "I never died." He looked right at her as if Dutch was not there. "You thought you were so powerful? That you could never fail at anything? But you did fail. Your spell didn't end my life. It only brought me here, just as I had planned."

She knit her eyebrows together. "I don't understand."

Achilles stepped closer to the cell. "You see, no one can just kill me that easily! I had my aging spell that kept me alive in your world, but I also have a few other spells."

Dutch and Jewel looked at each other, confused. She didn't know one could have more than one spell on themselves at a time.

"I had another spell that if I was to die in the outside world, I would just come back here, where I get my strongest powers." Achilles smiled at the space around him.

"What do you mean?" Dutch asked.

"I found this land a few weeks before killing your daughter, Jewel."

Jewel swallowed.

"I had heard stories of this land with its gem. I knew I would be unstoppable with it."

Dutch laughed under his breath. "You were unstoppable until a young girl put you in your place."

Anger grew in his eyes as they met Dutch's for the first time. "No! That girl would have died if it was not for you!" He glanced back at Jewel. "You were not part of my plan. If anything, I wanted you to live, but you kept getting in the way." He now stood in front of the cell. "You were the only person in town who welcomed me with open arms, but you *intervened*. So now, the plan changes. *You* will die! Tomorrow morning, you will be killed by me!"

Dutch pushed her behind him. "You touch her, and I swear—"

"Oh, Dutch," he said, almost laughing. "You have always been the least of my problems. You think you're keeping them safe, but you do nothing. You have never done anything to help them."

If his words hurt Dutch, he didn't show it.

"In the end, you won't be enough to save what you have. Just like you were not enough to keep Caroline and Jewel safe last year."

Jewel stood next to Dutch, holding his hand in hers. "Why are you here then? If you have been alive all this time, why not come after us?"

"Don't you see?!" Achilles yelled. "I have been strengthening my army, so I can come back to your world and get Caroline out of the way. There is something in that town so powerful that you could not even imagine." He mumbled that last part. "But now she is in my world, so the plan has changed."

He smiled and pointed at Jewel. "You should be worried, Jewel. What I did to you last year will be nothing compared to what I plan to do to your granddaughter now."

Zuly walked up behind Achilles with his hands behind his back and cleared his throat.

"Zuly," Achilles said, keeping his eyes locked on Jewel as he spoke, "tomorrow before the sun rises, take Jewel to the torture room." He glared at Dutch. "Where I shall end her life."

Jewel tried to hold back the wave of fear that might flood at any given moment.

"Wait," he said as he turned to Zuly. "If we find Caroline before the morning, I shall kill her in front of Jewel. If not, she will die alone."

Jewel reached through the bars, trying to hit him. "Don't you hurt her!"

Achilles turned and grabbed her face through the bars. "Look on the bright side. Dutch will have a lifetime alone in this cell."

She pulled her face out of his grasp.

"Achilles!" Dutch called out. "You won't win."

He laughed wickedly. "I already did. Enjoy the night."

****

Achilles could not believe his luck.

He walked into the throne room, passing his maids who lowered their heads as he walked by. On his throne, he sat, overlooking everyone as they worked. Not one soul dared to meet his eyes. He lifted his leg, placing his foot on the seat, as he rested his elbow on his knee.

He smiled, thinking about how everything had played out so much better than he could have ever hoped for. He no longer needed to go back to Duck for now. The amulet would have to wait till he could make his return.

"Sir," Zuly said, walking into the throne room. He bowed.

"What do you want?!" Achilles yelled, his voice echoing off the walls. He did not want to be disturbed, but here Zuly was.

Zuly put his hands behind his back and stood tall. "The guards have come in for the night."

His anger grew. "I gave you one order, and that was not it! Bring me Caroline!"

"N-no, I only thought that—"

"That's the problem, Zuly! You think you can overrule my orders!"

Zuly swallowed. "Why must we find this child? When I faced her in the—"

"You have faced her?!" Achilles stood from his seat, rage coursing through him.

"She is very strong and—"

He flicked his wand, making Zuly cry out and drop to his knees. Lightning kept flickering at the tip of his wand. "You are useless! A waste!" He grabbed a fist full of Zuly's hair, making him stand.

Zuly bit his lip, holding back a cry.

"Go find her! If you return without her, I will kill you slowly!" he hissed. He sent his fist into Zuly's ribs. "Now, get out of my face!"

Zuly's cheeks turned pink with embarrassment as he looked around as if to make sure no one had seen what had just happened. He wobbled on his feet. "Yes, my lord," he said, his voice shaking. He bowed and left the room.

Chapter 14

Caroline sat at the water's edge with her legs folded under her as she looked down, trying to find her reflection. The water seemed so unwelcoming since she couldn't see what was under it, but she still set the pot down next to her and put her hands in it. It was colder than she had expected. She cupped her hands and lowered her face, washing it. Without a mirror or a towel, she tried her best. Once she thought she cleaned most of the blood from her cut off, she looked up at the clear night sky.

In a clearing in the woods is where they had set up camp. Some trees stood around the lake, but it was so large that it made a clear circle in the sky. The yellow moon and white stars shined, softly lighting the land, but the lake didn't reflect the glow. She noted how bright the sky was with no other lights to dim it. *The village must still be so far away.*

She also wondered what Jewel was doing. She missed her already.

She knew she was closer to her dad, but her feet ached from the walk, and a part of her didn't want to do it all over again once she woke up.

She grabbed the pot, dunking it into the water. The

pot was small, but what she collected should be enough for the night. She made her way over to where Merlin was placing the logs that Sal had gathered for the campfire.

Sal stepped out of the woods with leaves, sticks, and anything else that would burn. "Should this be enough?" He set everything by the wizard's bag.

"That should be more than enough," Merlin said, placing a hand on his shoulder. "Thank you." He turned, noticing Caroline. "How are you feeling?"

Sal took the pot from her.

"Much better now that I've washed my face. I am going to need a new shirt though," she said, pointing to the stain.

"That is all right," Merlin said, still working on the fire. "You both need new clothes anyhow. We will reach the village tomorrow!"

Caroline pulled out her wand, pointing at the pot in Sal's hands to make the water safe to drink. "Waicl."

"That water is cold, so it will taste amazing," Merlin said.

"Can we eat tonight?" Sal asked as he set the pot down. His belly rumbled.

"I have been in the woods for years. All I need is a sharp stick and my wit!"

"Or I could just use my magic," Caroline said, making him smile.

"Yes. That sounds better."

Soon, the camp went silent as they ate their roasted ham with delight. No one spoke until everything was almost gone.

"Merlin," Sal said, making him look at him. "What has living in the woods been like?"

"Well, you learn things. It is also lonely."

"Were you alone all these years out here?"

"Yes," he answered in a much softer tone.

"I'm so sorry," Sal said.

Merlin looked into the fire's flames, seeming deep in thought. He stayed quiet for a moment before he spoke again. "I did not just lose my castle and my magic but all those I held dear. In the castle, many wonderful people worked so hard to make everything just right. I loved each and every one of them." He paused again. "I cannot even imagine what Zuly or Achilles did to them. Or if they are even still alive. But worst of all, I lost…" He closed his eyes.

Sal looked over at Caroline with sad eyes. It was so clear that this man had lost far too much. *Just like me.* She got up, sat closer to him, and rested her hand on his shoulder, encouraging him to share his story.

"I used to have an apprentice," he finally said, still not daring to meet their eyes. "She was a ray of sunshine, and I failed her. She died the day Achilles came here. Zuly killed her. He killed her!" His tone became harder. "I had felt as though I should be alone as part of my punishment for letting her down. I should have known she was not ready for that fight."

Caroline didn't know what to say. Loss—to her—sometimes felt like a scar. The pain would go away, but the damage would never leave one's heart.

"Didn't you say your friend killed her?" Sal asked.

"Yes. Zuly was my captain and good friend. Her friend as well."

"I'm sorry you lost her and everyone else," Caroline said. "And I hope you know you're more than just our map. We really want to help you."

Merlin smiled, but he still held sadness behind his eyes.

****

Much later, Caroline sat, looking at the small fire.

"May I sit with you?" Merlin's voice asked from behind her.

She looked back, seeing him holding his bag. "Of course."

He sat a few feet away, placing the bag between them. "Thank you for your kind words from before. I did not want to burden you with so much."

"It was not a burden," she said, meaning it with her whole being. "You and I have a lot in common. I've lost everything because of Achilles too. But I also have had good things happen because of him."

Merlin looked surprised. "How so?"

"I have a great bond with my uncle—the one you met—and his family because I lived with them for seven years. I see Edmund like a dad. I get to live with my grandmother, and if Achilles never came into my story, I would not have met Dutch or Sal."

"Well, I guess the good thing about all this," Merlin said, looking into the fire that lit up half of his face, "is that I met you and Sal."

She smiled. "Yes. I will add you to my list of good things because of Achilles."

After a few seconds of silence, Merlin spoke again. "I was really impressed by you today. I have never known someone who could hear a spell once and get it right on the first try."

"It wasn't always like that," she said, thinking back to her first days of training. "It was hard when I first started last summer."

"You only started last year?! I thought you have been

doing this your whole life." He laughed a true laugh that stunned her. "I should not be so surprised. You are a Smith!"

"Thank you," she said with a proud grin.

"If you do not mind me asking, how old are you?" he asked.

"I'm fifteen, sir," she said.

"So young and so gifted."

Caroline beamed. "My grandmother and my good friend, Dutch, trained me."

"You have great teachers."

She knew how proud they would be if they knew the king of this land, Merlin, was telling her these things. She made a mental note to tell them when she got back home.

"I would like to share something with you if that is all right." He reached for his bag.

"Yes—"

He yelped as he pulled his arm out. His face filled with pain. The little dragon from before was biting his hand, holding on to the raised arm.

"What in the world?" He gasped. "SAL!" He stood and walked toward a sleeping Sal, while the dragon still tried to eat his hand.

Caroline covered her mouth with her hands, trying not to laugh. *When did Sal put that thing in Merlin's bag?*

"SAL, wake up!" he yelled. "Explain yourself!"

Sal sat up, seeming a bit dazed. He looked at the little dragon on the wizard, and his eyes widened. "I know you said we couldn't keep him, but he was following us. So, when we stopped a while back, I put him in your bag."

Caroline laughed. He must had done it fast because she had no idea. The dragon let go of Merlin's hand, dropping next to Sal and cozying up to his side.

"Fine! You keep it!" Merlin yelled. "But I will not help you when that thing tries to kill you! In. Your. Sleep!"

Sal frowned. He looked down at the dragon, who was now eating some of the ham they had left. Merlin walked back over to his seat with his hands up in surrender before sitting next to her.

"It's so cute now," she said. She watched the dragon lick Sal's face, which made him laugh.

"Sure. If you say so," Merlin said, turning back to his bag. "Anyway, I want to give you my spell book." He handed her a large book with a green cover.

"You're giving this to me?" she asked as she held it in her lap. It was heavier than the spell book she had back home.

"It is filled with spells you might have never heard of before. In your world, magic is simpler, but I think you can master many of these. You have a gift, and you were born for great things," he said, making her smile. "We can work on them at night until we get to the castle."

"Thank you so much!" She opened it, reading the first spell she saw. She hadn't believed him when he had said that the magic she had learned was easy, but once she looked through the pages, she understood. "What is this one?" she asked, pointing at one of the pages. It had a photo of someone standing with no wand as if they were doing karate. "Do wizards here do karate?"

"What is karate? No. When someone is very powerful, they can use magic without a wand," he said. "I bet you can do it."

"I've done it once, I think." She stood, putting the book down with the pages still open.

"You must stand with your right leg out in front of you," he instructed. "Feel the earth underneath you and become one with the land." He stood just like the drawn person in the book.

She closed her eyes, trying to feel what he had told her. She felt grounded, that gravity was pulling her. "Then what?" she asked, opening her eyes.

He looked at her stance. "Now, reach both arms out in front of you and then pull them back." He did the movements next to her.

As she did what he said, power grew within her. Her body seemed as if it could not hold all the power she was making. "I'm nervous. This feels stronger."

"You are a Smith! You can do anything!" he encouraged. "Now, shoot your arms out again with your hands open toward where you want the magic to go."

Caroline did just that, and strong magic soared out of her hands. It pushed her so much that she thought she might end up on her back. The power traveled halfway across the lake, lighting up the night for a few seconds. She then dropped to her knees, breathing hard.

Merlin had a satisfying grin along his face as he helped her to her feet. "It is a very powerful spell that can hurt someone if you do it right. If you keep working on it, you will be able to reach across the lake in no time."

"You really think so?" she asked, turning to him with the biggest smile on her face.

"Yes, I do. That is only one of many things you can learn from this spell book." He put a hand on her shoulder. "In life, things can make you nervous, but never let it stop you from reaching greatness." He gave her a warm smile. "Try not to stay up working on this too late. We have a long day ahead of us."

With that, he turned away as a smile grew even more on Caroline's face.

Chapter 15

A few hours passed by, and everyone was sound asleep. The dragon slept like a puppy on its back next to Sal, Merlin slept a few feet away with his back to them, and Caroline slept the closest to the fire to stay warm. The only sound came from the crackling fire that still glowed in the middle of the field.

Until a calm male voice calling her name repeatedly filled her mind. She snapped her head up from where she lay, looking around to find the voice's source. She saw the others sleeping, clearly not hearing what she had. She turned to the tree line a few feet away from them, but there was nothing.

She had heard this familiar voice many times in her dreams, but tonight—out in a world she didn't know—it scared her. But it was probably nothing. She glanced at the fire before turning to go back to sleep, deciding it was just a dream.

As she lay her head back down, she noticed someone standing just outside of the fire's light. She jumped to her feet, her heart pounding in her chest. "Who are you? Show yourself!" She put her hand in her pocket, looking for her wand, but it was not there. *That's where I left it!* She searched around on the ground.

"I know you're here," the man said, stepping into the light to reveal the face of Achilles.

Caroline gasped, backing up. She lost her balance and fell onto her backside, staring up at him. "NO!" Her body shook. She crawled back, away from him. "You're dead! I watched you die! Grandma killed you!"

He took a few steps closer, kicking dirt into the fire. It died and left her in the dark with only the faint moonlight.

"Answer me!" she yelled, sounding much weaker than she wanted to. "How are you alive, Achilles?" His name was like poison in her mouth.

He stood right in front of her, bent down, and grabbed her neck. Her eyes widened as he pulled her to her feet, his nails digging into her skin. She grabbed at his wrist, trying to free herself from his grasp, but failed.

"I know you're here," he said once more. "I know you're looking for someone very special to you, but I will kill you before you even find them."

She looked over at her sleeping companions for help.

"Get ready, Caroline. You won't be so lucky the next time we meet."

She gasped, scratching at his hands and arms, as he lifted her off the ground. "Sal!"

"He is useless and won't help you when you need it the most." Achilles started walking toward the lake with her.

"Merlin!" she called out the best she could.

"That old man is weak! That's why he is out here, and I am in his castle." He held her over the lake, her vision darkening. "You will lose your life in this world!" He brought her closer to him and whispered, "My world."

With that, he dropped her into the cold water.

****

Caroline shot up from where she had been sleeping, out of breath. She was covered in sweat as she looked around the camp. Everyone was still sleeping, the fire was still going, and no one watched her from the shadows. It was just a dream.

She put her head in her hands. That dream had felt so much more real than it should have. She remembered how Jewel had told her that powerful sorcerers could send messages through dreams. *Is he alive?* She cupped her face with her hands, sobbing into them. The very last thing she wanted was to see Achilles again.

She closed her eyes, listening to the night's sounds. Bugs sang like they did back home, which brought her some comfort. The soft fire popped, and the dragon snored.

She grabbed her locket that Dutch had given her last summer. She opened it, looking at the picture of Jewel, him, and herself from the town carnival. After running her finger over the picture, she shut the locket and held it close. How she wished she could just walk over to the next room, wake her grandmother, and have her tell her that it was only a bad dream.

But as she looked around the camp and saw everyone else sleeping, she realized she was on her own.

Chapter 16

"It won't end like this! I won't let it," Dutch said, fidgeting with his hands. He looked over at Jewel, who sat on the floor with her legs pulled to her chest. Her eyes seemed unfocused on something.

It was clear that they were never getting out of this cell. But that fate seemed unbearable. He tried to pull the bars once more and then rested his head on them. It seemed like he could never save Jewel or Caroline, no matter how hard he tried. *Maybe Achilles was right.* His eyes burned with tears at the thought of losing the ones he loved the most.

"Dutch, can I ask you something?" Jewel asked, looking up at him.

He looked at her. He just wanted to hold her close one last time. The idea that she would be gone by this time tomorrow pained his heart. He moved and sat in front of her. "Anything," he said, putting on a strong face.

"When Achilles kills me…" She looked away from him, not meeting his eyes.

"Jewel—"

"Will you take care of Caroline?"

"Jewel, nothing is going to happen to you," he said in a stronger tone.

"Listen to me!" she snapped, looking back at him. "Please tell me that you will make sure she has a good life! That you will take care of her."

He didn't want to accept that he would lose her in just hours. "Jewel, please—"

"Promise me!" She held his gaze, making his throat tight.

"Yes! She will always have a home and someone who loves her!"

Jewel pulled herself closer to him, resting her head on his chest.

He wrapped his arms around her. "We will find a way out of this. You will go home with me." His voice shook as he tried to keep his tears at bay.

"Let Caroline know I love her."

"Stop talking like that. You're going to be okay!" He pulled her in a bit closer.

"Dutch, please!" Her voice was thick with emotions. "Tell her that I am sorry for not being in her life sooner and that she is my everything."

He looked up at the ceiling, wishing with all his heart that this was a dream.

She pulled out of his hug and looked into his eyes. "And I want you to know that I still love you."

"Jewel, I don't want to talk about the proposal."

"I have to tell you how sorry I am. You are my life."

"I love you so much," he said, rubbing her cheek with his thumb. He could look into her eyes forever.

"When Lester... When he got sick and d-died, he left me all alone."

He swallowed. "I know..."

Lester, her late husband, had been good friends with Dutch. The two would go fishing or anything else that seemed like fun every weekend. But he had heart problems that grew worse until his heart gave up on him. Jewel had been so broken for the next few years as she raised her daughters on her own.

"When he left me, that destroyed my world," Jewel continued, never taking her eyes off him. "I promised myself that I would never go through something like that again. So, when you asked me to marry you, I worried that I would lose you too."

Dutch pulled her back into a hug, trying to find the right words. "Nothing is going to happen to me. I would never leave you because I wanted to."

"When Zuly took you, I realized that I would suffer no matter what." She held his hand. "So, I'm sorry I made you feel terrible. I am also sorry that I am the one that will leave you forever tomorrow."

Dutch let a tear fall out of his eye, and she wiped it away with a loving hand that he melted into. "The agony... You're the one leaving me."

Jewel laughed under her breath. "I love you."

"I love you too."

They shared a lovely kiss that turned into another. He ran his fingers through her hair, but something poked him. He patted it and then opened his eyes, pulling out what he had found.

She pulled away. "Okay. What was that, Dutch?"

"You had a bobby pin in your hair this whole time and didn't say anything!" He held it, so she could see it. "I can pick a lock with this!"

Chapter 17

With a lack of sleep, Caroline dragged her feet the next day. Anxiety lingered in her, and her heart seemed as if it was trying to come out of her body, while her mind raced.

"Can we stop for a minute?" she asked Merlin after they had walked for an hour.

"Not for long," he said.

She took off to get away from the boys and to clear her mind. She sat by a little waterfall she found. Today, their plans were to get out of the forest and start going through the village. It also was going to be their longest day of walking, but the day had already taken a toll on her.

Caroline closed her eyes, listening to the water. But her mind went back to Achilles. If he was alive, and her dream was a warning, what had they done wrong the year before? How was he still alive?

"Are you all right?" Sal asked as he sat next to her. The little dragon sat on his shoulder, looking equally worried.

"No," she said as she watched a black leaf float down the stream. "I had a dream last night with Achilles. H-he said he would kill me. Sal, it was so real! I think it was a warning."

He took her hand in his. "It was just a dream, right? It's not true. You've said it yourself many times: Achilles is dead."

"But it felt so real. Sal, I am scared," she said, holding back a sob. "He made my life hell, and I can't do it again!"

"I know." He smiled weakly before kissing her forehead. "I hate seeing you unhappy about something that is out of my hands."

She blinked away her tears and stood, not wanting to waste more time. They still had a long way to go. "Let's get going."

"You're going to be all right," he said, taking her hand again and giving it a caring squeeze.

Merlin walked up to the pair, seeming in a fairly good mood despite the unplanned stop. "Is everything all right?" he asked, looking at them both.

"Yes," she said, giving him her best smile and hoping he wouldn't ask her anything more.

"Well, I believe we should get moving." He pointed toward the gray clouds that were visible through the treetops. "Looks like a storm is coming." He turned back and started walking.

"You should tell him," Sal whispered.

"No, not yet," she answered, not wanting to worry Merlin. She looked to her right, spotting something shining in the sunlight. "Is that...?" She moved forward to get a better look. "The mirror!"

Sal stopped in his tracks. "You mean to tell me that we're not even past the mirror?!"

"Yes. Did you think I would live close to where the guards roam?" Merlin asked.

No one answered. Caroline stared at the mirror with her mouth open in disbelief. Everything felt so much farther knowing that they were back where they had started.

"Let us go to the village," Merlin said, laughing as he started walking again.

Sal looked at the mirror one last time before grabbing her arm for her to follow.

****

Many hours crawled by. Storm clouds hung overhead but still held onto their rain. It was the longest walk Caroline had ever taken. Each step felt like they were walking on nails through fire. Her shoes pinched, making her wish she had brought better ones. She thought of taking them off but then thought that might not be the best idea while walking in a forest. Sal looked just as uncomfortable as she felt. Merlin would never say so, but Sal and Caroline both knew he had to be dying on the inside as well.

"Merlin, I was thinking," she said, wanting to lighten the mood. She walked next to him. "You met Sal because he fell. I met him the same way."

Merlin laughed. His smile lit up the woods. "Why must you always be falling?"

"I don't know. I hadn't even put it together till now," Sal said with a laugh.

"I was at the beach, and he fell next to me," she continued, recalling how he had hit the sand.

"At least he would not have died like when I saved him," Merlin said, turning to Sal. "You are quite the runner."

"You know, Caroline lit shoes on fire while learning magic!" he said, moving the wizard's attention back to her.

"Hey!" she said. "I was learning! But Dutch screamed so loud…"

"As would I." Merlin looked thoughtful. "The worst thing that happened to me while training was my apprentice made a cook fall down the stairs, and the food went everywhere." He laughed. "The castle smelled like fish for weeks!"

As the laughter died down, Sal spoke up. "Random question. What do we name the dragon?"

"Little monster of death," Merlin said.

"Come on. Something better than that."

"Do you think it will still kill us if it grew right now?" He looked at the creature with a bit of fear as the dragon looked at each of them.

"I would hope not."

"How about Fuego?" the older man suggested.

"I love that," Caroline said.

"That's fire in Spanish, right?" Sal asked.

"Yes. I know many languages. And the name seems only fitting since he tried to kill us with his fire," Merlin said, petting Fuego's little head.

Fuego closed his eyes, seeming pleased.

Soon, they stayed quiet, looking down at the ground while out of breath. Sometimes, Fuego flew over them. Other times, he sat on either Caroline's or Sal's shoulder since he got heavy just staying on one. Merlin even held Fuego like a baby for a while.

After an hour of silence, Merlin froze where he stood. "Wait. Stop!"

Caroline and Sal stopped in their tracks and looked at each other with fear. Her mind raced with possibilities of what was about to happen.

"Merlin," Sal said in a low, shaky voice.

Merlin didn't look toward him but at the ground.

"What is it?"

"Merlin?" Caroline whispered as the ground shook underneath her with a great force. Her eyes widened. "What is happening?"

"Run!" he said, but it was too late.

Roots from nearby trees moved like they had a mind of their own as the ground rose. Caroline and Sal ran left, while Merlin ran straight. The roots followed them. Fuego flew up to safety as a root grabbed Sal's ankle, pulling him back. He fell, slamming into the ground.

Caroline gasped as the root started to bring him back to a specific tree. That tree opened as if getting ready to swallow him. "Sal!" she screamed. Pulling out her wand, she flicked it at the root pulling Sal. "Fire itera!"

But the fire did nothing. She stood like Merlin had shown her the night before and did that spell. The magic slammed into the tree taking Sal, killing it and the others around it as they dried up. The roots dropped to the ground, lifeless.

Sal looked up to her from the ground. "Behind you!"

A root came up from behind her, hitting her shoulder. She dropped her wand as it wrapped around her chest and pulled her back. Sal raced to her wand, but Fuego was faster. He flew down, picked it up, and took it to her.

"Gepsic!"

Once more, everything stopped.

"Merlin!" She tripped over the root that had held her.

"I am here!" he yelled, sounding close.

"Are you all right?" Sal asked.

Merlin was strongly wrapped around his legs by one of the roots. Sal moved to pull the dead root off his legs.

"Yes. It had quite the hold on me," Merlin said.

Caroline ran up to them with Fuego on her shoulder.

"Are you both all right?" he asked, looking back and forth at each young face.

"I believe so," she said, feeling winded.

"What was that?!" Sal asked as they all stood.

"Someone in the castle must know we are trying to get there," Merlin said, sounding out of breath. "And they are trying to stop us."

He sighed. "How? How can they know?" he asked with a raspy voice.

"I do not know," Merlin said truthfully. "But we must be more careful because it is quite clear that whoever it is is determined we will never make it."

Chapter 18

When the tree line stopped and revealed a road, Caroline almost cried. She loved the open land and gray road that would take them to the village. The grass was still a dark color, but without the trees, it somehow didn't look as bad as it had before.

"We are near!" Merlin said.

"My feet hurt so bad! I can't wait to sleep!" she said, looking back at him.

He smiled. "We can keep working on your magic too. We do not have long before we make it to the castle."

She nodded, but sleep sounded so much more welcoming.

Sal dropped to his knees. "Halfway there!" Fuego flew over his head before landing on his shoulder. "You people should try cars out. Do you guys not have horses?"

Ignoring his comment, Merlin said, "The first shop is where I will find you clothes." He pointed to the village that was just out of sight. "You both will stay here."

"Why?" she asked, a bit disappointed.

"If one person sees you both dressed like…that…" He looked back at them with an unsure look, waving his hand in their direction. "Well, let me just say it will not be good.

The fashion where you come from is strange."

"Well, we don't have any money to buy clothes," Sal said.

Merlin laughed. "Do you have to pay for things to wear where you come from?"

"Well, yeah," Caroline said, finding his question odd.

Once more, he chuckled. "That is another reason why no one goes to your world."

Sal crossed his arms. "So, clothes are free here?"

"Of course. It is something every human and elf needs."

"Elf?" she asked.

"Yes, elf. Why would you have to pay for something that is needed? Nicer things do cost money, but simple things here are free."

Sal looked at her.

"Amazing," she said.

Merlin turned away with a wave. "I will not be long."

****

Caroline took off her shoes as she and Sal sat under a low tree branch. The gray clouds released the rain they had been holding at last, pouring down hard. They showed no sign of stopping anytime soon. The air turned colder the longer they sat still.

"I think Fuego is an amazing dragon," he said as he petted Fuego's belly. "Yes, you are!"

Fuego wagged his tail, clearly enjoying all the attention.

"There he is!" Caroline called out, pointing at Merlin.

Merlin walked toward them with two large paper bags in his hands. The rain made the bags almost break as he set them down in front of the pair. "I got what we need." He pulled out black pants for Sal, along with a long-sleeved white shirt that seemed a size too large and a dark blue vest to go over it. "And boots!"

Sal took his new clothes, and she flicked her wand at him. In a second, he was dressed in what Merlin had gotten him.

"Look at you!" she said, admiring the way he looked.

"I have something similar, but my vest is gold." Merlin smiled as he opened the other bag and pulled out a dress that left Caroline in awe.

It by no means was a princess dress, but it had three pieces. First, he pulled out an off-white plain dress. The sleeves looked as if they would only go down to her elbow with bell sleeves flowing around her arms. The second part was an olive-green skirt that would go over the first layer. He also pulled out what looked like a corset that matched the green skirt.

"I hope it fits well," he said, handing her some shoes that looked more uncomfortable than the ones she had with her.

"Thank you," she said, taking her new clothes. She pointed her wand at herself, putting the dress on in seconds. The corset squeezed her ribs.

She flicked her wand at Merlin, and he was dressed, looking more like a king. His dark complexion looked stunning with the gold vest. Everyone put their things into his bag. Once they were ready, they took off for the village. The unwelcomed rain poured down, soaking them.

"Caroline, do *not* use any magic in front of anyone," Merlin warned as they walked up to the village.

A sign that read *Welcome to the Village of Spotsyburg* greeted them. It looked run-down as if it had been years since anyone cared to paint it. Under the town name, faint wording could be seen, showing that the town used to be called Magically.

"Why?" she asked Merlin as she put her hair into a short braid. A few strands stuck to her face.

"Well, they might get scared and think you are with Achilles. It has been far too long since they have seen magic."

Sal nodded with an understanding smile. "No magic in the town. Easy!" He took her hand as she laughed under her breath.

The rain poured much heavier as they entered the large village. Gray cobblestone covered the road, and the color of the stones matched the stones used for some buildings around them. A handful had a wooden framework, making them stick out. Dark-colored plants grew up the sides of the houses and shops that lined the street. The buildings were stacked on top of each other with no space in between. Only a few had paths running between them.

It was still much busier than she thought it would be on this rainy day. Many people walked around with hoods and small umbrellas, trying to stay dry. She saw why Merlin had been so set on getting them clothes: Sal and Caroline now blended right in. The only difference was that their outfits looked brand new, while everyone else's clothes either didn't fit or looked like ripped rags.

"If clothes are free, why does everyone seem to have such old ones?" Sal asked Merlin, keeping his voice low.

"Achilles," Merlin said, barely above a whisper. "He changed the law!" He looked disgusted as his face turned red. "When I went to get our clothes, the man in the store said that villagers get something free to wear only once a year and that the children are not allowed to get anything for free!"

"Oh. That's awful," Caroline said as she stepped around a piece of trash. The muddy streets were filled with them.

Just by stepping into the village, she could tell how large it really was. Much like the forest, it felt like it would go on forever from where she stood.

Merlin's eyes snapped up to the guards walking their way. "Oh my. This way." He placed his hands on Caroline's and Sal's shoulders, guiding them around the corner and out of eyeshot.

"I see them too," Sal said, glancing at her and then looked toward someone yelling.

She followed his gaze. People screamed at each other from their windows across the street, near a mother and her child who were eating in the rain.

"Look what has become of my land and my people," Merlin muttered. "Achilles has turned this place into a mess."

"Where are we stopping today?" Sal asked, looking at Merlin as he walked right into someone.

"Watch it!" yelled the man as he glared at him.

"I'm sorry," he said as Fuego growled at the man.

"Sorry, sir. He was not looking at where he was going," Merlin said, putting a hand on Sal's shoulder.

The angry man's eyes turned on him. "You think it is acceptable that your boy does not look where he is going?"

Caroline glanced around, hoping he would not get too much attention on them.

"He did not mean it, sir," Merlin said, still holding onto Sal's shoulder.

The man looked them up and down. "You think that just because you can afford to get your kids new clothes that you are better than all of us?!"

"We already said we were sorry," Caroline said in a hard tone.

"Have a nice day!" Sal snapped as he made his way past the man.

"Stay out of my way!" the man yelled as they walked away.

"Ignore him," Merlin muttered.

She looked back and noticed that the angry man was speaking with one of the guards. "Merlin!" she said, poking his arm.

The guard looked at the three of them as the angry man pointed their way.

"Go to that inn!" Merlin instructed, pointing at a building on their left. "We can hide there!"

She hoped they could get lost in the crowd, but Merlin was tall, making her worry that he could be easily seen. The dead flowers next to the inn's stairway to get inside were not welcoming whatsoever. As they made their way up the wet stone steps, Caroline slipped with a yelp.

Merlin grabbed onto her arm, holding it tight. "Careful," he said, helping her back up.

"This dress is kind of hard to move in," she said, pulling it up to make the last steps easier.

"Put your skirt down," he said, looking around. "Remember what I said about your ankles! CHICKENS!"

He nonchalantly opened the door with a loud creak, letting anyone in the lobby know that someone had walked in. As the three of them looked around, the cold room gave Caroline chills. From deeper inside the inn, the sound of rain falling echoed. Sal closed the door behind them and looked out the dirty window.

"Hello," a lady said in a grumpy voice. She looked at Merlin with blank eyes.

"We would like two rooms: one for the lady and one for the boy and I." He walked up to her, resting his hands on the dusty counter.

"It is your lucky day," she said with no emotion in her voice. "We have rooms available."

"Oh good!"

"For three hundred each."

An awkward silence fell.

"That seems a bit much," he admitted.

"Do you have any money?" she asked.

"The rooms have never cost money before," he said in disbelief.

"Three hundred shells, sir! Or stop wasting my time." She rested her hands on the counter as if getting ready for a fight.

"This must be because of that rat Achilles!" Merlin yelled.

The lady's eyes widened. "Hey! I do not need someone hearing what you just said and getting upset! We all must deal with the changes that came with Merlin's death. Three hundred shells or leave!"

Chapter 19

In a shop to stay dry from the constant rain, Merlin, Sal, Fuego, and Caroline looked around at all the different items the store sold. The shop owner placed pots on the ground to collect dripping water from the leaky roof. The loud rain made the shop quite loud as well, and its cool air definitely didn't help warm them up. They each shivered, freezing.

Caroline had never seen anything like this store though. In the back, each aisle had amazing magical items. They were also cheap since no one had a need for them anymore. But that didn't stop her from looking at everything they had. She loved how normalized magic was here, unlike how she had to hide it back in Duck.

She found at least twenty different spell books. She opened one that called her attention. One page showed how to make large tornadoes and fatal earthquakes. She closed the book with wide eyes, putting it back. *Why would anyone want to make something so deadly?* But then she pulled the same book out again, curious to see what else was in it. On the floor, she read other dangerous spells.

Nearby, Sal looked at wands that sat in what looked like shoe boxes piled up on the floor. The boxes all had sizes labeled on the outside. "Look, Caroline."

She looked up. The wand he held had lovely woodwork. Beautiful light green details brought out the wood. But it was also very long, almost too long to hold well. "That's amazing. Want to know what I just read?! There's a spell to make a flood! Can you believe that?"

He put the wand back and picked up another box. "That's wild." He opened it, finding a smaller, light-yellow wand. "Look at this one!" he said to Fuego, bending for him to smell it from where he stood by his feet. The dragon opened his mouth as if to eat it. "It looks like it's for a child." He moved it away before Fuego bit down.

Caroline smiled as she put the book back and made her way to him.

"This is so cool!" he said, putting the wand back and looking for another. Fuego watched him close.

Down the aisle, Merlin put his hand over his stomach as his belly growled. He walked over to them. "Are you two hungry?" he asked.

Fuego nodded his little head, along with Caroline and Sal.

"Yes, I am," Sal said, looking from the boxes on the floor to Merlin.

"Me too," she said, stepping toward him and lowering her voice. "Can I make something?"

"We have to wait until we are away from the villagers," Merlin said. "Let me see what I can get in the meantime."

Caroline and Sal watched him walk over to where food was sold in the shop. He didn't have much to choose from. A box of oats read *Magically Yummy*, and a dented can of soup looked like it had pasta shaped like wands and pots for spells. They wouldn't be able to eat enough until Caroline could make them real food. But unless they found a place to sleep, they might not get a chance to use magic.

A shop worker walked up next to Merlin, writing something on a notepad as he looked at the shelves. "Do you need any help?" he asked, looking up to Merlin while sounding like helping him was the last thing he wanted to do.

"What can I get to eat around here that is free? I see price tags on everything," Merlin asked.

The worker laughed. "For free?" he said in a mocking tone. "Nothing!"

"We do not have anything to eat or money. Not even a shell." He pointed back toward the teenagers. "Surely you can give us something small to help."

"You want something to eat?" he asked, still with a tone of fake caring.

"Well, yes. That is all I am asking of you." Merlin sounded frustrated as a young lady in the shop looked over at them.

"Then get out of here!" The worker pointed at the door. "If you do not have any money, you are no good to me!"

Merlin looked down, red in the face. "I am glad I have no money! Because if I did, I would not want to spend it here!" He turned around. "Kids, let us go!"

The three of them headed to the door.

"And take your cat thing with you!" the man yelled as Fuego moved his little legs faster to catch up with the three of them.

"Merlin, this rain is never going to stop," Caroline complained, feeling even colder as the night started to fall.

Everyone who was out in the streets before were now back in their dry homes. The thought of them all eating with their families while having a place to sleep made her jealous. What she would give to have Jewel make her a hot plate of food right now.

"Let's not freak out," Sal said, but his voice divulged his panic. "We can always hide under something to stay dry, and Fuego can make us a fire in no time."

"And I don't care about scaring anyone," she added, looking at Merlin. "I'm making food!"

"Sir!" a young voice called.

They turned. The young woman from the shop ran over to them. She had her hood over her head, making it hard to see her face. It was clear that she was trying to stay dry as best as she could.

"Yes?" Merlin said as she got close.

"I heard you need something to eat. I might have enough food for you three at my house," she said with a kind voice.

"I would hate to intrude," he said, making Sal and Caroline look at him with wide eyes. Even Fuego made a grumbling noise at his answer.

"You would not be intruding at all," she said, fixing her hood. She gasped as her hood fell to her shoulders, her orange hair quickly becoming wet. "Merlin!" Her eyes filled with tears as she looked at him.

Sal and Caroline looked back, seeming confused by the turn of events.

Merlin studied her for a moment. "I do not recall who you are. Do I know you?"

She smiled, revealing a dimple on her right cheek.

"Athena..." he muttered, stepping closer to her.

She nodded. "Yes, Master."

Merlin's mouth hung open as he stared at her. "Athena!" He dropped the bag he was holding and pulled her into a hug, lifting her off the ground.

She laughed as he spun her in a circle before putting her back down. "Merlin, I never thought I would see you again."

He gently wiped away a tear that rolled down her face. "You are alive! I thought Zuly had killed you on that horrible day!" His own eyes were also filled with tears. "I felt no pulse."

Caroline smiled. This must be his lost apprentice.

"I have so much to tell you," she said. "I thought you were dead too!"

He looked her over again. "You have grown up so much. You must be seventeen now."

"I am twenty. And yes, I have grown up."

"That much is clear." His smile filled his face.

"Please come to my home. We have much to catch up on. And out of this rain."

"Thank you, young one!" he said as she put her hood back up. "This is Caroline, Sal, and Fuego." He pointed over to where they stood, smiling. "They are with me."

"Is that a dragon?" she asked, looking at Fuego in Sal's arms.

"Yes, it is," Sal said.

"And it is nice to meet you." She smiled at the dragon. "Let us go! I only live a few blocks away from here." She led the way.

****

"This is it!" Athena said as they walked up to the smallest building in the whole village.

Caroline only saw one window by the door. No flowers grew up the stone wall's side. Standing in the cold, she was glad she would have a meal and a roof over her head.

"Can Fuego come in?" Sal asked as Athena went to open the door.

It didn't move. She looked back at everyone, clearly embarrassed, before trying again. She then slammed her body into it. It creaked open. "Sorry about that, and yes, the dragon can come in."

Once inside, Caroline looked around. Athena didn't live in much of a house, just one small room. A small old-fashioned stove stood in a corner. She had a short table with a broken leg and pillows for seats. The small bed looked hard and uncomfortable. Caroline noticed one door that must lead to the bathroom. *At least, Athena's place doesn't smell.*

"Better than where we found Merlin," Sal said under his breath as if reading her mind.

Caroline smiled. Within seconds, she pulled out her wand, drying everyone off. Even Fuego. Athena warmed up some white rice for them to eat. Caroline then magically made some roast beef as a thank you. As they ate, Sal gave a little bowl to Fuego, who ate next to him on the floor happily.

"Please," Merlin said, turning to Athena once he was done with his meal. "Tell me how you survived. I thought Zuly had killed you."

Athena looked down at her hands. "That was the...the day my childhood ended." She met his eyes. "I am n-not even sure how I survived. Zuly h-hit me with such a painful spell. It still hurts sometimes. Like when the weather is bad. Like today." She placed her hand on her chest.

"The painful look on your face that day scared me in ways I had never known," Merlin admitted in a soft tone.

"I think they brought me back to life with magic," she

said. "To tell them everything I knew about you, Merlin. How you used your powers, what you did in your magic room, and where you could have gone to. I thought you had died. Because why else would you not save me?"

Merlin paled. "If I had known you were alive, I would have never left that day. I would have died trying to save you." His eyes burned with tears.

She nodded. "The day…the day Achilles came, they locked me up and almost never fed me. The maids and cooks would t-try to help me, but when Zuly would catch them…" She paused for a moment, taking a deep breath. "He would kill them. So, they stopped trying to help.

"Achilles left soon after…after he came here. I never really saw him back then. H-he set up everything with the guards and put Zuly in charge. Zuly… He acted like a king for years. He always asked me questions, but I would not talk, which made him m-mad."

"Do you know why they wanted to know so much about Merlin?" Caroline asked.

Athena shook her head. "They never told me why, but if I did not tell Zuly what he wanted, he would…do horrible t-things to me." She rolled up her dress' left sleeve, revealing a large black scar that looked as if she had been severely burned years ago. The spot looked dry, but the middle was red and painful looking.

Merlin gasped, horrified. "What did he do to you?! You were just a child!"

"Zuly did this to me a few…a few weeks after Achilles left."

Now that Caroline thought about it, Athena didn't use her left arm while cooking. Instead, she had held it close to her.

"That was the worst of it: my arm," Athena said,

covering her arm back up and holding it close once more. "Achilles had been gone for eleven years."

"He had been trying to kill me in my world," Caroline added.

"How did you get out?" Merlin asked Athena.

"I… I… Ach… Um… It is very hard to talk about," she said, looking down again.

"Athena, I am so sorry this happened to you," Merlin said as a tear slid down his cheek. "If I had known, I would have spent every day trying to get you out."

"I know," she said with a grateful smile.

Caroline knew just from listening to them talk that they loved each other like a father and a daughter. It made her miss Dutch.

A bright light popped in the room, making everyone turn. Caroline grabbed her wand. When the light disappeared, Jewel and Dutch stood in the room, looking wide-eyed at Merlin and Athena. Caroline and Sal looked at them in shock as Merlin screamed, and Athena jumped.

"Guys, it's my family!" Caroline said.

Jewel made her way over to them and pulled Caroline into a hug.

Chapter 20

"Grandma!" Caroline said in disbelief as she looked back and forth from Jewel to Dutch. Both looked awful with cuts all over their faces and hands. "W-what happened to you two?"

"It's a long story," Dutch said, sounding as if he had not slept in days.

"Are you okay?"

"I was so worried about you," Jewel said, pulling her into another hug.

Caroline hugged her back, hearing her softly cry. Her heart ached at the sound. She could not believe the stress she had put her grandmother in. Dutch joined in before everyone let go.

"How did you guys find me?" Caroline asked. "And why are you bleeding?!"

Jewel looked past her to everyone else in the room.

"Oh, this is Merlin," she explained. "He was a king. And this is Athena, his apprentice." She pointed to both Merlin and Athena respectively before pointing at her family. "This is my grandmother Jewel and Dutch."

Merlin walked over to them, putting his hand out to shake. "Nice to meet you both."

Athena waved.

"Hi!" Sal said, walking over from where he sat with joy on his face.

"Oh good. Sal was with you," Jewel said with an edge in her voice and sharp eyes.

He kept smiling anyway. "I never let her out of my sight. She has been in good hands."

"This young boy saved her from that dragon!" Merlin said, gesturing to Fuego who had his face in Sal's bowl and his butt in the air.

A silence fell over the room.

"Um," Caroline said, pointing to Merlin. "Merlin is a powerful wizard. He's helping us."

"It is very nice to meet you both," he said with a kind nod.

"Same," Jewel said as she looked over at Caroline. "I want to talk to you. Outside." She took Caroline's arm.

"But it's raining out there," she said.

Jewel didn't seem to care. "We just need a moment with my granddaughter," she said to everyone before walking out the door with her and Dutch right behind.

****

Once Jewel, Dutch, and Caroline were away from the house, and no one could hear them, they found a somewhat dry place to talk.

"Do you have any idea what we have gone through?!" Jewel snapped at Caroline.

"I knew this was coming," she muttered.

Dutch crossed his arms like a disapproving parent. "How could you have been so immature about all this? Leaving without telling us was wrong, and you know it!"

"I left a note, and Sal came with me. Besides, Edmund said it was okay."

Jewel's eyes went wide. "Edmund? What does he have to do with any of this?"

"Edmund told me I could go and gave me this." Caroline pointed to the bag with the marbles on her hip.

She crossed her arms. "Drop one. I want to speak with him."

"I don't want to waste them in case we need him. Like we've had."

"*Now,*" Dutch said.

Her mouth went dry as she reached inside to pull out a marble. She dropped it onto the ground.

Within seconds, Edmund stood between them. "Caroline, are you all right?" he asked. He was clearly getting ready for bed, already in his comfy pajamas.

"Edmund, did you tell Caroline it was okay to come here?" Jewel asked.

"Hi, Jewel. Dutch." He waved. "I told her she could come because she said you said it was okay. That's why I gave her the marbles."

Caroline's body tensed.

"I never said she could go in," Jewel said.

"What?" he said. "But she told me—"

"I asked her to wait."

He turned to Caroline and rested his hands on his hips. "Did you lie to me?"

Her cheeks became hot. With a big breath in, she looked away.

"Caroline, that is so wrong of you," Jewel said, sounding disappointed.

Caroline looked anywhere but their eyes, and Edmund disappeared.

"Well, would you look at the time?" She laughed awkwardly. "Bring your uncle back right now!"

"He was in his pajamas, getting ready for bed!" Caroline protested.

"Caroline," Dutch said sternly.

"Fine." Grabbing a marble, she threw it, and he appeared again.

"Jewel," he said, not even looking at Caroline. "I'm very sorry. If I had known you said she could not come, I never would have told her to."

Jewel's face softened. "I know that you're very good with Caroline and respectful to me."

He nodded before turning to his niece and speaking with a stern voice. "I hope you learn to treat those who care about you better. With the life you have had, I thought you would've been more grateful."

She didn't dare to meet his eyes. Tears burned in hers.

Looking back at Jewel and Dutch, he said, "I'm so sorry. If you two need me, use the marbles."

"Thank you for helping me with her," Jewel said.

"Let's just hope she never does that again." He looked at Caroline over his shoulder and disappeared.

"You betrayed my trust," Jewel snapped, turning back to her granddaughter. "I thought you were safe in the room next door. Not coming to this hellhole."

"Do you have any idea how much stress you caused us both?" Dutch asked in a dark tone that Caroline had never heard from him before. "We wanted to plan this with you. We were going to help you with this! Like we always do!"

"You could've been killed. I was almost killed! I'm lucky to still be alive."

"What?!" she asked with panic in her voice.

"You never think ahead of time," Jewel said after telling her everything that had happened since they came through the mirror. "Somehow, we found our wands on a nearby table and then teleported to you."

Caroline looked up, fighting back her tears.

"Caroline, listen—"

"I don't know what to say." Her voice cracked. "I'm so sorry. I never meant for this to happen. I got desperate, and I didn't want to wait."

Jewel softened her tone. "Caroline, we were worried sick. That pillow act you did gave me a heart attack."

She gave a soft laugh. "It used to work at George's house. I forgot you check on me."

Dutch grabbed her hand. "Let's move on. We're here now and will help you. Just don't do something like this again without us."

She nodded, blinking away her tears. "I promise." She looked at her grandmother. "Please forgive me. I regret it. So many horrible things have happened."

Jewel pulled her into a hug. "I'm just happy you're all right."

She rested her head on her shoulder.

"Do you know where your parents could be?" Dutch asked.

Jewel let her go and wiped away a tear that rolled down Caroline's cheek.

"Merlin said they could be in the castle," Caroline said. "That's where we're headed."

Jewel nodded. "Why haven't you teleported?"

"Merlin doesn't think it is safe. He has us going the long way, hoping there are less guards."

"So, what's the plan you have with that guy back at the house?" Dutch asked, pointing in the house's direction. The rain had eased up, letting the faint light from Athena's window be seen.

Caroline told them everything: the gem, Achilles

taking all the magic, Sal's new dragon friend, the new magic she was learning from Merlin, and who Athena was. "It has honestly worked out much better than I thought it would."

"You know, I understand your need to find your parents," Jewel admitted. "M-my mother died giving birth to me. I always thought it was my fault. That was the reason why my sister and I were fighting when I hurt her."

Her shoulders dropped.

"So, I know what you're feeling in a way. I would have given anything to bring my mother back."

"That wasn't your fault. Please don't think that. Your mother would have loved you so much."

Jewel's eyes watered. "Promise me that you will be smart going forward now."

Caroline nodded.

Dutch looked at Jewel, seeming hesitant. "Jewel, we have to tell her."

Caroline looked at him, and chills covered her whole body. "Tell me what?" she asked, looking back at Jewel.

"When we were in the castle..." Jewel said in a strange tone. "We saw him. Achilles. He's here."

"No!" she said, shaking her head and backing away.

"We spoke to him."

"No. You're lying!"

"I wish we were," Dutch said, "but Jewel is telling the truth. He is back, and he knows you're here."

Her dream had been a warning. "No, I don't believe you!" she said, finding it hard to breathe with her tight chest. "He can't be! I watched him die last year! Grandma, you...you...you killed him." Tears rolled down her face as she took fast, short breaths.

"Caroline, he had another spell to keep himself alive."

She didn't even know who had spoken. All she knew was that her mind was in a fog, running a hundred miles an hour. Her fingers went through her hair. "He can't be back."

"Breathe, youngin," Dutch said, her arms in his tight hold.

She met his eyes before melting into his arms, a sob escaping her mouth. Everything in her mind screamed so loud, but the loudest was yelling that Achilles was back.

Chapter 21

"Achilles is here!" Caroline said once they were back at Athena's house.

Merlin's face paled, Sal's mouth dropped, and Athena swallowed.

"Merlin, did you know this?" she asked, looking at the old wizard.

"I had only heard whispers," he said. "But you were telling me something different."

"This changes the plan!" Sal said, meeting her eyes. "We can't just walk into the castle anymore. What if he's waiting for you?"

"No," Merlin said loudly, making everyone turn to him. "We cannot back down because we are afraid. If we put the gem back, Achilles will be much weaker, and we all will have the power to fight him."

Caroline feared fighting him since her magic had been draining.

"Athena, is the gem in the castle? What did Zuly do with it?"

She froze, seeming as if she was put on the spot. "I was locked up. I did not see where they took it."

Everyone thought for a moment.

"There must be someone we can put a truth spell on to tell us where it is," Dutch said.

"We continue the journey like planned," Merlin said. "But once we are in the castle, the plan changes. We will split up since it will not be as easy to sneak around in large numbers. Caroline, Jewel, and Dutch will go find the parents." He looked at Caroline. "You should find them locked up in the dungeon. *If* they are there."

She swallowed at his *if*.

"If you find your parents, Dutch and Jewel should teleport away with them to keep them safe. If Achilles finds out we took them, it could get more dangerous. So, once they teleport away, meet us at the tower, Caroline. Since we do not have any powers, you can keep us safe as we work. Jewel and Dutch can then meet us there after the parents are safe."

"Athena, are you coming with us?" Sal asked.

She looked over at him with wide eyes.

"It is normal to be scared, young one," Merlin said, giving her a kind smile.

"I fear getting hurt again," she said in a shaky tone.

"Athena, taking back our land should be done together."

She fiddled with her braid. "But we do not have power, Merlin."

"Sal has proven to me that one can be just as powerful without magic."

Sal beamed. "Thank you."

"Our bravery is our power," Merlin said. "And I find that groovy! Did I use it right?" he asked as Sal laughed.

"Couldn't have said it better myself."

"Merlin," Athena mumbled. "I will help you."

"Perfect!" He embraced her for a moment before

turning back to everyone. "Athena, Fuego, Sal, and I shall put someone under a truth spell. I should still have enough magic to do that one spell. Then we will get the gem and meet everyone at the tower."

Caroline nodded. "Do you need a spell to put the gem back in?"

Athena spoke up. "No. The sun shall put the magic back in."

She swallowed. It was a huge plan, but she was ready for the fight of a lifetime.

Chapter 22

J ewel woke up a few hours after everyone had gone to bed, feeling that something was off. She was out of breath but not sure why. Caroline lay on the floor next to her, holding her hand. Fuego lay under Caroline's other arm with his head resting on her shoulder.

Then she heard it: a scream.

The more she listened, the more voices yelled not too far away. Sitting up and careful not to wake Caroline or anyone else, she listened to the outside commotion.

Athena lifted her head from where she lay, turning to Jewel with a confused look on her face. "What is happening?" she asked, propping up on her elbows.

Before Jewel could reply, bright orange smoke passed over the window, followed by much louder screaming. They stood, rushing to the window, as everyone else started to stir.

"Oh my," Jewel said, covering her mouth with her hand. Flames overtook the house across the street, and a pale woman was on her knees in front of the home, screaming. She noticed a few guards holding lit torches. "The guards did that!"

"Burn the whole village if you must!" someone ordered. "Find her!"

Athena turned back to the sleepy group. "Wake up!" she yelled. "Wake up!" She went over to Caroline. "How do the guards know you are here?"

"What?" Caroline asked, rubbing the sleep from her eyes.

"They're looking for you!" Jewel said, wishing the window had a curtain to close over it.

"Someone must have pointed us out," Merlin said, standing. "But I never thought this could—"

"What do we do?" Sal asked.

Caroline stood, looking out the window. The fire's light lit up her face. "I…I can't let this happen because of me." She shook her head. "I'll turn myself in."

"Caroline, no!" Dutch said, pulling her away from the window.

"I have to stop this," she said. Her chemise she had been sleeping in left her without a wand. Looking over to where the rest of her dress was lying, she snapped her fingers. Her wand flew from a pocket to her waiting hand. She flicked it and transported next to the screaming woman in the street.

Jewel watched through the window, her heart racing.

"That was not a good idea," said Dutch.

"Dutch, come on! We have to help her."

****

Caroline appeared in the street beside the screaming woman. She put her hands up, showing that she meant no harm. Out of the corner of her eyes, she saw the guards making their way toward her with their swords drawn. She flicked her wand, forming a force field around her and the woman. The guards slammed their swords into it. The shield shook, not as strong as it could have been.

She bent down beside the woman. "Is there anyone inside?"

"M-my daughter!" the woman sobbed.

Putting another force field around herself, Caroline ran into the building. Inside the house, smoke filled her lungs as her force field cracked. She found the young girl, unconscious on the floor, in a back room. The girl must've been about nine years old. Flicking her wand, Caroline lowered her force field with a cough. She pulled up her dress and knotted it up, keeping it out of the way. She then pointed her wand at the girl. The girl gasped and opened her eyes as the healing spell worked.

"I'm here to help!" Caroline said as she picked the girl up.

They both coughed as she put a force field around them both. Soon, they were back outside. The mother raced to her daughter.

"Mum!"

Caroline bent over and coughed again, out of breath. She had breathed in more smoke than she had wanted.

"Look at who is such a hero!" a familiar voice said, sending chills down her spine. His shoes stepped into her field of vision. "Hello, Caroline."

She looked up to find Achilles standing in front of her. "Why did you come here?" she asked with an edge in her voice.

He held his hands behind his back. "So brave. Hiding behind your tricks."

She flicked her wand, making the force field disappear. "I'm not scared of you! I beat you once, and I will do it again!"

"YOU CANNOT BEAT ME!" Achilles screamed. "YOU ONLY HIDE. THAT IS ALL YOU EVER DO!

YOU USE OTHERS TO FIGHT AND DIE FOR YOU. FIGHT ME!" He took a step closer. "Even when you were a child, your dad died because of you!"

Caroline's eyes narrowed at him. She had noticed everyone else—Jewel, Dutch, Merlin, Sal, Fuego, and Athena—standing off to the side and made a quick choice. She flicked her wand at where they stood.

"Caroline, no!" Jewel yelled as a force field that only Caroline could lower surrounded them.

"There! Is that what you want?" she yelled, never taking her eyes off Achilles.

Achilles looked over and laughed. "So, you think you can beat me. Why? You haven't done so yet."

She held her wand so tight that her nails dug into her palm. "Stone-soul!" she shouted. She knew she was not at her strongest, but the spell still came at him fast.

He waved his hand, and the spell was gone. "I see you have learned some things while I have been gone," he said, not sounding impressed. "One thing you should learn, Caroline, is that while I am here, I am stronger in arms"— he gestured toward his waiting guards—"and I have a right-hand man."

Zuly smirked from behind him.

"So, I would think before doing something you'll regret. Zuly." He looked back at him. "Keep your men back. This is my fight till I order you to dispose of her body."

Caroline blinked. The next thing she knew, she lay on the cobblestone. She gasped as pain poured into her from Achilles' wand. The spell he pushed into her was intense. After a moment, she pushed through and stood back up, ignoring the pain. "Fire itera!"

He sent the fire up and away. "Gepsic!"

"Teleportsheam!" She teleported next to Achilles and kicked the back of his knee, knocking him sideways. She pointed her wand at him. "Fire itera!"

Zuly grabbed her arms, restraining her.

She gasped, and her wand slipped out of her hand. "Get off me!" she hissed, trying to pull herself out of his hold.

Achilles stood and looked over at her with rage. "So arrogant." He put his large hand around her throat. "And now you will die so close to what you came for."

Her eyes went wide. "MY PARENTS! WHERE ARE THEY?!"

He rolled his eyes. "Sadly not here to save you."

A strong force hit him, knocking him off his feet. Jewel stood behind him, holding her wand toward him. Dutch stood by her side with his own wand aimed at Zuly. They had somehow brought down the force field. The guards lifted their swords, ready to defend.

"Zuly," Achilles said as he stood, fixing his hair, "you were right for once. Letting them escape brought us right to Caroline."

"Don't hurt them!" she yelled at Achilles, who acted as if she was not even there.

He flicked his wand toward Jewel, and strong lightning followed the path between them. Caroline's heart pounded. She kicked her leg back, hitting Zuly in the crotch. He grunted and let go of her. She then stood the way Merlin had shown her the other night and focused her mind on the ground under her feet. Dutch shot fire at Achilles, putting his attention on him. She raised her hands toward Achilles, pulled her arms back as power grew within her, and shot her hands forward.

The pure power knocked Achilles and every guard in

her path off their feet, throwing them into a nearby building. Breathing hard, she dropped her arms down to her side. Jewel and Dutch turned to her with wide eyes.

"She has done it!" Merlin said from somewhere.

Zuly grunted, standing behind her.

"Wand to my hand!" she said, making her lost wand jump to her waiting hand.

He swung his sword up, slicing her arm.

The cut burned as she grimaced. She flicked her wand. "Stone-soul!"

He froze with wide eyes and his sword held up close to her. She turned back to her people and teleported each of them away.

Chapter 23

"Caroline!" Merlin called out. "You executed that perfectly!" He grabbed her shoulders and shook her playfully with a smile along his face.

Caroline smiled too before looking around to see where she had taken them. The sun peaked out overhead, pushing the rain clouds away. They were still in the village, which was not safe, but she saw a new gate in the distance. They must be closer to the exit. The cut on her arm stung, sending pain throughout her body as she moved it.

"Are you okay?" Jewel asked, sounding as if she was trying to contain her worry. She gently placed her hand over the cut.

Caroline tensed at the touch, but in a second, the cut and pain were gone. The only evidence that remained was her ripped and stained sleeve. "Thank you," she said, hugging Jewel.

"When did you learn how to do that spell without your wand?"

"I taught her the other night," Merlin said, sounding proud. "You and Dutch have trained her well. Her mind is like a sponge."

"Thank you," Dutch said with a wonky smile as he

looked at Jewel. "She is very smart."

"She is a Smith after all," Merlin said, patting Caroline's shoulder once more before walking toward the new gate.

Athena looked back at the village.

"Are you coming?" Sal asked.

"Y-yes," she said. She slowly turned around and walked next to him as they left the village.

****

Achilles sat up, blinking away the black dots in his vision. His brain felt clouded as he woke beside the rubble. He coughed, noticing dust and small pebbles on his face. Raising his hand to his face, he felt blood oozing from his forehead. He pushed the debris off him as he stood.

Never in his life had he expected Caroline to do such a powerful spell.

He looked at the guards around him. Some moved, while others did not. Taking a deep breath, he coughed, waving his hand in front of his face. He looked out the large hole in the wall that he had gone through and saw Zuly frozen. Anger grew within him like wildfire.

"Zuly!" he yelled as he stormed out of the broken building.

He looked around the cobblestone street. Everyone had left. Caroline was gone. He also noticed that the sun would show itself soon. It had been entirely dark before; he didn't even want to know how much time had passed since she had escaped.

"Zuly, you insignificant waste!" He snapped his fingers, and his wand came to his hand in seconds. "Freezenone."

The spell unfroze Zuly, making his body relax as he

took in a deep breath. "Thank y—"

Achilles sent his fist into the other man's face. Zuly dropped his sword as he fell backward, holding his nose with a gasp.

"Get whatever guards who are still alive out of that building!" Achilles ordered. "We are going back to the castle." He kicked Zuly hard in the stomach as he tried to stand. "So far, you have been useless! You have one last chance to prove yourself. Or I will give you a slow and painful death!"

Zuly looked up at Achilles, slowly standing on his feet. Blood poured out of his nose as Achilles turned his back on him.

****

As blood dripped down Zuly's chin, and pain shot through his body, a thought came to his mind for the first time in years. *Merlin would have never done this to me.*

He looked at the other man with hate.

****

By the time Caroline's group made it to the end of the village, the sky had cleared up, and the sun warmed them after the cold morning. Songbirds sung their morning song as the village came back to life.

"There!" Athena called out.

Caroline looked at what she was pointing to. A short man with a large hat and an unpleasant look along his face stood by the closed exit gate as they walked up. Luckily, she had already cast a spell, adding a dress and corset on top of her chemise. She also had changed Jewel's and Dutch's clothes to match the village's culture since she now knew their style. So hopefully, the guard wouldn't recognize them.

"What is this?" Merlin asked Athena.

"They were placed here after Achilles," she explained. "They will not let us leave if they do not like the reason."

Merlin looked puzzled. "But no one was at the entrance when we came in…"

The guard raised his hand. "Stop right there!"

"Good morning," Sal said in a cheerful voice.

The guard didn't look his way. "It is a bit early for such a big group to leave now, is it not?"

"We are heading to the castle. Achilles wishes to meet with us," Merlin said, sounding so sure of himself.

"All of you?" The guard raised a giant eyebrow.

"Yes."

He looked at each of them with disgust before he spoke again. "There was an attack last night. How would I know you are not running off after you did the attacking?" He crossed his arms. "Besides, no one just goes to the castle. Achilles does not let peasants inside."

Athena rolled her eyes. "Let me handle it," she whispered before stepping up to the guard.

Everyone watched in silence as she stood in front of the guard and spoke in a low voice. Caroline could not hear her, but whatever she had said worked because a smile grew on the guard's face.

He looked over to the group. "Go on," he said, opening the gate with a loud, extended sound.

"Thank you," Athena stated coldly.

Without another word, the guard closed the gate once they were all through.

Merlin spoke in a low voice. "What did you say to him?"

"I just reminded him what would happen if Achilles

knew it was him that stopped an order of the king."

Caroline felt breathless as an endless black field stretched out in front of her. She also noticed a large body of water that looked like it went on for miles.

"We have to cross all of that?!" Sal asked, keeping his voice low. "My feet already ache."

Dutch seemed to be thinking the same thing as he looked at Sal with a tired face before looking back at all they had to cross.

"Do you or do you not want to get to the castle?" Merlin asked, turning to Sal.

"Well yes, bu—"

"Then we start walking! No more said."

"There should be a boat we can take at the lake, or Caroline and her family can use their magic to get us across," Athena said as they began their walk.

"How can we use our magic to get across?" Jewel asked, putting her hand to her forehead to keep the sun out of her eyes. "A teleport spell?"

Merlin giggled. "No. In this world, we have many more spells to make life easier."

She looked up at Merlin with a smile. "Really? Like what?"

"Thousands."

As they started walking back down a hill, Athena's feet slipped on the wet grass, and she yelped out.

"Be careful," Dutch said, grabbing her good arm to keep her from falling.

Caroline watched as Sal stopped at the top of the hill, looking down. He put one foot in front of the other like he was surfing back at the beach, letting the wet grass take him down the hill. He yelled out, laughing as he zoomed past a surprised Merlin and Jewel. Fuego flew down fast, trying to keep up with him. Once he got to the bottom, he turned around. "Try it, Caroline!"

Caroline, still at the top, placed her feet just like Sal had done and slid down. She smelled the wet grass as water splashed onto her legs. The cool air brushed past her. She slid into Sal's waiting arms. As her body slammed into his, knocking them both off their feet, they laughed. She smiled before kissing his lips quickly. His cheeks turned pink as she pushed herself off him.

They made their way through the hilly field, laughing and sliding down each hill. Even Athena joined in on the fun.

"Youth," Jewel said as she watched with a smile along her face.

****

Once they reached the dark-colored lake, Merlin set his bag down and pulled out a spell book. "Here you go," he said, handing the book to Caroline. "Read page forty-five."

She took it, sitting on the damp sand and placing the book in her lap. Her dress lay around her.

Dutch sat next to her, watching as she flipped to page forty-five. "What is that?"

"If there is no boat, Caroline, Jewel, and you will have to get us across," Merlin explained, pointing at the open page. The drawing showed someone using their wand in front of them as they stood like the other spell Merlin had shown her with their feet on the water.

"Hmm," Jewel said, sitting and reading over Caroline's shoulder.

"We are going to see if there are any boats around here," Merlin said as Fuego landed on his waiting arm.

Caroline watched as he, Sal, and Athena walked off but then looked back at the spell, sighing. With her wand out in front of her, she would have to make a wave that they could ride to the other side of the lake. The photo made it look like she would make a solid platform with the water. But since it was not just her, they would have to make the wave big enough for all six of them.

"That looks wild," Jewel said. "But fun at the same time."

"Let's just hope Merlin finds a boat we can use," Dutch said, ripping the book out of Caroline's lap.

"Dutch!"

His face dropped. "If you do this wrong, you can drown!"

"Where did you read that?!" Caroline asked, pulling the book back. The last thing she wanted was to drown when she was so close to the castle. Especially not after Achilles tried to drown her last year.

"Right here." He pointed at a small print of words under the picture.

Jewel squinted her eyes to read it. "For the one doing the spell: you shall not get distracted; for it can turn on you and pull you far under the water."

"That sounds great," Caroline said sarcastically before looking back up, hoping the other group had found a boat.

"What the heck is this spell?!" Dutch said.

"We're weaker as well. We've been here for a long time," Caroline said, swallowing hard.

"Why not just teleport across?" Jewel asked with panic in her eyes. "How wide is the lake?" She stood to get a better view. "It must be more than twelve miles. I can't see the other end."

A long silence followed as they looked out toward the

dark choppy water. Twelve miles was a long time to not get distracted.

"Is there no other spell to get across that won't kill us? I don't even know how to do this," Caroline said, flipping through the book.

Athena walked up to them. "I bet you can do it easily. If you are all Merlin says, you can do anything you put your mind to." She gave them a sweet smile. "But we can also work on the spell if that makes you feel better."

Merlin and Sal were close behind with disappointed faces.

Caroline sighed as she stood. "I'm guessing you didn't find a boat."

Sal shook his head. "Nope. Not a single one! It seems we don't have a choice."

Fuego flew off Merlin's shoulder, landing on Caroline's. She patted his little head, much to his liking. She then looked out at the water and bit her lip.

"I would not have asked you to do this spell if I did not think you could do it," Merlin said.

"Just talk us through it a bit first please," Dutch said with a nervous laugh in his voice.

"Do not worry." Athena reached for the spell book and opened it to page forty-five. "Step one is to hold the wand in front of you like so." With her free hand, she pointed to Merlin, who mimicked the pose.

****

"You are ready," Merlin said, looking back at the three sorcerers as the sun started to set behind them. "Jewel first, then Dutch, and then Caroline." He turned to Sal and Fuego, waving his arms for them to join them by the water. "Come on!"

Sal put Fuego on his shoulder, grabbed Merlin's bag, and headed over to the water's edge.

Jewel took a deep breath before standing in front of the water. Caroline stared at her, holding onto Dutch's arm. Slowly, the dark water lifted and formed a wave. Athena nodded to Dutch. He stood next to Jewel, pulling out his wand. The wave grew higher and expanded toward him. Caroline was scared to even breathe too loud; she didn't want to distract them. Once the wave looked stronger, Merlin lightly pushed her toward Dutch's side. Taking one last look at Jewel's and Dutch's concentrated faces, she closed her eyes.

The wave expanded, becoming a big enough platform for everyone to ride across the lake. It stood a foot or so over the lake, making a deafening rushing water sound. Jewel, Dutch, and Caroline got onto the water platform first before everyone else. As Caroline stepped onto it, her foot didn't get wet. They had created a solid surface. Through the murky shade, she couldn't see any creatures or their own reflections.

Once everyone was on, the wave moved down the lake. It was not super fast, but it was fast enough. The wind lifted her hair, letting it flow behind her. A few minutes went by without any problems. It seemed like luck was on their side for once during this journey.

But that luck ran out fast.

"Sal, are you all right?" Merlin asked somewhere to her left.

Caroline's muscles tensed, but she tried to keep her concentration strong, only looking ahead. She couldn't drown.

"Are you feeling ill?" Merlin added.

"T-There is something in the…the water," Sal said.

Out of the corner of her eyes, she saw Merlin lean over, looking down. He whispered something she couldn't hear. She forced her eyes back on the water ahead. They weren't too far now. She just needed to focus.

"It looked like an octopus with really large arms!" Sal said, pointing at the water a few feet away. "I saw an arm or something come out of the water."

"What?!" she asked, sounding worried. As she spoke, the whole platform shook, which made everyone yelp.

"Focus!" Merlin snapped.

She put her energy back into the spell, and the wave leveled out, more stable again. Focus. She just needed to focus. She couldn't help but notice Athena walking over to Sal and Merlin though. Even Fuego seemed concerned.

Only Sal spoke loud enough for her to hear. "I can still see the water moving by where it was."

Out of the corner of her eye, a large tentacle shot up from the water a few feet away. She stayed quiet as her eyes widened. Fuego backed up from the platform's edge, lifting his wings. The tentacle lifted higher and higher, casting a long shadow over them.

Caroline looked ahead, not wanting to know where the tentacle came from. She couldn't think about it. *Almost there. Focus.*

Jewel turned and gasped. Dutch turned too. Before any of them knew it, the wave they had been riding on disappeared. They yelled as they all fell into the dark water.

Chapter 24

The water wrapped around Caroline, pulling her down further. Hard. Her ears popped as she went deeper. She opened her eyes, but all she saw was darkness. She couldn't even see her own body. Her lungs burned as if they were going to explode if she didn't get air soon.

She flicked her wand hard, wanting to teleport out of the water. But nothing happened.

Dots filled her vision as her panic grew. Her hand moved to her bag of marbles on her waist. It was still there. She feared opening it and losing what was left inside, but as her lungs screamed for air, she didn't have much of a choice. She reached for a marble. Her eyelids grew heavy, and she closed her eyes.

Something strong grabbed her waist and pulled her. She couldn't tell in what direction.

But the second her head broke the water's surface, she gasped and coughed as something hit her back. Her lungs burned with every breath she took in.

"What's happening? Are you okay?" Edmund asked, pulling her off his shoulder to meet her eyes.

She couldn't have been gladder to see him. "Y-you

have to help Dutch and Grandma!" she said through her coughs.

He let go of her, diving back under the water. Sal's head popped up a few feet away, along with Merlin and Athena. They all looked frantically around the water.

Dutch's head appeared. He took a deep breath and looked around. "Where is Jewel?!"

Jewel and Edmund came into view. Her coughs echoed as he clapped her back.

"Edmund?" Dutch said, sounding confused.

"Is everyone okay?" Merlin asked, sounding raspy from the water.

Fuego flew overhead, looking down at everyone, and Edmund disappeared.

"What was that thing?!" Jewel asked, looking at Merlin.

"A Dunkopus," he answered, looking around at the water.

"What is that?" Caroline asked with wide eyes.

"Something bad! Teleport us!"

Athena screamed, and fear overtook her face. "It got me! Help!"

Merlin moved to swim toward her before anyone else.

"I do not want to die—" She screamed again as something pulled her under water.

"NO!" he yelled, looking at where she had just been. Another tentacle appeared in the same spot.

"What do we do?" Sal asked with fear in his eyes.

"No! No! No!" He took a deep breath and dove under the water. But he came back up with nothing.

"Is there a spell I can do?" Caroline asked.

Athena popped out of the water a ways away from everyone. A tentacle held onto her body. She disappeared just as fast as she had reappeared.

"Say Lifterit!" Merlin yelled.

Caroline reached for her wand but lost focus as Athena came back up with her arms flailing, trying to take hold of something.

"Help me!" her scream echoed. Her fearful voice was almost unrecognizable.

Jewel, Dutch, and Sal swam toward her, but she was pulled back under.

"Caroline!" Merlin yelled.

Caroline grabbed her wand with both hands. "Lifterit!"

Everyone and everything in the water lifted into the air, floating as if they were in space. Even fishes swam around midair like nothing had happened. Caroline could not believe what was under there: fish, boats, glass bottles, and the Dunkopus. The Dunkopus' large body was maybe fifty feet long, and it had a mouth full of sharp teeth. From its body, many long tentacles waved about except the one with a strong hold on Athena, who was still struggling to break free.

"Teleportsheam!" Caroline called out.

She opened her eyes and lifted her head up to see everyone back on dry land, taking in deep breaths. What had been flying moments ago fell right back into the black water. The Dunkopus fell last, making a large splash that shot up into the air. Dropping her head back down, she welcomed the black spots that filled her vision.

****

"Is everyone all right?" Sal called out.

Before anyone could answer him, Merlin yelled, "Athena!" He raced to her side as she gasped for air a few feet away. "Breathe in slowly! You are all right."

180

She sat up, meeting his eyes. "I never want to do that again!"

"Caroline!" Jewel said with panic in her voice.

Merlin looked over to find Caroline's eyes closed. He rushed over to her, kneeling by her side and placing his fingers on her wrist. "She is alive! After all that magic, she is too weak. It took a heavy toll on her."

Fuego lay next to her and licked her forehead. Jewel moved a lock of wet hair out of her face.

"So, she's okay?" Sal asked with worry etched across his face.

"She is more than fine," Merlin said, standing. "She just needs to rest. I suggest we find a place to stay for the night. Sal, are you all right?" he asked as he turned to face him.

"For the most part." Merlin rested his hand on his shoulder, sighing with relief. His eyes were filled with care.

"The castle is a few miles that way," Athena said, pointing toward the forest behind them. Her voice sounded raspy.

Merlin thought for a moment. "There is also a village northeast from here, right?"

She nodded. "I do not know how welcoming they are to new people, but I know Achilles has not touched them. I do not think he knows about it yet." She brushed some sand off her arms.

Dutch scratched his head. "How can he not know about a village that's on his own land?"

"It is not on his land technically," he explained. "It is on the outskirts of our land and not on any map. Someone like Achilles—who is not from here—would not know about it."

Dutch looked down at Caroline. "If she'll be safe there…"

"Achilles or his guards will not find her there."

He bent down, sliding his arms under her legs and her back as he picked her up. Jewel made sure her head was well rested on his shoulder.

Sal grabbed her wand. "Come along, my dragon."

Fuego did as he was told as they walked away with Merlin in the lead once more.

Chapter 25

As the sun set, the stars and the moon guided everyone as their only light. No one hardly spoke until the villages' light shined through the trees. Soft sounds of music and laughter traveled from there.

"So, do we all just walk into this village?" Dutch, still holding on to Caroline, asked.

"Yes," Athena said.

"Athena, go find someone trustworthy who will give us a place to stay," Merlin said.

"Can I go with her?" Sal asked.

He nodded.

Sal patted Fuego's head as he sat on his shoulder. He started to make his way through the trees when a hand grabbed his arm, pulling him back.

"Are you taking the dragon with you?" Jewel asked, meeting his eyes. She looked as though she was trying not to laugh.

"No. I don't think that's a clever idea," he admitted. He put his arm on her shoulder, letting Fuego walk over to her.

"Oh, o-okay," she said as her body tensed. She moved her head as far from Fuego's as possible while tentatively petting Fuego's head.

He giggled. "He won't hurt you." With one last smile, he turned and headed into the village with Athena.

****

"What is taking them so long?" Dutch asked as he sat with Caroline still in his lap. Her head rested on his chest. It had been more than an hour since Sal and Athena had left.

"Do you think the villagers took them?" Jewel asked from where she sat with Fuego sleeping by her feet. Her eyes kept drifting over to Caroline. Seeing her so vulnerable like that broke her heart.

"Why would they take them?" Merlin asked, staring at the ground.

"Music is still playing, so they didn't draw too much attention," Dutch said.

"Maybe they are roasting him over a fire."

Everyone stayed quiet for a moment as his words sank in.

"What?" Jewel asked.

"I am not saying that is what is happening, but there is a reason this village is not on any map."

"They eat people?!" Dutch asked as his eyebrows shot up.

Merlin nodded. "I would not put it past them."

"Guys!" Sal's voice broke through the awkward silence. Athena was close behind.

Jewel raced over to him, pulling him into a hug. "They didn't eat you! That would have been so weird to tell your grandma!"

He looked at her, confused. "What? No. We found someone."

"She says she will let us stay with her for the night," Athena said. "She is by the tree line."

"Good job!" Merlin said as he stood.

"Wait," Jewel said, making everyone look at her. "What if this person is tricking us?"

Sal shrugged. "She seemed pretty trustworthy."

"Take me to her. If Sal comes back and gets you guys, it's because it is safe. If no one comes back in five minutes, come and get us, deal?" She looked at Dutch, who nodded.

"Sal, hope to see you soon," he said with a small smile.

Jewel and Sal made their way through the woods, following the village's lights and sounds.

"This village is much smaller," he said, looking down at his footing.

"Did she know who Merlin was?" she asked, looking over to him.

"No. She didn't seem to know very much about anything happening here. Only that Achilles is back."

As they made their way to the edge of the forest, he pointed at a woman who stood with their back to them. "There."

She held a basket by the nook of her elbow as she looked out toward everyone else dancing in the village. Her hair was pulled up into a long ponytail with many loose curls. Jewel noted that her dress was much cleaner than anyone's in the village before.

Sal cleared his throat, making the woman turn.

The basket she was holding dropped to the ground, all the fruits rolling out. She gasped, cupping her hands over her mouth. "Oh my!"

Jewel took a step back, pale as if she had seen a ghost.

"Mother!" the woman cried.

"Is it really you?" Jewel asked, looking over the woman's every feature. Her green eyes and light brown hair were much like Caroline's. Her pointed nose was also familiar. "Lucy?!"

The woman nodded, holding her hands to her heart. Jewel took two steps toward her before pulling her into a hug. They both sobbed as they held onto each other tight.

Jewel pulled away first and cupped her daughter's face. "I've missed you so much!" she said, wiping a tear off Lucy's cheek. Holding her youngest daughter once more seemed as if it was a dream. She feared that if she looked away from her, she might lose her once more. Her heartbeat loudly with joy and disbelief.

"How can this be?" she asked, holding her mother's arms.

"Caroline, she—"

"Caroline!" She gasped, looking around. "Is she here?"

"She is okay but needs help," Jewel said, grabbing her hand.

"I want to see my daughter!"

"That's why we need a place to stay," Sal muttered as he stood off to the side.

Lucy looked at him as if she had forgotten he was there. "Who are you?" she asked in a sweet tone.

"He's her friend. His name's Sal," Jewel explained. "Well, they are going steady."

Her eyes went wide. "What—"

"I can't believe it's you," Jewel said, hugging her once more.

"My house is the white one behind me," she said, holding her mother tight as if she too feared losing her. "Bring Caroline and everyone this boy said are with you." She pulled out of the hug. "I want to see my daughter."

****

Lucy's house was a bit larger than Athena's with two bedrooms and an actual table with four chairs. Dutch put Caroline down on Lucy's bed as Lucy moved to sit next to her.

"Look at how grown up you are," she whispered. She touched her face with the back of her hand softly as if she might break her. She leaned over, kissing her forehead. Her eyes filled with tears again as she noticed how her Caroline was so grown up; she was almost unrecognizable to the young girl she had last seen.

"She's all right," Dutch said from beside her.

"Dutch…" She sighed and stood to give him a hug. "I never thought I would see you again. It is so good to see you."

He hugged her back with a smile. "When Sal first told me, I didn't believe it." He then sat at the foot of the bed. "She's a lot like you," he said, looking at Caroline.

Lucy smiled, wishing she would wake up so that she could meet her.

"The only difference is that she has not taken anything from my backyard," he added, making her laugh. "She has also made her way into my heart just like you did back then."

Her smile widened.

Jewel walked in. "Everyone has eaten and is now asleep." She hugged Lucy once more.

"How did you find this place?" Lucy asked as she sat in a chair in the corner, still close enough that she could see Caroline.

"Caroline," Dutch admitted. "She found the mirror, a door to this world."

Her eyes widened. "There is a way out of here?"

187

"Yes!" Jewel sat by Caroline, taking her hand. "Did you think you were stuck here?"

Lucy nodded. "Even if there is a way out, I will stay until I can get Dilandro out."

"Dilandro is here?"

"I do not know anymore," she admitted in a heavy tone. "A year after we were put in this world and locked away in the castle, there was a prison break. So many people got out, but it was full of violence. The guards were the worst." She looked down at the ground. "It was a real mess, but Dilandro and I saw that as our moment to escape and get back to her." She glanced at Caroline. "This monster of a man with a bun started killing everyone he could reach. Because of Dilandro, I got out. I do not even know how he did it, but he made sure I was free. He could be dead or still locked up. But I have not dared to go back to the castle and throw away his sacrifice."

"I understand," Dutch said with sad eyes. "We were here to look for you and Dilandro. Caroline said she heard his voice in this world."

Lucy's body tensed. "Wait. She heard Dilandro?! That could mean he is still alive!"

"That's what she believes," Jewel said, meeting her daughter's eyes. "But if there is no magic, how could he have cast a spell for her to hear it?"

"Dilandro is smart. Even in those cells, he would find ways to make insignificant amounts of magic come to him." She stood, walked over to Caroline, and brushed her hair with her fingers. "When she was younger, much younger"—she quietly laughed with clear pain behind it—"she was so wise. Much wiser than any other four-year-old I knew. When I sent her away that day, I somehow knew she would find us again." She smiled up at Jewel, blinking away tears. "Her father would be so proud of her."

Jewel smiled back.

A thought poked at Lucy's mind. "I sent her to my sister." She looked over at the pair, reading the room. "But she clearly lives with you now. What happened?"

"She never really talks about Tilly. I don't know if she was too young to remember or if she just doesn't want to talk about it. She didn't stay there long," Jewel said. "But she lived with Edmund for years and then George for a few more years."

Lucy leaned forward, soaking all this information in. She wanted to know the most she could about her daughter.

"She is very close to Edmund and his family. She sees him like a father. He comes by every few nights to have hot chocolate with her. Norna even sleeps over occasionally."

She looked up at her mother with a warm smile. "Sounds like she has a good life with you."

"We're both happy to live together. She is a ball of sunlight."

Sitting back down, Lucy asked, "What about Tilly? Why did she not live with her for very long?"

Jewel let out a heavy sigh. "She doesn't talk to me anymore. So, I don't know."

Her eyebrows furrowed. "What? Why not?"

"She blamed me for your death."

"What?!"

"She said that if I had never taught you magic, maybe you would have stayed in the house, and Achilles would not have killed you."

Lucy rolled her eyes. "I would have done anything to keep Dilandro safe, magic or not!" Then she softened. "So, you really have not seen her in years?"

"The last time I saw her was at your and Dilandro's funeral. She yelled at me in the parking lot. Told me it was all my fault. I cried, begging to have Caroline for the summers, but she just said so many awful things. I never saw Caroline again until last year."

Lucy sat back, taking everything in. A part of her didn't believe her mother, but she also recognized that a lot had changed since that day. "I am sorry."

"Don't be sorry. You did what you had to, and the past is the past. Let's not dwell on it."

She sadly smiled as she got up to hug her mother tight.

****

Sunlight peeked in through the small window. Caroline could feel its warmth across her face. With her mind feeling like gelatin, she tried to open her eyes.

"Caroline," an unfamiliar voice spoke, sounding far away.

She forced herself to open her eyes, taking in the room. For a second, she thought she was back in her room. That was until she saw a young-looking Jewel smiling down at her. The face slowly became clearer.

"Mom…?" she said. She saw her mother looking back at her with a loving smile, but her mind became clearer and reminded her that her mother was dead. *Am I dead?* She must have drowned in the lake. The last thing she remembered was needing to breathe in the dark water. "I died!" she yelled, pushing herself up. Her head hit the headboard. "Grandma!"

"Caroline!" her mother said, reaching for her arms.

"Grandma! Dutch!" she called out for reasons she was unsure of. If she was dead, there was no way they could help her. Her throat tightened.

"Calm down, Caroline," her mother said, keeping her in the bed as she tried to get up. "Everyone is all right!"

"What's going on?" Jewel asked as she and Dutch rushed into the room.

Caroline looked at them, completely lost.

"She thinks she died," her mother explained.

"Sweet girl," Jewel said, grabbing Caroline's arm, while the other woman backed away. "You didn't die. We are all here, and look who is here now with you!"

Caroline took a deep breath before turning to her mother. Her *alive* mother. "Mom?" She jumped into her arms and gave her a hug.

Chapter 26

Everything seemed like a dream. Caroline's tears of joy did not stop till her mother asked to get some fresh air with her. Her mother held out her hand, and she never wanted to let go. If she did, she feared she would wake up, and all of this would be a dream.

"So, Mom tells me you are powerful," Lucy said, looking at her daughter with nothing but joy along her face. Caroline could not help but notice that her mother spoke like Merlin and Athena.

She looked up at the many fluffy light gray clouds that filled the sky like cotton candy. "Why have you not left this place to come find me?"

"I did not know there was a way out of here. Besides, your father could still be alive in the castle. I told myself that I will not leave without him."

"I plan to go to the castle and free him."

"You must know that he could be dead."

She hated that everyone told her that. It was like a punch to the gut. "I know."

"Please tell me everything about your life. I want to know it all." Her mother sat on a bench by the forest. The leaves behind her moved in the soft wind, making a calming sound.

Caroline sat close, still holding onto her mother's hand tight. "Like what?"

Lucy smiled a smile so filled with life. "Everything. Let us start small!" She looked out toward the people walking in the village. "What is your favorite color?"

"Yellow."

"What is your favorite food?"

"Grandma makes the best pancakes, but there is also a donut shop that Dutch and I enjoy a lot. Oh! And cherry pie."

Lucy looked around as if thinking of what to ask next. Caroline smiled as she watched her eyes move from building to person to Caroline's necklace.

"What is in your locket?" her mother asked at last.

With her free hand, she grabbed her locket.

"You do not have to show me if—"

"Here," she said, taking it off and handing it to her. She smiled as Lucy opened it to find Jewel, Dutch, and herself. "There was a carnival in town, and we took this picture there."

"Who is the boy?" her mother asked, handing her back the locket.

"Who? Sal?" Caroline asked as she put it back on.

"Yes, Sal."

Her cheeks turned red. "He's incredibly special, a real gentleman."

"Have you been happy?" Lucy asked, seeming almost scared to ask.

"I have had a really hard life. I can't lie about that."

"You seem as if you have enjoyed living with my mom."

It was true. Before living with Jewel, Caroline had never been as happy as she was now. "It's amazing. In a way, Grandma has become like my mom, and Dutch has helped train me. He is like a dad to me."

Tears of joy filled Lucy's eyes. "Do they work together to train you?"

"To train me and in life. Whenever I need advice, they both are more than ready to hear me out. Dutch sometimes picks me up from school, and Grandma helps me with my homework most nights." She lowered her voice. "But she's not good at math."

A small child ran by with his father close behind, calling after him. They both watched as he picked the child up, and the boy laughed with delight.

She turned back to her mother. "I am happy now and while living with Edmund and his family, but I have missed you and Dad so much."

"I miss him too," Lucy said, looking saddened. "I have spent every day thinking about you and the life I have missed. You are still four in my mind, but here you are, all grown up. *And* you like a boy." She stood, leaving Caroline on the bench. "It breaks my heart to think of everything I have lost with you. Like how I did not know you like pancakes. You used to like cupcakes." Her eyes filled with tears once more, not daring to meet her daughter's eyes.

Caroline stood next to her mother. She noted that her mother was only about a foot taller. "We lost a lot of years because of Achilles, but let's not let him take any more time from us. Besides, now I want to know what your favorite food and color is."

Lucy gave her one more tight hug. "I like scones, and my favorite color is green."

They both sat again, talking about anything they could think of. Caroline didn't want to tell her about living with George. At least not yet. But she told her all about

Edmund, her sleepovers with Norna, the best donuts in Duck, Jewel and Dutch going steady—which came as quite the shock—how hard high school could be, and anything else she could think of. Lucy told her what life in the mirror was like, and to her surprise, it was much more peaceful than she thought it would be. The hidden village worked well to keep her a secret as well. They talked for what seemed like hours as the sun hit its highest point in the sky.

"You are so much like your father!" Lucy said as she laughed. "He would make the same faces you do as he talked." She took a deep breath. "What is the world like now? I am guessing no one dresses like us here."

Caroline looked down at what they wore. "No, not at all!" She had so much to tell her. So much had happened in ten years that she feared she would overwhelm her. "A few years after you and Dad left, World War II ended. A polaroid camera came out, and Norna and I loved it. 1950 was a good year! We have coast to coast telephones now, which are awesome because I can call my family. Some television shows have color! Queen Elizabeth II was crowned queen, and—"

"Wow," Lucy said, laughing. "Slow down. That is a lot of stuff. How do you dress now?"

"Short puffy skirts and ponytails. Sometimes pants if your day fits it better."

"Caroline!" Athena called, standing by Lucy's house. She looked anxious, holding her bad arm close to herself.

"We should go in," Lucy said, standing and taking Caroline's hand.

As they walked up to Athena, Athena looked around and spoke in a low voice. "Merlin wants to leave now."

"What?" Caroline asked.

"He does not want you to run out of magic. He says we cannot waste the day here."

Athena's words made sense, but she didn't want to listen to her or Merlin. She knew she would have to leave her mother, and it pained her to do it so soon.

"I will go with you," Lucy said.

Caroline shook her head. "You can't. Achilles cannot find you. It's not safe." Her words physically hurt to say, but she didn't let go of her mother's hand.

Lucy looked down and nodded. "I-I understand. You must go. I would not be much help without magic anyway."

"I want to stay with you," Caroline said, blinking away the tears forming in her eyes.

"Caroline, you cannot," Athena said with a kind voice.

Lucy cupped Caroline's face and kissed the top of her head. "Just bring your dad home, and we will have the life together that we were always meant to have."

****

Once they were deeper into the forest, and the night had fallen, they set up camp. Fuego started a fire, and everyone had a small bite to eat from Jewel's magic.

Merlin pointed off into the distance, but nothing could be seen. "The castle is just a few feet out of the woods that way."

Everyone stayed silent, listening to the animals in the woods.

Caroline looked at each face. She knew they had to be worried about what was going to happen in the morning. "Can we go over the plan once more?" she asked, looking up to Merlin.

"Yes. I think that is a promising idea," he said, looking up from the fire.

She found that she remembered little of the plan. "How do we get into the castle?"

"There should be a space big enough for you to fit under the front gate's bridge," Athena said, patting Fuego's head. "I found it when I was a kid. It is directly under the bridge. But you have to be quiet. Someone is always watching the gate above there."

Soon, they had gone over the full plan, and everyone understood what had to happen the next day. One after another, they fell asleep with full bellies and tired minds.

But as Caroline lay on the ground between Jewel and Athena, she found it difficult to fall asleep. It had been impossibly hard to leave her mother. Her mind kept thinking about the castle and her father. He had to be there, meaning both of her parents had been alive her whole life. It was a weird thought to think of, one her mind could not understand well.

She watched the stars shine down through the trees. It would have been peaceful if she had been back home. After a while, she sat up, spotting Dutch sitting by the fire. His eyes focused on the flames as if in a trance. He did not seem to notice her. She lifted her arm high above her head, waving it. His head snapped over to her, and their eyes met in the dark. A smile grew on his face, letting her know that she could come over. Careful to not disturb Jewel or Athena, she made her way to him.

"Can't sleep?" he asked, keeping his voice low.

"No," she said as she sat beside him. "I keep thinking about tomorrow and my mom. I can't believe she is alive." She glanced over at him. "Why are you still up?"

"I'm keeping watch, but I am worried for you," he

said, keeping his eyes on the fire. "What if your dad is gone after all of this? I don't want to see you suffer anymore. You're important to me, and it hurts to see you sad."

She grabbed her locket. "I've been thinking about that a lot. I hope he is still alive."

They both stayed quiet for a moment, watching as the fire popped and crackled.

"Are you okay after everything with Grandma?" she asked.

"We haven't really had the chance to talk about it." He looked at her warmly. "I was hurt and couldn't understand it before, but we're okay now. Being with her here helped somehow." He looked over toward where Jewel was sleeping.

"I'm glad."

Fuego moved, catching their eyes.

"I heard you made him that small," Dutch said.

"Yeah. Merlin told me what to do."

He paused. "Merlin has shown you a lot."

"He has. He wants me to have his spell book."

"Well, you were trained by the best." He smiled, rocking into her as she playfully rolled her eyes.

"I was. Grandma is amazing!"

"HEY!" He laughed a bit too loudly, and they both tensed as they watched Merlin move in his sleep. He lowered his voice as he put some small sticks into the fire to keep it burning. "It will be fun to have new things to show you again. But tomorrow is a big day, and we need you on top of your game."

"I know, but this dress is awful to sleep in," she said, standing.

"You think this is comfy?" He gestured to his vest and high boots.

She didn't want to sleep in those either. "The fashion here is so outdated."

"Tell me about it," he grumbled.

"You can't even guess how many layers I have on right now!" she said with a laugh. "Love you, oldie."

"Love you more."

Chapter 27

Caroline gasped as everyone froze. "Wow!"

The most beautiful castle—that seemed to have come out of a storybook—appeared. Its sandstone shined as the sun hit it, and its roof was a strange color of gray, matching the clouds almost perfectly. It had many tall pillars and windows. A courtyard stood in the middle. The tall mountains in the background made the castle look even more stunning.

It was so much bigger than she had ever imagined it to be. She looked up to see that the highest point seemed to disappear into the clouds.

"Oh wow!" Sal said. A smile grew along his face as Fuego landed on his shoulder. "It must be so big up close."

"It's beautiful!" Jewel said with delight.

Merlin had tears in his eyes. "I never thought I would see it again," he said, barely above a whisper. Athena walked up to him and grabbed his hand. He hugged her, picking her up and spinning her with joy. "We are almost there!" He laughed as a big smile grew on her face.

He then set her down and walked over to Sal and Caroline, resting a hand on their shoulders. "You two came into my life so randomly. Sal quite literally fell into my life." He let out a small laugh. "But in the few days that I have gotten to know you both, I have never felt so grateful. I will never forget what you both have done."

"And we will never forget you," she said, meaning every word.

He pulled them into a hug, and Fuego pushed his body between their legs, joining in. "Now, this is going to be groovy!"

Caroline and Sal both laughed.

****

Everyone walked up as close to the castle as they dared, staying out of sight in the overgrown bushes and woods by the main gate. Caroline knew they had to act fast and stay quiet to keep their presence a secret. At least as long as they possibly could.

"Caroline, Dutch, and Jewel," Merlin said after they stopped behind another bush. "Remember, try not to use big spells. Small magic will keep your energy up for longer."

They all nodded.

"Is everyone ready?" he asked, looking at each person.

"Yes," Sal said.

Everyone else gave a thumbs-up.

"Great." Merlin looked over at the castle as the guards, standing with swords by the front door, were changing shifts. He turned to Caroline. "You should start heading under the bridge."

"Thank you," she whispered.

"For what, dear?" he asked.

"For everything. I could not have gotten this far without you."

Fuego flew and landed on Merlin's shoulder. He pet

his small head. "I pray Achilles left your father alive and that you are reunited with him soon."

"Next time I see you, you shall be king again."

He smiled at her words. "And your family will be whole again."

Caroline hugged him, and he held her back tight. She then walked over to Sal.

"Be careful," he said, pulling her into a kiss.

"I will. I promise."

"Just remember that I can't live without you. So, come back to me in one piece." He winked, and her love for him only grew.

"I promise!"

"Good. Now, get your dad."

"Go while the guards are talking," Merlin hissed, looking over at Jewel and Dutch.

After one last kiss, she went to their side and headed under the bridge. Dutch reached his hand out, guiding her into the cold, deep water. She clung onto him. Looking at the water's dark color, she couldn't tell what was underneath its surface.

"Come on," Jewel whispered, looking uneasy a bit further up ahead.

Caroline's foot slipped on an unseen rock, sending her crashing into the water. A loud splash filled the air, and they each froze.

"What was that?" one of the guards asked, sounding jumpy.

Dutch slowly pulled her back up to the surface to not make another loud noise, and they both looked at each other with wide eyes. She held her breath as the guards above moved.

"What did you hear?" another guard asked.

Dutch moved as fast as he could, quietly grabbing Jewel and pulling both her and Caroline under the bridge, out of sight.

"I heard a noise in the water," the first guard answered, still sounding spooked.

Time seemed to freeze as they waited for the guards to go back to what they were doing. They stood under the bridge, only inches away from being seen. The shadows were their only hope. The long pause lasted a lifetime.

"It is probably nothing," the second guard said. "Might be those killer fish Achilles placed in the water the other day."

"Oh right. They do jump a lot."

Caroline's eyes widened even more as she looked at Dutch and then at Jewel.

The guards' conversation changed to something unimportant, and she let out a quiet sigh. She turned, spotting the hole in the wall that Athena had mentioned the night before. She pointed at it, and they all slowly made their way to it. The fear of the killer fish didn't help as they inched their way over, not wanting to disturb the guards again. One by one, they stepped out of the water and onto a small patch of grass, trying not to make any loud dripping sounds.

She rested her hand on the wall and investigated the hole they had to go through. It was much smaller than what Athena had made it sound.

She pushed her body through the narrow hole. Her body scraped across the ruff walls. Pushing her through, the castle's cold air chilled her, filling her arms with goosebumps. She pulled herself out of the hole and onto the other side.

Once inside, she couldn't see much through the

darkness. The only light that filled the space came from the hole, but when Jewel got into the tunnel, the light went away. Caroline pulled out her wand, dried herself with a simple spell, and then used it as a flashlight. Jewel walked up next to her, turning to help Dutch. Caroline knew he was too big; she was the smallest of all of them, and she had a challenging time.

"I don't fit!" Dutch muttered under his breath, but the sound echoed.

"Shh!" Jewel scolded.

They both reached for his hands and pulled him as best as they could. Halfway through, it was clear that he was too big to go any further.

"Forget this," he whispered. "Can you teleport me in?"

Jewel grabbed her wand and flicked it, making him appear next to her. "Could you be any louder?" she said, sounding like a disappointed mother, but he didn't seem to hear her as he cracked his back and looked around. As she used her wand to light the space up, he did the same. "This is the same place we were locked up in."

Caroline flicked her wand at them both, drying them.

"Where is everyone?" Dutch asked as they walked deeper into the space. He looked back at Jewel. "There were others, right?"

Caroline could see just how lost he was in the faint light. But she had more pressing matters to worry about. She leaned over, looking into the next cell and hoping to see a familiar figure.

"Don't get too close to the bars, Caroline," Dutch warned, gently pulling her away from the cell. "The copper makes your magic stop working for a while."

She nodded and walked a bit faster, looking into each

cell. Her breath strained as she noticed how empty they all were. Merlin had mentioned that this was the only cell room, the only room her dad would be locked up in. Her heart raced. *He's dead! He's really gone!*

Again, she looked into all the cells. Empty.

"Merlin was wrong?!" she hissed once she made it to the other end of the room. She turned back to Dutch and Jewel, who walked up to her as they looked in each cell as well.

"What did Merlin tell you?" Jewel asked.

"He said that there was only one room like this, but that can't be true!" she said, trying to stay calm. But as the seconds went by, it became harder and harder to hold back her emotions. Tears formed in her eyes. "He has to be here." Her voice cracked. "Dad is alive!"

She looked into the cells again. Not caring if she got too close to the bars, she frantically looked for any sign of her dad being down here. But each cell turned up empty.

How can this be? She had heard her father's voice. He was supposed to be here, waiting for her. Her mother had said he was here, and she refused to believe otherwise. She turned back to Dutch and Jewel, who looked at her with tears in their eyes. *Why are their eyes watery? My dad is here. We just need to find him.*

"I heard him," she said, holding back a sob. She didn't want to cry. She would not cry! She wanted to find him, and crying would only slow her down.

"Caroline." Her grandmother spoke soft as if trying to hold back her own emotions.

"My dad has to be here!" Caroline said, looking away as a tear rolled down her cheek. The longer she stood in the dungeon, the more it dawned on her that her dad was gone. That Achilles or Zuly had already taken his life.

"Maybe you heard someone who sounded like him," Dutch said gently. "Mayb—"

"NO!" she yelled, tears streaming down her face. She wiped them away angrily. "He can't be gone. I need him."

Jewel walked up to her and pulled her into a hug, rubbing her back.

"He is here!" she said, sounding choked up.

"Caroline…" Dutch said, meeting her eyes.

She put her face into her grandmother's shoulder, feeling like her whole world had broken in half and that she had no way to fix it. Her mind suddenly seemed as if it was opening to what they were saying.

Dutch joined the hug. "It's going to be okay, youngin."

But how was it going to be okay when her dad was dead? She was never going to see him again.

"Caroline," Jewel said, pulling her out of the hug and cupping her face with her hands. She wiped away her wet cheeks. "Let's go."

Anger stormed in Caroline. Why did everything bad always happen to her? Life was so unfair, and she was sick of it! She held her wand so tight that her nails dug into her palm. She yelled out in frustration, flicking her wand at the ground. But her body tensed as something shot out, shooting to the floor.

Jewel looked back at her with warning eyes as the floor shook underneath them. Not a word was said as the floor gave out, dropping them into the darkness.

Chapter 28

"That is the best way in," Athena said, pointing up at a window on the fourth floor.

Sal looked up, trying to imagine any way they could climb up without being seen. A guard walked by, making her, Merlin, and him drop low to the ground. He held his breath as the clueless guard passed. Once the guard was out of earshot, he asked, "The fourth floor is the best way in? Really?"

"Yes," she snapped. "The fourth floor."

"Do you have any idea how hard that's going to be? You're in a dress!"

Merlin poked him, probably reminding him to keep his voice down.

"I know what I am talking about," she said. "That is the kitchen window. Achilles and Zuly never go there! Only the cooks and some maids. We will not get caught by the wrong people that way."

He rolled his eyes.

"Maybe one of them will be kind enough to tell us where to look," Merlin said.

"And how do you plan to climb with one good arm?" he asked, making her sigh. He looked up at the window that seemed so high from where they sat. "What about your arm?" he asked again in a more sincere voice.

"I do not see you coming up with better plans!" she snapped.

He opened his mouth to protest, but Merlin interrupted him. "Shh! Stop this at once, both of you!" he said, keeping his voice low and making Sal feel ashamed. "It is childish to fight now! We listen to Athena. We will go in through the window like she said."

"How do we get to the window and have enough time to climb up without being seen?" he asked, hoping she had thought that far into her plan.

Merlin looked past him, and he followed his eyeline to Fuego laying in the grass. He was using his paws to catch something small on the ground, probably a bug.

"Well," Merlin said as the small beast lifted his paw to see if he had caught anything. "We use the dragon."

A wide smile spread across Sal's face. "You brilliant wizard, you!" he said, playfully punching Merlin's arm.

"That little thing will not do much," Athena said, looking at Fuego.

The dragon must have felt all their eyes on him because he looked back at everyone. His curious expression turned uncomfortable as if he knew their plan.

"I might have one last spell left in me," Merlin said with a smile, reaching into his bag to pull out his wand.

"Will it hurt him?" Sal asked, concerned.

"No more than it did before."

"Get down!" he hissed, putting his hand on Athena's head and pushing her down. He dropped down to hide as well.

Four guards walked by a few feet away, much closer than the last guard. Each had a sword resting on their shoulders. Sal, Merlin, and Athena waited for them to pass. Each second seemed as if it lasted a lifetime. The guards walked past, heading far out of sight.

Merlin looked around once more. "They are gone," he said. "Bring me the dragon."

****

The two guards who stood by the front gate stayed silent until the one on the left's stomach growled.

"Did you miss lunch?" the right guard asked, looking over at him. He pushed his oversized helmet back to see the left guard better.

"No," he answered, sounding a bit uncomfortable. He grabbed his stomach. "It is the eggs we had this morning. They never sit right with me."

They stayed quiet once again until an even louder vibration filled the air.

"What in the world, man?" the right guard said, turning to the left one with wide eyes.

"What?" the left guard asked. Any sign of discomfort had now turned into annoyance.

Another loud vibrating noise filled their ears, making them both jump. Their armor clanged against themselves.

"If that is your stomach, you need help!" the right guard said.

"How can that be my stomach, Christopher?" the left guard asked, crossing his arms.

"Those eggs messed you up, Neal!"

His face turned red. "That was not me!" He opened his mouth to protest some more, but a loud, orange light made them both jump.

A strong burning fire lit the grass a few yards away. Their bickering stopped as their mouths dropped. From where they stood, they could feel the heat on their faces. Both looked up and gasped.

A purple-scaled dragon flew above them, filling the sky. His large wings opened as he breathed down more fire. The grass burned at an alarming rate.

****

Sal and Athena quietly laughed as the guards' screams echoed. Sal could hear as both men pushed each other through the gate. He watched as every guard ran to the gate with their swords tight in their hands. Fuego flew back to the grass, almost smirking. This would clearly give Sal, Athena, and Merlin time to make it up the wall without anyone noticing them. The three of them stood and made their way toward the castle wall.

But Merlin dropped to the ground.

"Merlin!" Sal said with panic in his voice.

Athena stopped running, looking back. "Are you okay?" she asked.

"That was a big spell," Merlin said on his knees. "But I shall be fine. Get to the wall. I will be right behind you."

Sal shook his head. "No, we are not leaving you." He took his arm, pulling him to his feet.

Athena rushed to his other side, and Sal looked around to make sure their presence was still unknown. They helped Merlin walk as fast as they could and made it to the wall. Fuego's mighty roars filled the sky once again. Sal looked up, noticing how high they had to climb.

"We do not have all day," Merlin muttered.

"I'm so proud right now!" Sal admitted, smiling. "Look at my dragon all grown up and defending his daddy."

Merlin shook his head with a smile.

Bending over, Athena reached for her skirt, pulling it in between her legs. She then pushed the fabric into her belt, making it almost like pants. Her brown shoes had sloppy knotted laces. Her off-white socks went up halfway to her knees, and Merlin looked around, seeming a bit uncomfortable. She grabbed hold of the wall, pulling herself up.

"Please be careful with your arm," Sal said, coming up behind her. He noted that even with only one good arm, she climbed the wall with little to no problems.

"And the chickens!" Merlin said with one last look around.

Before they knew it, they were at the fourth-floor window. Sal looked around as smoke filled the air. Fuego's distraction worked beautifully. Athena looked into the window before knocking on the glass. Sal and Merlin tensed, looking up toward her and holding their breaths. Seconds later, the window opened inward.

"Athena!" a voice with a thick Italian-esque accent said. He sounded happy but a bit confused. He took her hand into his pale one and pulled her inside. Once she was in the kitchen, he reached down to help Sal and Merlin up and turned back to her. "What are you doing child?!"

"No time," she said.

Sal looked over and noticed that everyone in the kitchen looked at them with a smile. Each cook wore stained white outfits, and the maids wore long dresses. Athena had been right.

As Merlin closed the window, a collective gasp filled the room. The workers all went on one knee with their right fist over their heart.

"My King!" the one who had opened the window said.

Merlin looked toward each person in the room.

"Please not yet. I must redeem myself first."

"Redeem? For what, my King?"

Merlin froze, seeming shocked. "I was not strong enough, and everyone has suffered for that," he said, making everyone look toward him with a raised eyebrow. "Please get up. I have done nothing for you to bow to me."

Sal noticed that with the way they looked at him, it was clear no one seemed to think that.

"You have always been our king," a blond maid in the back said. "No matter what."

"Thank you. We are going to make things right though," he continued. "I promise. When I am king once more, I will make up for all the years of suffering you have had."

Everyone stood back up, smiling even wider.

"But first, I need something from you," he admitted.

"Anything!" a tall dark young man to his right said.

"Do any of you know where the gem is located?"

Sal watched as their faces changed from helpful to clueless. The room fell silent, and Fuego's roar echoed behind them. Sal's heart lurched at the thought of him possibly getting injured.

"Are you putting it back?" the one who helped them through the window asked.

"Yes. That is the plan," Merlin said. "But I need to know if it is still in the castle."

Sal noticed one short maid looking away, not meeting their eyes. He pointed toward her. "She knows."

"Do you know?" Merlin asked.

She met his eyes and shook her head. "If Achilles or Zuly finds out that I told you, they will kill me. I cannot tell you."

Merlin nodded, pulling his wand out of his pocket. As

he flicked it toward her, her eyes went wide. "Do not worry. This is just a truth spell. It will not hurt."

Her face became neutral as she spoke. "It is locked away in the lower levels. There are two guards."

He flicked his wand again, removing the spell. Her face turned horrified as Merlin smiled kindly. "Thank you. Does anyone have an—"

Zuly's voice filled the room. "Faith!"

The air became tense. The workers all jumped and got back to work. Pots banged together, while maids whispered as they got what they needed. A wall full of aprons covered where Merlin, Athena, and Sal stood, not letting Zuly see them. But he sounded as if he was heading toward them.

"The closet," the worker who had opened the window whispered, pushing Merlin and the two teenagers into the back closet. He shut the door, leaving them in the dark.

"Where is Faith?!" Zuly demanded in a cold voice.

Sal looked toward Merlin. Though he could not see him, he knew he must've been feeling faint. He had used a lot of magic today.

"I do not know where she is," he heard the one who had opened the window say in a calm voice.

"I did not ask you!" Zuly snapped.

"I am here, sir," a soft shaking voice said.

"How many times have I called you?!" he yelled.

"I—"

"More than once!" Silence followed for a moment. "Achilles was putting on his armor, and there was dust on it. Was it not your job to clean it?"

"I—"

The sound of a smack filled the room, making Sal jump. "Go now!"

The young woman's footsteps faded away.

"Useless!" he yelled after her before the room filled with the sound of work once more. "You are all useless! And replaceable!"

Sal held his breath as everything went quiet.

"Something is wrong," Athena whispered.

Merlin's hand covered Sal's mouth, and he put a finger to his lips, telling them to be quiet. Sal nodded, trying to make his breathing as calm as he could.

Zuly's footsteps walked toward their closet door. Sal's eyes went wide as he remembered that Zuly was able to smell where he and Caroline had been hiding when they first came into this mirror world.

Slowly, the doorknob turned.

Chapter 29

"**Z**uly!" a guard called out, sounding winded as he ran into the kitchen.

"What is it?!" Zuly demanded with his hand still on the doorknob.

Sal watched the doorknob turn back, but he still heard Zuly right outside the door. He looked and noticed a frying pan hanging inside the closet, just next to the door. He took it, holding it like a bat. It was heavier than the ones he had back at home, which was perfect. The heavier, the better.

Merlin must've seen him grab the frying pan because he grabbed a rolling pin. Athena, who stood behind them, took hold of another pot and held it like Sal. Each looked at each other, ready to attack Zuly if needed.

"Zuly, the dragon is wreaking havoc on us," the guard explained. "We cannot beat it. It killed some of our men and is flying too high for the cannons to hit it."

"Deal with it!" Zuly hissed.

"Yes, sir! But we could use your help." As the guard spoke, everyone in the kitchen fell silent.

"You dare—"

The castle shook, making everyone gasp as multiple

pots and food fell to the ground. Merlin grabbed Sal's shoulder as he lost his footing.

"I will go get Achilles. He can deal with this," Zuly said, sounding farther away. "Clean up this mess!" he ordered, and the room fell back into the rhythm of movement once more.

Sal looked at Merlin with worry in his eyes. "Fuego!" he whispered.

The worker who had opened the window for them now opened the door. "Go now while they are dealing with the dragon."

"Thank you," Merlin said as the three of them put down their weapons. He turned to Athena. "It is time to get the gem."

She nodded. With one last smile, the three of them left the room.

Right outside of the kitchen, Sal's mouth dropped to the floor. The great hall stretched before them. A beautiful chandelier with candles took his breath away. He walked up to the railing, looking down and then up. He counted about five more floors with a gasp.

"Sal, come on," Athena called from over her shoulder.

"This place is beautiful," he said, walking fast to keep up with her.

"Imagine what it looked like before," she added with a smile. Their quiet voices echoed off the walls, along with their footsteps.

"Quiet. Both of you," Merlin whispered, walking at a quick pace.

The castle shook once more, dust falling from the ceiling.

"This way," she said as she pointed to the end of a hallway that had a set of stairs.

Chapter 30

"Is everyone okay?!" Dutch asked as he moved stones that had fallen on top of him. Dust filled the space, making him cough painfully as he sat up. A warm liquid dripped from his head. He touched it and pulled his hand back, realizing it was blood. His head pounded, but he forced himself to stand as he looked around in panic. "Jewel! Caroline!"

He noticed movement a few feet from him that made him snap his head in that direction. Caroline's small hand reached through the stones.

"Caroline!" he yelled, climbing his way to her. He took her hand in his. "I'm here!" He felt for his wand in his pockets, but he did not find it. A few feet away, he saw Jewel slowly getting back to her feet, seeming dazed. "Wand to hand!"

His wand came to his waiting hand. He flicked it at Caroline, and in a second, she sat next to him. "You okay?" he asked, noticing a cut on her lip.

She nodded, but her eyes seemed dazed.

"Good," he said, taking a deep breath in. "What the heck was that?!" he snapped, waving a cloud of dust away.

"Is everyone okay?" Jewel asked as she looked to where he and Caroline sat.

"We're okay," he said as he pulled Caroline to her feet. Her legs wobbled.

Jewel gasped. "You're bleeding, Dutch!" She put her hand to his forehead, and in a second, the cut disappeared. She turned to Caroline, running her hand down her back to heal any pain she must have felt.

"What now?" he asked, looking around at all the destruction.

"We regroup with Merlin," Jewel said as if it should have been obvious.

"Do we teleport or find them?"

"Teleport. That is the safer idea."

Caroline sighed.

"Caroline, are you ready to go?" Jewel asked, turning back to her granddaughter.

She froze, looking over toward the far right. "There is a door over there," she said as she walked closer to it.

****

Caroline noticed that the door had a key already in its keyhole. *Strange.* Faint mumbles from someone talking to themselves came from the other side.

"I bet a monster is in there," Jewel said, walking up behind her.

Caroline was over everything creepy about this mirror world and did not want to fight another monster. The more she stayed in this world, the less she thought that this land was peaceful since so many things had been trying to kill them. "Who's there?" she asked the darkness.

Jewel and Dutch stood by her side, ready.

The whispers stopped, covering Caroline's arms in chills. She flicked her wand, and a soft light shined from its tip. "Hello?" she called out into the shadows.

She flicked her wand harder. The candles that had long melted on the wall reversed, coming back to life like they had never been used. They lit the room in a soft glow, letting them see the door better.

A small, barred window was toward the top of the door. Caroline held her wand tighter as she walked up to it. She stood on her toes, looking into the dark room. Only a little light came in through the barred window. She noticed a sickly looking man on the floor, just outside of the light. "There's a person!"

The man held his shaking hands over his face. "Please! I have not done anything to get a beating today." His voice shook.

The three of them looked at each other. Caroline and Jewel softened their stances, but Dutch still pointed his wand at the door.

"It might be a trick," he whispered.

"We are not going to hurt you," Caroline said to the stranger.

The stranger's wrists had been chained, holding him to the far-right wall. They made a metal-on-metal sound as he moved. She looked around and wondered why anyone would be locked up all the way down here. After realizing he was more scared of her than they were of him, she put her wand in her pocket and unlocked the door with the key.

"Caroline!" Jewel warned.

"He needs help," she said, glancing back at Jewel. The door made a loud creaking sound as she cracked it open.

"Caroline, stop!" Dutch spoke in a strong voice.

She stopped in the doorway, not daring to take one step closer. The smell was not as bad as Merlin had smelled when she had met him, but she could tell that this man had been here awhile.

"Listen to me," Dutch continued. "I don't tell you what to do much, and you know that!"

She removed her hand from the door as she looked at him.

"It can be a trap! Leave it and let's go."

"Sorry," she muttered. "I just thought—"

"Let's *go*," he said.

The door slammed open, pushing her out of the way.

"I will not let you hurt me!" the stranger, now standing, yelled. His chains yanked him back, making him stay where he stood.

Dutch and Jewel raised their wands as Caroline got back to her feet.

"Don't give us a reason to!" Jewel warned, keeping her wand aimed at his face.

The skinny stranger's body shook. Dry blood from the chains covered his wrists, and his long beard reached his chest. Taking a few steps back, he covered his face with his hands. "I know you… Jewel?"

Caroline pulled her wand out, pointing it at the man while walking next to Dutch.

"Who are you?" Dutch asked.

"I don't mean any harm." The man's voice cracked. "Achilles locked me away years ago. I just want to be with my family again." He looked at Jewel, seeming puzzled. "I know you."

"Why did Achilles lock you away?" she demanded.

"I'm a Smith! He hates us!"

Caroline's body turned cold. "Smith?"

"Yes, wh—" The man looked at her for the first time and froze. "Caroline?" He sounded as if he was holding back tears.

His voice sounded so familiar when he spoke her name. It filled her soul with hope.

"Caroline!" he said once more. "Is it really you?!"

"Not so fast!" Jewel said, narrowing her eyes. "Why should we believe you?"

The man looked desperate. "My name is…" He looked puzzled, putting his hands to his head again. "It's been so long since I used my first name." He turned toward Jewel with red, puffy eyes.

"So, how do you remember your last name?" Dutch asked, pushing Caroline behind him.

"Because Achilles uses my last name."

Caroline put her wand away, moving toward the man. "Dilandro Smith was my father."

"Yes! Dilandro! That was my name!" His body shook once more, seeming as if he could fall over at any minute.

She tried to contain any excitement she felt. This man was clearly not in the right state of mind. "Tell me something only my father would know," she said, keeping her voice even.

Once more, he put his hands to his head. "Two days before the masked man came and took us from you, we— your mother and I—had just finished making your big girl room. You fell, cutting your lip."

A forgotten memory formed in her mind. She recalled the flower wallpaper, the bed on the far wall, and the large windows that let in the afternoon sun. They had just put up the last picture on the wall, and the floor was still a mess from everything they had done. Excited, she had raced out of the room, getting her toys to show them the room. She had tripped over the rolled rug and slammed her face onto the floor, cutting her lip open.

"He could have made that up!" Dutch said, taking her away from her memory.

She kept her eyes on the man. "Mom healed me," she said in a small voice. "I cut my lower lip open, blood was everywhere, and she healed the cut."

"Anyone could have said that," he said, "if they saw you with the scar."

"Dutch, *Mom* healed me. No one outside of the three of us knew that happened." Tears built in her eyes. "No one would have known but my parents!"

Everyone stayed quiet for a moment. Then Jewel flicked her wand toward his wrist, and the chains disappeared. Caroline ran, closing the space between them, and hugged the man in front of her. Her father.

"You're here," he said. Tears rolled down his cheeks, leaving clear marks through the dirt.

"Are you all right?" she asked, holding him tightly. She feared that if he let go, she would lose him once more. He felt so fragile.

"My sweet girl!" he said through his tears.

"How?" she asked, pulling just her head back to look him in the eyes. "I never thought I would see you again."

He had a huge smile as he tightened his arms around her again. She laughed through her tears, thinking about how wild this felt. All her life, she was so used to losing everything that she never thought she would get something back.

He pulled back, cupping her face and wiping away a tear with his thumb. "I cannot believe how much you have grown! How did you know I was here? Did you get my message?"

Her heart beat wildly in her chest. "I found the mirror.

When I accidentally came in, I heard your voice. But how? How did I hear it if you're here?"

"You heard my voice! You heard the message!"

"Yes. But how did you make it so I could hear you from across this world? It was so clear."

"My magic is not as strong as it once was, but when I feel strong every few days, I try to reach out to you. I might not live for much longer. I feel as if the end is near."

She froze.

"I know my days are numbered, but I wanted to reach you. I prayed for one last chance to see you again."

"But I am saving you. You're coming home with me and Mom," she said, refusing to believe what he had just said.

"Lucy? Is she here?" he asked, looking around. His eyes watered when he did not find her. "You mean to tell me that she is still alive?"

"She's somewhere safe. I can't tell you here. But you're not going to die. Grandma can heal whatever is wrong with you," she said, meeting Jewel's eyes.

"I can try," Jewel said, walking up to him. She placed her hand on his boney chest, but after a moment, her legs wobbled, and only a little color returned to his face. "I am not strong enough. I'm sorry. I could only do so little."

"Jewel! The world's best mother-in-law!" He gave her a hug, closing his eyes. "How I have missed you!" He pulled away, breaking into a coughing fit.

Caroline's heart broke.

"When I have my magic fully restored, I will heal you. I promise," Jewel said.

"What have they done to you?" Dutch asked as Dilandro caught his breath.

"Achilles liked to torture me for fun. Used magic in

sick ways," he explained. "My heart has been slowing with each passing day. I have been ill for weeks."

"We have to take you to Lucy," Jewel said.

"Yes," he said with an adoring smile.

The ground shook. Caroline knew that Merlin had started his part of the plan and that she had to join him. He had risked his life for her to get to this moment. She owed him everything.

Dilandro coughed once more.

She looked over at him. "Dad doesn't have a wand and isn't strong enough to face Achilles." She turned to Jewel and Dutch. "Stick with the plan. Teleport him to Mom, and don't let her come this way."

"You cannot beat him alone. I am staying with you," Jewel said as Dutch nodded.

Caroline lowered her eyes, frustrated. She didn't want to be alone, but she wanted them to take her dad away. "Guys, please just get him to safety and then come back to help us put the gem back and fight Achilles." She turned back to her dad. "Please don't let Mom come here."

Dilandro looked at her as if she was speaking another language. "But what about you? I want you to be safe too. I will not lose you again!"

"I will be fine. I promise!"

He nodded, giving her a tight hug.

"I want to stay," Jewel said.

"Grandma, please," Caroline begged. "Just get them to safety and then come back."

She hesitated but then nodded. "Be careful," she said with worried eyes.

"I promise. We will see each other again," she said as Dutch gave her a concerned look before taking Jewel's hand.

"Our girl's got this," he said.

She nodded. Together, they teleported themselves and Dilandro, leaving her alone in the cold dungeon.

Chapter 31

Merlin, Sal, and Athena headed down a spiral staircase, holding onto the railing as they traveled down the steps fast. The castle shook again. The shaking was far worse than before with pebbles and dust falling from the ceiling and dropping around them.

"Wait!" Athena said, putting her good arm out to the side to stop the boys from going past her.

They stopped and listened, hearing at least two guards talking. *Oh no.* Merlin grabbed her and Sal's arms, pulling them down the last few steps and behind the stairs. They all sat on their knees, out of sight.

"What do we do now?" Sal asked. He poked his head around the stairs.

Merlin peeked over as well. On the other side of the room, two husky guards talked as they guarded two large metal doors that the gem must be locked behind.

"I have a plan," he said, turning back to the pair.

"What is it?" Merlin asked, his voice barely above a whisper. At this point, he was open to anything.

"All I need you two to do is get into that room. Okay?" He looked at Athena and then Merlin, who both shared a face of puzzlement. He then stood and walked out of their hiding spot.

Merlin reached for his arm but missed, grabbing the air instead.

"What is he doing?" Athena asked.

"Hey!" Sal called out.

Merlin froze. *Oh lord...*

"Who are you?" one guard, who sounded intimidating, asked.

Merlin heard the guards draw their swords, but footsteps raced back up the stairs.

"Come and get me you ankle biters!" Sal called.

"Stop right there!" a guard called as they both chased after Sal, leaving the door alone.

"*Genius,*" Merlin muttered under his breath.

As Sal raced up the steps, Merlin and Athena ducked deeper under them, not wanting to be seen as the guards chased him. Once the thundering footsteps quieted, they moved from their hiding spot.

"Not something I would have thought of," she said.

Merlin nodded. He grabbed the door's large handle and pushed. With a loud creak, the door opened to reveal a room with no windows. The only light came from the gem as it faintly lit the space with its green glow.

"Here it is," he said as his eyes landed on the gem. It was even more beautiful than he had remembered. He walked over to one side, while Athena walked over to the other. They both took hold of it. "You look pale," he noted, looking up at her face.

"I-I am nervous," she admitted, keeping her left arm close. "How heavy is it? I do not know if my arm can do this."

"We can do it! We take the gem out on three," he said, getting a good hold on it and looking up as the green light lit her face.

She nodded and grabbed the gem.

"One. Two. Three!"

They lifted the gem, and it popped right out of place. She gasped. They both struggled to hold onto it.

"We got it!" Merlin encouraged, sounding strained.

They made their way out of the room and up the steps.

****

Sal ran through the castle, not sure where to go. His only plan was to not get caught by the two guards running behind him. He ran even faster than he had back in the woods, and that was saying something because back then, it had felt like his legs were going to fall off. His legs burned now.

The two guards kept up with him, which was surprising. He had thought they would have given up long before now.

As he passed the throne room, he looked over, finding Achilles talking angrily to Zuly. His heart jumped even faster. If Achilles saw him, he knew he'd be dead.

"Sir!" one of the guards yelled down the room, stopping.

The other guard continued to chase Sal. Sal knew Achilles must have seen him since another set of feet thundered behind him. A quick glance over his shoulder let him know that Zuly had been teleported to him. The guards pulled out their swords.

Sal glanced out a large window as he rushed by and saw Fuego flying outside. A smile grew along his face. He looked back, saw that Zuly and the guard were far enough behind him, and stopped. The window opened with a hard pull.

Sal looked down and noticed how high up he had gotten. His stomach flipped. He glanced back. Achilles walked behind his running guards, getting closer.

He turned back to the window. "Fuego!" he called out, hoping his dragon heard him over all the loud sounds around them.

Fuego's big eyes looked over toward him, and the dragon made his way to the window. From where Sal stood, the strong wind made by Fuego's large wings pulled the air around him.

"Enough, boy!" Achilles yelled.

He didn't give it another thought. He stepped up onto the window's frame and let himself drop. Fuego flew under him, and he landed on the dragon's back with a thud, making him gasp. He looked up to see Achilles' angry face in the window.

"Good job, boy!" Sal said once air returned to his lungs. "Let's go find Merlin!"

Chapter 32

Athena and Merlin made it to the base of the tower without being seen, which was a surprise to Merlin. Everyone was outside fighting Fuego; that part of the plan had worked out better than he had thought. But even though everyone was busy, they worked as fast as they could, trying not to push their luck.

Athena cried out, losing her grip on the gem once more. "My arm! My arm!" Pain filled her face.

"We have to keep going," Merlin said, though his heart ached at her pain.

"I know!" She blinked away her tears fast.

They continued walking as fast as they could, though she had to stop more than ten times because of the pain. After what seemed like a lifetime, they made it to the tower. Merlin looked up at all the steps they still had to climb—at least four hundred—to get to the top of the tower.

"Where is Caroline?" Athena asked. "She should have been here by now."

"I do not know," he said, taking one last deep breath before stepping forward. "I do hope she is all right, but we must hurry."

Athena cried out in pain. "I do not know how much longer I can do this!" she grunted as her face turned red. She put the gem down, holding her arm close.

"I know, I know…" he said sadly.

After a moment, they started to make their way up the spiral stairs together.

"Watch your step," he said more to himself than to her as he could not see the steps with the gem in front of him.

Athena took another backward step up the stairs and looked over Merlin's shoulder. "Caroline!"

****

Caroline looked up as Merlin and Athena set a hefty green gem down on a stair step and looked at her with one hand still on it to keep it steady. She gasped. "Wow! It's so big!"

"Did you find your father?" Merlin asked, his dark skin seeming flushed.

"I found him!" she said with a huge smile.

"Groovy!" he cried out, hugging her with one arm while keeping the other on the gem.

She looked over at Athena and noticed her friend's absence. Dread filled her with terrifying possibilities. "Where is Sal?" she asked with panic in her voice.

"He is fine," Merlin said quickly.

"He distracted the guards," Athena said.

"But we must hurry, or someone will find us!" he added. "Teleport us up to the top, Caroline." He pointed all the way up the stairs.

"Merlin, I don't know if I can," she admitted. "I feel very weak. It was hard teleporting here."

"One last spell, and the gem will be back in place," he reminded her with a warm smile. He turned to Athena. "Grab the gem tight."

She held her arm back. "It hurts too much!"

"I know, but we are so close!"

As Merlin and Athena took hold of the gem once more, Caroline pointed her wand at them. She knew that after this spell, she would feel awful, but the promise of the gem helping her feel better again was great.

A strong pain—like nothing she had ever felt before—filled her body. She yelled out in agony. She dropped onto the steps, rolling down the few steps she had climbed.

"Caroline?!" Merlin gasped.

Her dress lay in a mess around her. She inched her eyes up just as Achilles stepped over her.

"You think you can just get away with this?!" he yelled toward Merlin and Athena. He kicked Caroline, putting his foot on her back.

Her wand rolled out of her hand as she gasped out in pain.

"And you!" he said, looking down at her. "Your family ruined my life! Now you want to help take what I have here?!" He grabbed her arm, pulling her to her feet.

He put his wand to her throat, ready to do the worst, but Merlin flicked his wand, pushing Achilles into the wall and away from her. She dropped to the ground. He placed the gem down as he raced toward her.

"No!" she cried out as he tried to help her up. She grabbed her wand, and her voice cracked. "You have to go!"

"I will not leave you," he said, pulling her to her feet.

Achilles pointed his wand at Merlin. Pushing Merlin away from her, she flicked her wand at him, teleporting him. She then flicked her wand at Athena with the gem, sending her to Merlin at the top of the tower.

Achilles grabbed the neckline of Caroline's dress from the back, throwing her into the wall. "You little rat!" he yelled as she forced herself to stand.

With Merlin and Athena putting the gem back, she could not let Achilles stop them. She had to fight. And she had to win. Pushing all the pain and tiredness she felt to the back of her mind, she stood tall.

"Zuly!" Achilles, never taking his eyes off Caroline, yelled as Zuly came up the steps. "Go up there! Do not let Merlin put that gem back. K-kill them both if you must!"

"NO!" She pointed her wand at Zuly, but Achilles beat her to it.

He flicked his wand, teleporting his captain to Merlin and Athena.

"Zuly! He's coming!" Caroline yelled as hard as she could up the stairs to them. "Zuly is coming!!" Her voice echoed off the stone walls.

Achilles flicked his wand. She turned, face-to-face with him. Her feet lifted off the ground as her heartbeat wildly in her chest.

"You will die by my hands!" He grabbed her neck and squeezed.

Panic filled her mind until she recalled a spell that Dutch had taught her months ago. "Heatlingn." Her body became hot, burning under her skin.

Achilles yelled, dropped her, and pulled back his hand. Painful boils could be seen on it. He flicked his wand. "Hucabufs!" he called out.

Pain shot through her body much like before. Her vision blackened. As her feet lifted off the ground once more, she moved fast through the window. Gasping, she dangled more than seventy feet from the ground. Achilles held her there with his wand. Pain held her body, numbing her mind. He snapped his fingers, taking her wand from her hand.

"No, Achilles!" she gasped. Her mind slowly took in what was happening.

He smiled. "So…" He stood in the window's frame, resting both of his hands on the frame by his head. The sun shined down on him. "This is where your story ends. With no one around who cares. No Grandma. No Dutch. No Sal. Not even your uncles."

His words made her mind snap back into focus. "Achilles, wait!"

"You want me to save you?" he hissed. "You deserve nothing in this life!"

Suddenly, she fell through the air, screaming full of terror as her stomach flipped. The air rushed past her. She closed her eyes, waiting for the worst.

"Caroline!" Sal's voice yelled.

Sal? She opened her eyes as Sal reached out, grabbing her waist and pulling her onto Fuego's back. As she landed in his lap, she pushed down her skirt, and he held her tight.

"No!" Achilles yelled from above.

As Fuego flew up the tower, she grabbed two marbles and threw them at Achilles. She heard Edmund's voice.

"Hey! How's it going?"

She held onto Sal tightly as the dragon flew. She found it hard to catch her breath.

"Are you all right?" he asked, resting a hand on her back.

"I think so."

"Where do you need to go?"

"Take me to the top!" She pointed at the top of the tower.

"What about Edmund?" he asked.

"He only has a few minutes. We better hurry." She reached for her pocket. "Wait. I don't have a wand!"

"Here," Sal said, pulling his out of his pocket and handing it to her.

"What about you?" she asked, taking it.

He laughed. "I don't need a wand! I have a dragon!"

Caroline couldn't help but smile as they reached the top of the tower. "I don't know what's taking Grandma and Dutch so long. But they did have a hard time teleporting before. Can you please go get them?"

Fuego lowered himself beside the tower, letting her jump off next to Merlin and Athena. Zuly looked over at the dragon and then to Sal with wide eyes.

"Please be careful," Sal said before Fuego flew off.

Caroline noticed blood on Zuly's sword right away. She ran to Merlin, who held his right arm. Athena lay on the floor—motionless—with her back to Caroline. The gem was on the ground behind Merlin.

"Zuly, stop this nonsense at once!" he said.

Zuly stood in front of where the gem had to be placed with his bloody sword drawn. His eyes were set on Merlin. Caroline, while looking toward Zuly, slowly made her way to Athena. She bent down, placing her hand on Athena's neck to check for a pulse. Athena looked so still.

"Back away from her, child!" Zuly snapped. Anger filled his voice.

"What did you do to her?" she asked, not fearing the man with nothing but a sword.

"Nothing she did not deserve!" he said. "This is bigger than you know, girl!"

After feeling Athena's pulse, Caroline walked back to Merlin's side.

"Zuly, you must listen to me," Merlin said, daring to take a step forward.

Zuly held his sword tighter, his knuckles white. But

something in his eyes was off. "I am warning you! One more step!"

But Merlin did not show any fear as he kept his eyes on Zuly. "Caroline, please put your wand away."

She looked at him, confused. "But Merlin—"

"Caroline," he said, keeping his tone calm. He looked back at her with pleading eyes.

She put her wand in her pocket, hoping Merlin was not making a mistake.

He turned back to Zuly. "I only want to talk. I do not want to hurt you."

"I do not promise the same to you!" Zuly snapped but still did not move to attack.

"Zuly, what has Achilles given you that I did not?" Merlin asked.

The question seemed to take Zuly by surprise, though he tried to hide it well. She saw the wheels turning in his head. His face showed a battle going on in his mind. Merlin dared to take another step toward Zuly. Every part of her feared what could happen next.

"We have known each other for years," Merlin said, sounding as if he was choosing his words carefully. "You were very young when you came to work at the castle. In fact, I was young myself when I met you." He laughed despite himself. "You were the only person I had ever thought of as a friend."

Caroline saw Zuly's grip had lightened up.

"You used to be one of the most powerful people in this land. Now, you just run around doing what Achilles tells you."

Zuly's face softened.

"Do not pretend that I cannot see the bruises on your face. Zuly, please tell me what I did that made you seek out Achilles?" His eyes watered, but he blinked them away.

"I will not speak with you of such things!" Zuly yelled. His voice cracked. "I-I will kill you if you take another step!" His grip on his sword tightened once more as his eyes narrowed.

Achilles teleported behind Caroline, jabbing his wand into her back. "Smart trick to send your uncle to do your dirty work," he said in her ear. "I did not think you were smart enough to make such a move." The wand dug deeper.

She looked at Merlin, who shared her fear in his eyes.

"Then again, you always have those you love die for you."

Her body went cold. She turned her head to meet his eyes. A wicked smile played across his face, which made her fears worse.

"Go to him," he said in a dark voice. He pointed at Merlin with his other hand. "This does not concern you, Caroline."

He lowered his wand, and she turned around completely to look him in the eyes. A thin smile sat on his face. She found no words.

"I'll find you later," he said, looking down at her.

She glanced at Merlin, who nodded. They held each other's gaze for a moment until she looked back at Achilles, whose smile had not faded.

"Yes. Run along, Caroline."

She made her way to the stairs, her heart beating fast in her chest. But before she could make it, Achilles whispered, and she dropped to the floor.

****

Merlin jumped at the sight of Caroline collapsing.

"Well, now," Achilles said, turning back to face him.

"The bystander is out of the way for now. We can finish this once and for all." He moved in front of Merlin with his wand pointed at his chest.

Merlin stood with his back to the gem, between Zuly and Achilles. He glanced at Caroline once more. She had fallen much like Athena had years ago. It seemed like history was repeating.

He looked his enemy dead in the eyes. "I do not fear you, Achilles! I never have. You will have to kill me if you think you can stop me!"

"That is where you are wrong, Merlin. You should fear me." Achilles looked at Zuly while keeping his wand pointed toward Merlin. "You're as useless as ever," he hissed. "I told you to take care of this."

Merlin met Zuly's eyes before Achilles turned back to him.

"I will give you two opportunities, Merlin," Achilles said, taking a step toward the other man. "One is you give up now and die here like the coward you are. Or you can go ahead and try to put the gem back, so you can die a hero."

Merlin laughed under his breath. "Those are awful opportunities."

Athena started to sit up, her arms shaking as she pushed herself off the ground.

"Oh! Look, Merlin!" Achilles laughed. "Are you going to let her do all the work for you like last time?" He pointed his wand at her.

"NO!" Merlin yelled.

She dropped back to the ground, as still as before.

His heart stopped. "She does not need to be a part of this."

Achilles laughed again. "Surely you did not make her come all this way to die. Like last time."

He saw her chest barely rise and fall. With somewhat of a piece of mind, he glanced back at Zuly. Two against one was not what he wanted coming into this. A part of him wished he was back in his cave. Safe. But another part noticed how close he was to putting the gem back. He could not give up hope now.

Grabbing his wand from his pocket, he flicked it at Achilles. "Recanio!"

The spell bounced off Achilles weakly. He tried to teleport with the gem but was weakened by the first spell. He only made it halfway to where he wanted to be. A laugh broke out, and he struggled to stay on his feet.

"I see you've chosen the second opportunity: to die trying to help your hopeless cause." Achilles took a few steps toward where Merlin had dropped.

His breath was heavy as he pushed himself off the ground. His body leaned on the gem as the sun burned down. "If I am to die, I would like to go down fighting!"

"If you wish—"

Smack!

Merlin punched Achilles in the jaw, and Achilles took a few steps back in shock. Zuly moved toward the wizard, swinging his sword. Merlin lowered himself and kicked his legs, making Zuly drop his sword as he fell on his side. Acting fast, Merlin took the sword, pointing it at Achilles.

Achilles flicked his wand. "Fire itera!"

Merlin gasped, moving away from the flames.

Achilles shot lightning, making Merlin drop to the ground with a grunt. "Zuly, you useless piece of crap!" he yelled.

Zuly stood, holding his arm in pain.

Achilles pointed his wand at him, who had wide eyes. "You will die slowly! I want you to suffer for now till I have the time to kill you with pleasure!"

Merlin stood, swinging the sword at Achilles.

Achilles took a step back to avoid the hit. "Look at the powerful wizard fighting like a weak human." He flicked his wand toward him, sending fire his way.

Merlin—who had not felt this alive in years—moved out of the way fast enough to make another swing at Achilles.

Chapter 33

Merlin breathed in deep and heavy, holding Zuly's sword tight. He stood across from Achilles, who had a cut on his chin. Blood dripped down, staining his vest. Zuly stayed back, holding his arm and staying by Achilles' side.

Achilles pointed his wand at Merlin. "You put up more of a fight than I thought you would, old man!" he said angrily.

Merlin smiled. "And I thought you would be much harder to fight. Caroline made you sound like you were a monster."

Achilles' face turned red. "Fire itera." He sent spell after spell toward Merlin. "You were a fool to think you could get your kingdom back!" He lowered his wand.

The smoke from all the spells cleared. Merlin lay on his hands and knees. The sword had dropped to his side.

"The gem's magic and this land are mine!" Achilles yelled as he walked toward Merlin and flicked his wand, sending more waves of pain through Merlin's body.

His whole body jerked as he dropped to his side. His dark face became paler with each passing second. Out of the corner of his eyes, he noticed Zuly look away.

"You will die today," Achilles said in a calm tone. "I want you to know that you left your people powerless and weak. And *we* will make them suffer for years to come because of you." He bent down and grabbed ahold of Merlin's hair, turning his head to face him. "But your death will be in vain."

Merlin met his eyes.

"I will make sure no one knows what you tried to do today. Ready to die?" Achilles roughly let go of Merlin and stood. His wand pointed straight at Merlin's heart.

Merlin closed his eyes, waiting for Achilles to take the shot and end it all, but a loud grunt and bang filled the air instead. He snapped his eyes back open. Zuly was on top of Achilles, trying to grab his wand with all his might. On the ground, they both fought each other with closed fits.

"How dare you!" Achilles said through clenched teeth as he punched Zuly's shoulder.

Zuly flinched but never let go of the wand. Somehow, Achilles rolled, taking Zuly with him. Now, he was on top, punching Zuly in the face multiple times. Zuly pushed his hips up, making Achilles lose his balance. He then clawed at his face and landed a punch to his jaw before digging his thumb into the other man's eye.

Achilles yelled out. His hold on his wand loosened, and Zuly pulled it from his grasp. Merlin stood with his own wand as his old friend stood with Achilles' wand. They held each other's gaze for a moment, both seeming hesitant to make the next move.

Achilles' face filled with rage as he stood, bruised and beaten. Blood oozed out of a cut on his eyebrow. "You dare to side with the fallen king?"

"I was wrong to trust you so openly and to never question what you made me do," Zuly said, holding

Achilles' wand so tight that his fist turned white.

"You came looking for me, boy!" Achilles said, raising his voice.

Merlin picked up Zuly's sword, standing by his side.

"Everything you made me do," Zuly muttered. "All because I let you fill my mind with fear! Hurting the people in this kingdom and my friends." He pointed to Athena, who lay by the gem.

"You burned her arm on your own will!" Achilles hissed. "I never gave you that order! I never would have done that to her." A vein popped out of his neck.

Zuly snapped his wand in two as if it was nothing more than a twig. He threw it at Achilles' feet.

"A real man knows when one has lost, Achilles," Merlin said.

"A real man, you say?" Achilles said, shaking with rage. "This world's power… Everything here is mine! I found it! I took it! It's mine. I will not let you, Merlin, and this worthless man stop me!" He lifted his hands, and lightning shot out, making both men move out of the way.

They both went behind the gem to shield themselves.

"Your gem cannot keep you safe!" Achilles yelled.

"We need to put the gem back!" Merlin said, shooting what little magic he had at Achilles. He missed as he moved.

"If we put it back, we might stand a chance!" Zuly said, placing a hand on the gem. His shoulder rested oddly by his side. "But we need him out of the way first."

"If you will not come out and fight, things might end badly for you," Achilles growled.

****

Caroline, dazed, slowly pushed herself up.

Achilles grabbed her shoulder. "Nice of you to join us!" he hissed in her ear as he pulled her in front of him. He wrapped his arm around her neck, turning back to the gem. "Come out, dear King."

All the fuzziness in her brain faded as Merlin popped his head around the gem.

He gasped. "Caroline!"

"Come out and nothing happens to her because of you!" Achilles threatened.

"Merlin, no!" she yelled.

He tightened his hold on her. "Don't try anything, Merlin! This girl will be dead within seconds if you do." He looked straight at Merlin. "I can feel it. You care for this child as much as you *cared* for Athena."

Merlin swallowed.

Caroline stared at him, mentally trying to tell him that her life was not worth the land.

"Zuly," Achilles continued in a hard tone, "if you knew what was best for you, you would come back to me, and maybe I will act as if this never happened."

No one moved. No one said anything.

Caroline's eyes never looked away from Merlin's. The wind grew stronger, moving her hair around wildly. "Wand to my hand!"

Achilles reached for her hand to take the incoming wand. Merlin handed Zuly his sword, and Zuly raced toward Achilles, slicing his arm. He dropped Caroline, who raised her arm just in time to take Sal's wand back. She was unsure why Zuly was on their side, but it hardly mattered now.

She stood, turning to face Achilles. "Teleportsheam!"

The spell hit him, and he was gone. For now.

"GO!" she yelled at Merlin, who took hold of the gem.

"Help me!" he pleaded.

Zuly dropped his sword with a loud clang, running to the gem. Caroline got close behind.

"On three!" Merlin shouted as each grabbed a side.

Achilles reappeared, yelling, "Recanio!"

Caroline pointed her wand at him. "Gepsic!" She missed him as he made his way to them. His spell missed her by inches. "Teleportsheam!"

Once more, he was gone.

"One!" Merlin counted.

"Two," Zuly said.

"Three!" she shouted as they all lifted the gem. It was so much heavier than she had thought. "Hurry!" They moved as fast as they could.

"We are almost there!" Zuly gasped.

The sun beat down on them as the winds grew stronger.

"Look out!" she shouted as Achilles appeared behind Merlin.

He held a new wand in his hand, and his eyes were full of hate. She removed a hand from the gem, but he was faster. In seconds, he put his wand to Merlin's back, causing Merlin to scream a scream so full of agony that she would never forget it.

Merlin's face twisted. He dropped the gem, sending Zuly and Caroline off-balance. The gem dropped.

"NO! Merlin!" She flicked her wand at Achilles, hitting him with lightning that made him gasp. She then sent wind toward him, knocking him a few feet back. She almost launched another spell, but Zuly grabbed her arm.

"No. We are almost there!"

All they had to do was set the gem over a foot, and it would be back in place. They grabbed it.

"No!" Achilles yelled.

The gem sat back in its rightful spot. But nothing happened. Caroline's eyes filled with tears. *How can it not work?!*

A bright sunray—brighter than anything she had ever seen—shined onto the gem. Everyone closed their eyes, protecting them as the sun filled the gem for the first time in eleven years.

"Get down!" Zuly warned as he grabbed her arm and pulled her to the ground.

She covered her head with her arms as the light created a strong wind that threatened to send her away.

As they lay with their faces down, he put his arm over her. "Hold on!"

The wind shoved everything around. Achilles' screams echoed, becoming farther away. But the light soon died down, along with the wind.

Zuly helped her to her feet. She first noticed how the gem shined a bright shade of green within the sun. She blinked a few times, still adjusting to the light. Her body felt stronger, more energized. By the look on Zuly's face, he felt the same way.

She looked around. Achilles lay on the ground, motionless.

Grabbing her wand tighter, she took a step toward him. He would die for everything he had done to her family and to the people in this kingdom. She took another step, but Merlin's gasps caught her attention. She turned.

Merlin lay a few feet away, holding his chest.

"Merlin!" she cried out, running to him.

Zuly ran too, close behind her, and crouched on the other side of him. "My King, my friend."

Merlin looked so pale that it scared her. He coughed

hard. His lips were a light shade of blue.

She grabbed his hand, which sat heavy in hers. "What did he do to him?" she asked, fighting back tears. She glanced up to see Zuly's face full of fear. Her heart pounded. "Can I heal him?"

He didn't respond.

"Zuly! Can I heal him?" she asked again. A part of her felt as if he did not deserve to help Merlin; he was one reason he was like this.

He didn't meet her eyes. "No," he muttered as if he was scared to say it any louder.

"W-what. Why not?" she asked with a shaking voice.

Merlin coughed. To her horror, blood came out.

"He hit him with a black poison," Zuly explained.

"What?"

"It is unhealable."

She shook her head, tears streaming down her face. "No. There must be a way!"

Merlin reached up to her face, and she melted into his touch. He held no fear in his eyes. "Caroline, it is going to be all right," he said weakly. His words came out quiet.

But how can any of this be all right? "No. This land needs you! You can't die," she said, feeling desperate.

"Athena can"—he coughed—"run the kingdom." He rolled his head to look over at her. A weak smile formed. His eyes closed.

For a horrible second, she thought he died. "Merlin…"

"Zuly, I am sorry," he said, opening his eyes and turning to Zuly. "I-I am sorry for what I did to make you seek out"—he coughed again—"A-Achilles."

Zuly shook his head. "No. Do not be sorry, my King. I am so very sorry for what I did to you and to your kingdom." His voice cracked. "I-I brought him here, I helped him, and you trusted me."

Merlin gave him a weak smile. "I forgive you," he said to Zuly, who looked as if he didn't want his forgiveness. "Please forgive me, my old"—another cough—"friend." Merlin extended his hand to Zuly, and he took it in his.

His hand then reached for Caroline's. She took his as he held hers tight. She had never felt more helpless as she watched his life start to leave his body. It was clear that he was fading every second that went. She had never seen something so terrifying.

"Take the b-book, Ca-Caroline," he said as he fought to keep his eyes open.

"I will," she said, not knowing what else to say. She wanted to thank him for everything he had done for her. Her life would never be the same now that she had known him. She wished there was a way to let him know that. But as he smiled one last time, she had a feeling he knew.

"O-oh," he said, opening his eyes as best as he could. "Tell S-Sal that he has a br-bright future and that Fuego…will not e-eat him. I was wrong. H-he is a loyal one."

Somehow, she managed to lightly laugh through her tears. "I will."

"Sir," Zuly said, and Merlin's gaze moved to him, his breaths short. "Athena is workin—"

Caroline screamed as Achilles ran Zuly's sword through his chest.

"You never should have double-crossed me," he hissed.

Caroline stood, backing away in disbelief. Zuly's face filled with torment before becoming completely emotionless as he dropped to Merlin's side. Merlin turned toward her, and his eyes shut. His weak smile fell from his face.

Chapter 34

"You think you can take everything away from me?!" Achilles yelled, looking at Caroline. Zuly's blood covered the sword.

"You're a monster!" she screamed, her voice hoarse. "You wrecked my life and everyone's who live here—"

"Shut up!" he demanded as he threw the sword down with a bang.

"You will die just like they have! And at last, I will live in peace." She pulled out her wand, pointing it at him with a shaking hand. Magic—like nothing she had ever felt before—coursed through her. "I will kill you for Merlin!" she hissed, meaning every word.

He pulled out a wand of his own. He shot the same spell he had killed Merlin with at her, but with one wave of her wand, the spell disappeared. She stood the way Merlin had shown her. For a second, his eyes went wide as the spell was sent to him.

He yelled as he fell out the side of the tower. Without a second thought, she teleported to the bottom of the tower where he made himself softly land. She shot lightning and water his way. Yelling, he made her magic go back toward her. Teleporting out of the way, she stood like

Merlin had shown her before, but Achilles' wand pointed at her, and a green light shot into her, giving her a wave of pain.

She sat on the ground, breathing hard, as she looked up at him. He walked over to her, holding his wand so tight that she saw the veins in his fist. Slowly, she moved her free hand toward the bag of marbles on her hip. She didn't know how many remained, but one would be enough.

"Your story ends now, Caroline Smith!" he said, pointing his wand at her face.

"Achilles! Enough!" Jewel's voice said from behind her.

Caroline's heart beat wildly, but she didn't dare look back. Achilles looked past her.

"Touch her, and you die!" Dutch said.

A thin smile grew along Achilles' face. "This couldn't be more perfect," he said with a strange delight in his eyes.

"Step away, Achilles!" Jewel ordered.

"Dutch, Jewel, you always come to the aid of this child," Achilles hissed, keeping his wand pointed at her, but his eyes were glued to Dutch and Jewel. "If you dare send anything my way, I will kill her."

Caroline reached into the bag of marbles, never taking her eyes off Achilles.

Dutch laughed. "We have a dragon, Achilles."

"Do you really want to play with those odds?" He rolled his eyes. "I am not backing down because you made one of my dragons turn on me."

Dutch laughed under his breath. "Unwise. It's three against one, and it seems that the gem is back in its place. So, we can handle you."

Caroline glanced around. She had hardly noticed how

green and lovely everything around them was now. She then grabbed what was left of her marbles. "Make it four against one!" she yelled as she threw them at the wall behind Achilles.

Edmund showed up, ready to fight.

"You again!" Achilles said as he whipped around to face him.

Edmund sent powerful spells toward Achilles, who sent back stronger spells. Even with the gem back, he still had a lot of power. Jewel teleported herself, along with Dutch, next to Caroline.

"Are you all right?" he asked.

She shook her head. "Where is Sal?"

Seconds later, she spotted Fuego flying overhead. Sal held on tight as he landed near them smoothly.

"How can we help?" he asked, still on the dragon's back.

Fuego's eyes followed Achilles and Edmund. He opened his mouth, sending a wave of fire toward Achilles. Edmund put a shield around himself, and everyone else shielded their face from the heat. Achilles sent lightning toward Sal, but Jewel blocked it as Edmund punched Achilles' chest.

"Sal, I need you to go up to the tower and help Athena," Caroline said. Dread filled her as she thought of him finding Merlin's body. "Merlin's gone." The words burned out of her.

Jewel and Dutch ran off to help Edmund, leaving her with Sal's broken eyes.

"H-how?" he asked under his breath.

"He's up there. Be ready."

His eyes filled with tears as Fuego lifted into the air.

Caroline raced to where Edmund, Jewel, and Dutch

were putting up a good fight, sending spell after spell toward Achilles. Achilles yelled out, trying to keep up with everything they sent.

Standing as Merlin had shown her, she sent Achilles into the castle's wall.

"Fire itera!" Jewel called out, pointing her wand at him as he stood.

The fire hit him, making him gasp. He waved his wand to make it disappear. With a hard flick, Dutch sent lightning to him, and he teleported a few feet away.

Edmund turned to him. "Stone-soul!"

"Enough!" Achilles yelled as Caroline sent the same spell.

Slamming his foot down, a wave of power went through the ground, knocking everyone off their feet. Jewel stood and pointed her wand at his head without missing a beat, but it was not fast enough.

Achilles sent out wild and deadly spells that Caroline had never seen before. "You will die! All of you!"

Dutch and Edmund jumped, making a force field around the four of them. The hurtful spells broke after contacting the force field.

"What do we do?" Caroline asked, never taking her eyes off where Achilles stood as he sent endless spells their way.

"When we take this down," Dutch said, holding his wand tight along with Edmund to keep the force field up, "everyone is going to send a stone-soul spell at him."

Everyone nodded.

"It should freeze him in place and give us the upper hand."

Achilles banged his fist on the force field. "Fight me!"

Caroline backed away. "This better work," she

muttered. Her hands shook as she adjusted her hold on her wand.

"It's the only shot we have," Jewel said, never taking her eyes off Achilles.

"Cowards!" he screamed.

"Everyone ready?" she asked, standing in a line with Dutch and Edmund.

Caroline followed, standing next to her.

Edmund looked over to her, winking like everything would be all right. A faint smile grew on her face.

"Now!" he yelled as he and Dutch removed the force field.

Achilles stepped toward them and pointed his wand straight at Caroline. The spell hit her face, making her drop to the ground. Unconscious.

****

"Stone-soul!" Jewel, Dutch, and Edmund called out.

Achilles, with his wand still pointed toward Caroline, froze like a statue.

"Caroline!" Jewel ran to be by her side.

Caroline had her back to Jewel, laying as still as ever. Jewel dropped next to her with shaking hands and rolled her onto her back. She gasped as she saw black marks marking the side of her face. They reached across like long, wicked fingers. She put her finger to Caroline's cheek, feeling how ruff the marks were. She looked up. Dutch and Edmund sat around her.

Edmund put his head to Caroline's chest. After what felt like a lifetime, he said, "Her heart is beating! It's faint!" His body shook.

"Help her!" Dutch cried out.

Desperate, Jewel looked back at Caroline's face. She

put her shaking hands to her granddaughter's face, doing a healing spell. After a moment, she removed her hands.

A wave of terror overtook her as the marks still stretched across Caroline's face.

"Caroline," she whispered as she shook her. She looked back up. "I don't know what he did to her!"

"Youngin," Dutch said, lightly slapping Caroline's face. "Come on. Wake up. You can't leave us." He lightly slapped her face a few more times, but nothing happened.

"She needs help!" Edmund cried as his voice cracked.

Fuego landed a few feet away with Sal and Athena.

"Achilles!" Athena gasped as she saw him frozen. She slid off Fuego's back, making her way to him.

Sal glared at him. "Send him to the dungeon! He should pay for killing Merlin!"

She flicked her wand, and Achilles was gone.

He turned to everyone surrounding Caroline and froze at the sight of her still and pale body. "Oh my god," he muttered, stumbling over his own feet.

Edmund disappeared as Sal took his place.

Chapter 35

"I have had all the guards sent to the dungeon," Athena told Jewel, Dutch, Lucy, and Dilandro once they were back in the castle. "I insist that you all stay here until Caroline is healthy enough."

Workers moved all around them as Achilles' things were being removed from the castle. Bags filled with his clothes were taken, followed by seashells sculptures he had and artwork in the halls.

"The spell that hit Caroline is strong. I have no idea how to remove it."

Jewel swallowed.

"I never should have left," Dilandro, now fully healed from any illnesses thanks to Jewel, muttered as Lucy held her husband tight.

"Is there anyone who can help her here?" Jewel asked.

"Y-yes. I believe so," Athena said. "I shall call for them."

Jewel looked down the hallway, watching her leave. Sal walked out of Caroline's room, seeming lost. She walked over to him as his watery eyes met hers.

"I can't believe Merlin is gone," he said, holding back tears. "And n-now this…" He broke down.

She pulled him into a hug, holding him close.

****

Caroline woke up with a gasp. Everything seemed foggy, unknown. The only thing she understood was that she was in horrible pain. Her whole face hurt like she had the worst headache of all time.

"I am here to help. I am a healer," an unknown voice said.

As her vision cleared, she saw the healer standing beside her as her family stood around her. The healer was a short man with a long and pointed nose.

"Who are the parents again?" he asked, opening a large bag and pulling out a magnifying glass.

Jewel opened her mouth to speak, but Lucy said, "We are."

The healer nodded, looking back at Caroline and holding the glass by her face.

Caroline had never felt so overwhelmed. "Grandma?"

"I'm right here," she said, resting a hand on her foot.

"Oh my," the healer muttered under his breath. "That is never good."

"What?" Dutch asked with worried eyes.

The healer pulled away from Caroline, putting his tools back in his bag. "I cannot heal what Achilles has done to her, but I can help her in a way."

The room became deadly silent for a moment.

"What happened to her?" Jewel asked.

"Caroline has been cursed." His words hung heavy in the room. "Achilles put a curse on her that will cause her much pain."

"What do you mean?" asked Dilandro.

"Her body will become weak and painful."

"Is there a cure?" Lucy asked.

"Not really. Her magic will not be as strong, so you must keep an eye on her. But there is a way to help with it." He reached into his large bag, pulling out a small bottle of purple liquid. "Caroline, you should take this potion once a day. It will help make it not unbearable."

She took the bottle as the healer spoke with Lucy and Dilandro. With tears in her eyes, she looked up at Jewel. She had never wanted something like this to happen to her.

"You're going to be all right," Jewel said, sitting on the bed and taking her hand. "We will figure this out."

Caroline nodded. She took the lid off the bottle, put the bottle to her lips, and drank a sip.

****

A few days later, they said their last goodbyes to Merlin.

Caroline had thought the whole week was hard, but that day was one of the hardest ones in all her life. The sun set the day as they held his ceremony. Many people, rich and poor, filled the courtyard. She knew that Merlin would have wanted this: his people united and with magic. But it saddened her to know that he had to die for it to happen.

"Are you ready?" Sal asked, meeting her at the window.

She nodded. He took her arm and helped her down to the courtyard, where Athena and a small Fuego waited. In the middle of the courtyard was a gold coffin. She swallowed at the sight of it.

Athena stood in front of it. She wore a black dress with a long train that moved behind her gracefully. After Sal and Caroline stood at the coffin's sides, she flicked her wand, and the coffin lifted a foot off the ground. As she walked, it followed.

Caroline watched everyone bow as the coffin passed.

Up ahead, she saw her parents, Jewel, and Dutch by where they would stop. Sal kept his head low, his eyes burning with tears. Fuego flew sadly behind them. Everyone stayed silent as they made their way through the courtyard.

When Athena stopped walking, the coffin stopped, along with Sal and Caroline. Fuego flew to Dilandro's shoulder, making him jump a bit.

Athena turned around to face the coffin, lowering it back down. "Merlin died for us," she said loudly for everyone to hear. "He was a kind soul who would do anything for those he called his friends."

Sal swallowed, and Caroline took his hand.

"Merlin was and forever will be our king. He died so that you have your magic. Till his last breath, he thought of nothing but his people." She took a deep breath. "The captain of the guards, Zuly, aided Merlin in the end. He helped put the gem back and is a large reason you have powers tonight. I know he did a lot of bad things, but Merlin cared about him very much, and he died a hero next to Merlin. So, recall him as one. And let us be thankful to Merlin, our fallen king."

Everyone bowed. Caroline looked at Sal, whose face was a light shade of pink. She grabbed his hand tighter.

Athena flicked her wand toward the coffin, transforming it into a lovely stone statue of Merlin. His face had a kind smile.

Caroline placed a flower below it before she was told to go inside along with her family and friends.

Chapter 36

Athena's voice filled the hallway. "Jewel!"

Jewel turned to see Athena walking quickly with a large book in her hands. She stopped to let her catch up. "I was looking for you."

Her hair was in a loose ponytail that bounced with each quick step. She was dressed in a much lighter colored dress than Jewel had seen her in since she became queen. But she was still in different tones of black. Once she was by Jewel's side, Jewel walked alongside her.

"I brought something for Caroline," she said, handing the book over. "Merlin wanted her to take this with her back to her world."

Jewel took the spell book. "Are you sure you don't want to keep it?" she asked, feeling bad for taking something from him when she was so much closer to him.

"Yes. I know he really wanted her to have it. Why were you looking for me?"

"Each of us now knows how to make the potion for Caroline. I think it is time we head home," Jewel said.

Athena had said that she would not let them leave until everyone knew how to make the potion. And after a few days, everyone could make it without the instructions.

"I am so glad she is better," Athena said. "And I feel much better knowing you all know how to make the potion. When do you want to leave?"

They stopped walking in front of an open balcony door. A light wind from the lake blew inside.

"Would tomorrow be all right?" Jewel asked. "I feel so bad to leave you after everything that has happened."

"I will be all right. It will take time, but time heals."

****

Before Caroline knew it, everyone was dressed, ready to go back to Duck. Athena had gotten a royal carriage to bring them to the mirror. As the carriage pulled around the castle, Caroline slipped away from her family. She made her way to Merlin's grave and looked up at the blue sky filled with white puffy clouds. The green leaves and grass made a peaceful sound as a light wind blew by.

"Merlin, I hope you know how much you mean to me." She rested a hand on the statue's cold stone. "I will never forget you."

She looked over to a rose bush by the grave and picked a flower from it. She rested it on the statue's foot, not knowing what else to say. A part of her knew he would never understand how much he meant to her. She closed her eyes, wishing she could see him one last time and talk to him about her curse. Would he find it a big deal or not?

"Caroline!" Dutch called.

She turned to go, feeling the curse's weakness on her body. She looked over her shoulder at the grave one last time. "Goodbye, Merlin."

Chapter 37

"You got the spell book?" Athena asked, taking hold of Caroline's hand as they stood a few feet away from the mirror.

The carriage ride had gone by so much faster than anyone would have liked. Caroline had found it very enjoyable to see everything they had walked by full of life now. The water had been the brightest blue she had ever seen, and everything else looked so green.

During the ride, Athena had talked about how Fuego would stay with her. Sal was not too pleased with the idea, but a dragon would stick out in Duck. As the mirror came into sight, the carriage had stopped, and now everyone stood to say their goodbyes.

"I have the spell book in Merlin's old bag that you gave me. Along with his wand. Thank you, Athena," Caroline said as Dilandro put the bag over his shoulder.

Caroline found this goodbye bittersweet. It was hard to say goodbye to Athena, Fuego, and this world that she had found to love. But no one seemed more ready to leave than her parents.

"Oh, heaven! I almost forgot," Athena said, putting a hand in the pocket of her large dress. Its long sleeves flowed with each movement. They rested on her mid-shoulder, showing her many freckles. "I cannot believe I almost let you leave without this!" She handed her a small piece of rolled paper. "This is how to make more potions for your—"

"Thank you," Caroline said, holding the paper tight. She had a knot in her throat.

"Athena, thank you," Lucy said, walking up and resting her hand on Caroline's shoulder.

"I feel sorry to leave you all alone," Caroline said as she looked up to Athena.

"I will be all right," she said. "Fuego will keep me company."

Sal petted Fuego one last time, and Fuego licked his cheek. He hugged him tight before Fuego flew over to Athena's shoulder. "Take good care of him."

"I promise." She patted his little head.

"I hate to say it, but I like the little guy," Dutch said.

Sal shook his head. "You and Merlin both." He gave the dragon a sad smile. His eyes watered, but he blinked the tears away fast.

Caroline rested her head on his shoulder, looking up with an understanding smile. Athena opened her arms, giving both Sal and Caroline a hug.

"Are we ready?" Dutch asked, smiling back at them.

"Yes, we are!" Caroline said, looking back to see Dutch and her grandmother holding hands and her parents standing close together. She was more than ready to start the next chapter of her life with them. She patted Fuego's head before turning to leave.

"Caroline," Athena said. She gestured for Caroline to come closer with her hand.

Caroline looked back at everyone. "Give me a minute."

She heard her parents sigh as she made her way to Athena. "What's wrong?" she asked, keeping her voice low.

"I need you to do one thing for me. I was not going to, but I know I must." Athena seemed so unsure of herself, which Caroline found odd.

"What is it, Athena?" she asked as Fuego looked down at her from where he sat.

Athena took a deep breath and spoke fast, as if ripping off a bandage. "I need you to break the mirror."

"What? Why?"

"Listen, once you have gone through, you must break it!"

"Athena, why?" A wave of emotions coursed through her. "Did I do something wrong?" Caroline asked, unsure why she would request this of her. Breaking the mirror meant that she could not come back.

Athena gazed at the trees around her as if she was looking for something before meeting Caroline's eyes once more. "N-no, you did not," she said as her voice cracked.

"Why do you want me to break it?"

"What if Achilles finds a way out of the dungeon? With the mirror broken, he will be stuck here with me and my guards. We can take care of him before he becomes a problem to you," she said, taking Caroline's hand.

"That makes sense," she muttered.

Athena nodded. "I know it is a lot to ask, but I am doing it for you to be free of him forever."

Caroline looked back at her parents, who were holding hands and talking. She had suffered so much without them because of Achilles. Keeping him locked in this world meant none of her cousins would suffer what she had, and she would never have to again too. "I understand."

Athena squeezed her hands before letting go.

"Goodbye, Athena," she said before turning to face her family.

She took hold of her parents' hands. Leaving the mirror with her parents as she was now was the most surreal moment. She came here, hoping she would leave with them, and here she was, walking home with them.

"Are you ready?" she asked them both with a smile that they shared back.

"Ready for a life with my girls," Dilandro said, looking from his daughter to his wife.

With a deep breath, Caroline took a step and followed them into the mirror.

****

Athena watched from aside as Sal turned to her with a smile.

"Take care of Fuego," he said.

"Of course," she replied.

Jewel went through the mirror next to Dutch, who nodded toward Athena before they too disappeared.

"Goodbye, Sal," she said as he turned to the mirror and jumped through the glass.

"I must say…" Achilles' voice filled the woods as he stepped out of the tree line.

She wiped away any tears that she had let fall before.

"That was some pretty convincing acting you did these past two weeks."

She turned to him with an adoring smile.

"I am impressed with you, my dear," he said as he made his way to her.

Fuego flew off her shoulder and into the sky fast, but she hardly noticed as she looked up to Achilles' face. Once at her side, he placed his hand on the small of her back.

"Thank you, master," she mumbled.

He ran his hand through her hair as she locked her lips to his. He responded to her affection aggressively.

Chapter 38

Caroline closed her eyes as she traveled through the mirror. Her feet felt the ground change, and she opened her eyes, seeing the familiarness of Achilles' old house. The house was mostly dark with a bit of sun coming in through the windows in the other room. Dust still moved in the air. It was not a welcoming place to come back to, but she didn't care.

She had done it, and her parents were back.

Tears burned in her eyes. "I can't believe I did it. I missed you guys so much."

Her parents wrapped her in a hug and held her tight.

"We love you so much!" Lucy said.

As they released from the hug, Jewel and Dutch stepped through the mirror.

Dutch wrinkled his nose and laughed. "I forgot how bad this place smells."

Seconds later, Sal came through the mirror fast. "I'm going to miss that world."

Caroline looked at the mirror behind him, feeling its pull once more. "We need to break the mirror."

Everyone collectively gasped.

"Why?!" Sal asked.

"Is that what Athena talked to you about?" Jewel asked.

Caroline nodded. "She asked me to for a good reason." She told them everything Athena had said, and their faces seemed understanding.

"If that is what she wants," Sal said with a sigh, "then we must listen to the Queen."

Dilandro opened Merlin's bag, handing her Merlin's wand. She held it with two shaking hands, her eyes filled with tears. She could not believe how caring Athena had been to give her so many of Merlin's things. She also could not believe that she had become so close to Merlin in such a short number of days.

With a deep breath, she lifted the wand to the mirror, and everyone stood back. She looked back at her reflection in the glass. She thought of Athena and all she had lost because someone had come through the mirror. She then thought of Merlin and how he had lost his life because someone came in. She owed it to them to make sure that didn't happen again.

She closed her eyes as she sent the spell. The glass made a loud cracking sound as it went everywhere in what seemed like slow motion. But the shards never hit the ground. Instead, before they got close to the floor, they disappeared, turning into golden flakes.

Only one small piece landed on the floor by her feet. She picked it up, putting it in her pocket. She then looked back up at the broken mirror. No more magic pulled her closer. All that remained was a gold frame, a reminder of the beauty within a world that was now out of reach.

****

Sal went back to his grandparents' house to answer the

hundreds of questions they had. They were far from pleased that he had disappeared for weeks with nothing more than a note. Afterward, he gave Caroline a goodbye hug on his doorstep.

"I'm sorry," she said as Patti stood in the doorway with her arms crossed.

"So what if I'm grounded?" he said. "I kept you safe…"

She noticed how his eyes fell. "Hey, listen," she said, grabbing his arms. "The curse was not your fault or mine. You did keep me safe!"

He nodded and pulled her in for one last hug. "I love you."

She froze for a moment. He had never said that before. Neither of them had. "I-I love you too."

After he locked his lips to hers, Patti called out, "Sal, come inside!"

****

Caroline opened the front door to her house, and her mouth dropped. "Edmund?"

He pulled her into a hug and lifted her off the ground. "I didn't know what had happened to you. I tried to teleport, but my wand couldn't find you. I was so worried! Are you hurt?" He breathed in a shaky breath as she hugged him back.

"Uncle Edmund, I'm mostly okay. I'm sorry it took so long to come back."

"As long as you're okay," he said, kissing her cheek before setting her down. He turned to Jewel. "Jewel, I hope you don't mind that I was staying here."

"Not at all," she said.

Then he froze as his brother walked through the front door. "Oh my God!"

Dilandro gasped. "Edmund!"

They held each other tight, not daring to let go. Lucy smiled behind them, and Edmund reached out, pulling her into the hug.

Caroline watched with tears in her eyes. She had made her family whole once more.

About the Author

After years of vocal training and after graduating from high school in 2020, Vianlix-Christine's goals were to start a career in Broadway. But the pandemic hit, and like most of the world, she got stuck at home, wondering what would happen to her dreams and her career. Her first book, *Seaside Magic*, took her out of the world for a few hours a day. It brought joy and blessings with it as a new career started. It later won first place in YA – Fantasy at The BookFest. She also has a children's book, *Puffy Ball!* Vianlix-Christine lives in Virginia with her supporting family and her two dogs, Hershey and Oreo.

Acknowledgments

Everyone always says that they don't have a favorite child. That they can't pick a favorite. But this book is my favorite. Every time I had to read over it and edit it, I did so with a smile on my face. I want to thank everyone who picked up my first novel, *Seaside Magic*, and loved the characters so much that you went and got the sequel. Thank you for your support.

I also want to thank my mom. Without her, my stories would stay hidden with no deadline in my computer. My dad, for cheering me on and keeping me safe at each book signing event. Both of my parents have given me so much support that I don't think there will ever be enough words to say how thankful I am to them.

I want to thank my grandparents for their love and support in this series, along with my brother, Christopher, for helping put the pieces of this story together once again. Also, a shout out to my dogs, Hershey and Oreo. They always keep my feet warm while I work.

Mostly, I want to thank Robin LeeAnn. You are such a talented editor, and once more, you helped me make my story something deeper and beautiful. Lena Yang, you outdid yourself with this book cover. I love it!

And finally and most importantly: to my readers, THANK YOU for letting me take you through Caroline's journey once more.

Coming Soon

Ingram Content Group UK Ltd.
Milton Keynes UK
UKHW010850100323
418370UK00004B/463